When he is not in the office giving legal advice, or at home writing on a new book, Nick's favourite activities are flying light aircraft and scuba diving. He has a commercial pilot's licence and is an enthusiastic photographer. After living in the Netherlands for several years, Nick is now based in London. *Death of a Diplomat* is his first novel.

DEATH OF A DIPLOMAT

Distinguished British diplomat Sir John Little seems to be living out his days quietly in retirement. But then, at his beach house in the Bahamas, he goes for a swim — and doesn't come back. Was it an unfortunate accident, suicide, or a well-planned murder? British Foreign Office employee Michael Burton and Bahamian detective Chester King are given the job of finding out. With little to go on, and still less volunteered by the diplomat's enigmatic wife and the unexpected heir who practices black magic, Burton and King discover that all is not what it appears.

NICK GREAVES

◆

DEATH
OF A
DIPLOMAT

Complete and Unabridged

ULVERSCROFT
Leicester

First published in Great Britain in 2011 by
Robert Hale Limited
London

First Large Print Edition
published 2012
by arrangement with
Robert Hale Limited
London

British Library CIP Data

Greaves, Nick.
  Death of a diplomat.
  1. Murder- -Investigation- -Bahamas- -Fiction.
  2. Diplomatic and consular service, British- -Fiction.
  3. Detective and mystery stories. 4. Large type books.
  I. Title
  823.9'2–dc23

  ISBN 978–1–4448–1065–3

Published by
F. A. Thorpe (Publishing)
Anstey, Leicestershire

Set by Words & Graphics Ltd.
Anstey, Leicestershire
Printed and bound in Great Britain by
T. J. International Ltd., Padstow, Cornwall

Prologue

It was early evening and the setting sun was disappearing into the aquamarine ocean across from Old Fort Bay. One end of the beach, where the sun still warmed the sand, was an untidy patchwork of towels and sunbathers. Despite the now rapidly cooling air, the more tenacious tourists were determined to make the most of the last rays of sun, before the dark-grey storm clouds, gathering in the distance, brought in the rains. Almost nothing was visible in the expanding shadow which had swallowed half of the shore and was slowly completing its conquest.

Amongst the screaming children, courting couples and sun-worshipping singles walked a man dressed in a pair of brief swimming trunks and a short-sleeved check shirt. On his head was a beige sun hat, on his feet brown leather sandals. His eyes were shaded by an expensive pair of designer sunglasses, below which a neatly trimmed salt-and-pepper moustache adorned his upper lip. He barely looked round as he trudged past the happy families, heading away from the crowd, each step shovelling a fine spray of sand in front of him.

As he reached the shaded section of beach, the man removed his hat and brushed some strands of grey hair from his forehead. He then removed the sunglasses, folding the arms in, and groped in first one shirt pocket and then the other. Finally, his hand emerged with a glasses case, into which he inserted the folded sunglasses. Once finished, he placed the glasses case in the hat and, clutching both in his left hand, reached down with his right to unfasten the sandals. He kicked the sandals off, bent down to pick them up and continued on his way, quickening his pace.

Without the direct heat of the sun, the beach was much cooler. He could feel the beginning of the nightly land breeze, which would pick up during the evening as the island cooled down and became relatively cold compared to the sea. He breathed deeply, savouring the clear air. The notes of cigarette smoke, fast food and suntan lotion, which had tainted the air in the more densely populated part of the beach, were gone. A hint of diesel oil, from the endless traffic of boats around the islands, was just starting to creep in.

When he had walked for about five minutes, and the cries of the playing children had died down to an occasional fleeting whisper heard above the perpetual hiss of the

2

waves breaking against the shore, he threw down the hat and sandals, and began to unbutton his shirt, revealing a scraggy torso and a slight belly. His body had not yet run to fat, but the loose folds of flesh suggested he had once been far more muscular. About half a mile of sand now separated him from the bulk of the people inhabiting the beach, and he stole a furtive glance towards them, as if checking that nobody was watching him. He folded his shirt quickly and placed it on top of his sandals, glanced at his watch, a golden band around his tanned wrist, and strolled towards the sea.

His feet entered the foamy surf that was climbing slowly up the beach, and he felt immediately the cool touch of the dominant sea. Striding defiantly over the small waves, he felt his body stiffen as it sought to acclimatize. He momentarily felt his heart pound irregularly, wondering briefly if, by some curious quirk of fate, he was to be spared his last, onerous duty by a failure in the pump that coursed life through his body. This fear — or was it a perverse hope? — was dashed as his heartbeat regained its habitual regularity.

The water now reached his knees. Although the light, clear waters of the Bahamas owe these characteristics to their unusual lack of overall depth, he knew that in this part of the island he wouldn't have to go very far before the bottom fell away sharply. As he walked on steadily, he looked to his left. In the distance, he could still make out the people on the beach, and behind them the buildings of the Old Fort Club. The shadow had crawled still further along the shore and now covered three-quarters of the beach; the only vestige of the sun that had heated these now cooled sands was the glow of its tangerine disc slipping rapidly below the horizon.

The man breathed deeply as the beach sloped away and his crotch submerged. The sudden change in temperature momentarily took his breath away, and he was aware of a heightened sense of touch, as if his nerves were intensifying everyday feelings. He sank to his knees, allowing the cool, velvet touch of the ocean to flow over his body, before starting a strong, lazy crawl away from the shoreline. His stroke was meticulous and capable, although flawed: unable to fully submerge his head, he tended to swing it alternately side-to-side, giving the misleading appearance that he was desperately gasping for air.

After several minutes, he turned onto his back, and watched the sun as it sank further behind the rolling azure expanse that he knew was to become his grave. He looked again at the beach, his eyes scouring it for the signs of anything that might change his mind. He was now a considerable distance out, and tiny figures ran like a colony of ants away from the rapidly cooling beach. The sandy expanse was almost deserted now; the thinning crowds sloped off as the sun dropped behind its watery curtain for the night. They would be back tomorrow, he thought; he would not.

He resumed his facedown position, and began to swim as strongly as he could to overcome the yearning that he felt to return to the beach and simply accept the consequences of his actions. But he knew that he could not do that. To him, it was not simply a matter of his position, reputation and indeed liberty, but also those of the organization which he represented and to which he had given the best years of his life.

He stroked further away from the shore, further away from life. He looked back one last time. The sun had set and the island was covered in a blanket of darkness.

Although anathema to him, he began to greedily breathe in the ocean. In his mouth, the water tasted dank, salty and bitter, and he fought the urge to retch. His nose stung as droplets of sea water found their way in. It required huge willpower to continue ingesting the foul-tasting liquid, but he managed to persevere until he felt his lungs were full.

The next thing he knew, he was coughing and spitting out sea water, and there was suddenly brightness where there had been darkness. He felt his chest expand involuntarily as his lungs drew in as much air as they could. Drops of salt water irritated his throat and started more coughing fits.

He tried a couple of times to drown himself in this fashion, but each time as his consciousness began to waver, his body's natural yearning for life would gasp the necessary air in time. He began to wonder if it would ever work. Panic set in, not the fear of being helplessly overwhelmed by the water and having his life snatched away from him, but rather the humiliation of not even being able to commit suicide successfully.

After several more failed attempts, he realized that he would have to prevent his body's natural reaction. For a second he considered, then breathed in slightly, and began to swim downwards as far as possible. For what seemed like minutes he struggled against his own buoyancy, increased by the intake of breath, before finally making headway. To aid his descent, he breathed out gradually. On his skin, he felt the water turn suddenly colder, and in his legs he felt the stinging of his thigh muscles, which, without fins, had to work hard to move sufficient water to propel him at any reasonable speed. In his chest he felt a burning feeling as if his lungs were about to burst. He swallowed again and again as he fought off the initial urge to breathe, struggling to put off the manic gasp for breath he knew would be coming. Gradually, his whole body was overwhelmed by the effort required to keep going. When he could go no further, he opened his mouth and inhaled.

1

'He wants to see you.'

Michael Burton looked up from the chess puzzle on which he was concentrating and glanced at the secretary — the bringer of bad tidings — through several strands of longish brown hair that had fallen over his eyes. The girl shook her head at him, unconcerned, as oblivious to Burton's fate as she was the last time and the time before that. She disappeared, leaving the door open. What on earth had he done now to deserve the old man's wrath? The secretary had left before he had had the chance to ask her, so he had no choice but to go straight to Reardon's office. He picked up a notepad and located a chewed blue biro under a wad of paper. Thrusting these under his arm, he walked through the open doorway and headed for the stairs.

'Sir Anthony Reardon OBE, High Commissioner of Jamaica' read the ostentatious engraved gold on wood plaque outside Reardon's office on the second floor of the High Commission building on Trafalgar Road. Burton contemplated knocking but then decided against it, pushing the door open and walking in.

Reardon was seated as always behind his expansive oak desk, which had a burgundy leather centre decorated with gold leaf. As Burton entered, Reardon gestured dismissively towards one of the two leather chairs facing the desk. As Burton was contemplating which chair to sit in, Reardon launched into a heated, impassioned speech about responsibilities. Burton was momentarily taken aback, only then noticing that Reardon was talking on the speakerphone, gesturing wildly as if this would help him to get his point across.

Burton pulled the furthest of the chairs away from the desk and sat down, positioning himself to benefit from the view over Reardon's shoulder. As he sat down, a hiss of air escaped from the leather cushion. The chair was soft and comfortable, and certainly not what he was used to in Jamaica. Behind Reardon's desk were two generously sized windows affording a reasonable glimpse of the city and, in the distance, far beyond the tops of the surrounding buildings, the ocean. On one wall was a photograph of the Queen, the official head of state, which looked as though it might have been taken in Jamaica, but at least a couple of decades ago. On the other wall was a painting from an artist whose name and qualities were unknown to Burton and, judging by this particular piece of work, likely to remain so.

Apart from the desktop computer on Reardon's desk, his office seemed surprisingly void of any work-related objects. There were no bookshelves, no filing cabinets and no cupboards. A small coffee table bearing a very old leather-bound document, which was clearly intended for decoration rather than reading material, was the only furniture the room had to offer other than the desk and chairs. The clutter normally encountered in all other government offices must have been stored elsewhere. Probably in some poor secretary's room, Burton mused.

Reardon appeared slightly agitated as he flustered his concerns to whomever he was talking to. At first, Burton tried not to listen, and concentrated instead on the constant din from outside, the sounds of the everyday hustle and bustle of Kingston life that the windows were unable to keep out. This was, however, difficult to maintain and he soon found himself subconsciously tuning in to the terse, excited discussion. Beyond gleaning that both Reardon and his absent nemesis seemed to be arguing about who should be doing what, Burton was unable to follow the conversation, having obviously missed some key points earlier on. He can't have invited me in here to watch this farce, thought Burton. He stood up to leave, planning to come back later. Reardon waved him back, indicating the seat Burton had just left. He exhaled deeply and sat down again, allowing his thoughts to wander.

'Michael, hello, sorry about that. Lots to sort out at the moment.'

Burton started, realizing suddenly that Reardon was talking to him. He looked up at the older man, whose soft, flabby face, normally pasty and expressionless, was now etched with concern. Reardon had always given Burton an impression of cold, calculating intelligence, but now his normally impassive brown eyes seemed to exude emotion.

'I assume you know Sir John Little,' Reardon began, looking for confirmation. His eyes seemed to take on a penetrating demeanour, and Burton looked away. He had never felt completely at ease with Reardon, whom he'd always felt to be sanctimonious and unfeeling, but now something had definitely thawed the older man. He glanced back at Reardon, noting his greying hair, tidy but uninteresting, and his neat grey suit. Despite the heat, Reardon had not removed his suit jacket. The overall image was of a stone man, a grey man, a statue hewed from a rock face. But today something had breathed colour into his veins.

'I know *of* him. And I've met him once or twice. Yes, I'm sure I met him at one of the receptions at the High Commission. And at some charity event earlier this year, I think.' Burton struggled to remember what he'd said to Sir John on that occasion, if anything. What was this all about? Had he made a fool of himself whilst talking to him?

'Well, he's dead.' The voice was gruff, matter-of-fact and emotionless.

'Oh,' murmured Burton, thinking to himself that Reardon was fairly blunt for somebody supposedly skilled in the art of diplomacy.

Reardon reached forward and selected a large cigar from a wooden box with a faded yellow and red motif on the top. His hand fished around in his jacket pocket for a while before emerging with a guillotine-style cigar cutter, which he fitted thoughtfully over the tip of the cigar. With an unhurried, deliberate motion, he removed the end of the cigar and dropped it into a bin under his desk. He remained silent as he tipped a match out of a box on the desk and ran it along the striking surface. The match lit towards the end of its run, and Reardon lifted it slowly to the end of his cigar, rolling it across the wide, freshly cut tip of the cigar. The episode took a couple of minutes, and Burton was surprised by the deliberation shown by a man who had always come across as coldly efficient, but more so by the fact that Reardon was smoking at all. Burton had never seen him smoke before, and the office was officially non-smoking, although the Jamaican interpretation of this was fairly loose.

'Sir John was a colleague, but also a friend, a very good friend. I worked with him when he was High Commissioner, when he was showing me the ropes, and it was a sad time for the High Commission, indeed for the Foreign Office, when he retired. And, let me tell you, my boy, following in his footsteps here was no easy task.'

Reardon took a large puff of his cigar and let the smoke curl out of his mouth and up towards the ceiling, undisturbed by any breeze. The old air-conditioning unit was working overtime in the heat, as evidenced by the incessant rattle, but the room was stifling, and the windows remained firmly shut. The smell of cigar smoke was swift to pervade the enclosed space; Burton felt sure that there had been no trace of smoke in the air when he had entered.

'Anyway, at the moment the death is being

treated as suspicious. I gather that most deaths of this nature are. Unexplained deaths of noteworthy ex-diplomats, I mean, although they don't happen very often, thank God. At the moment there doesn't seem to be any evidence to suggest that anything untoward happened, but, of course, the incident will be fully investigated.

'You're probably wondering what happened. Well, this is what we know so far. Sir John apparently decided to go for one last swim in the ocean outside his beach house, late yesterday afternoon. He was seen by several eyewitnesses walking along the beach, and then entering the water. They all thought, quite understandably given the circumstances, that he was merely taking a swim as he was wont to do in the late afternoon. Well, maybe he was, but he never came back, or at least not alive.

'Nobody even realized that anything was wrong. Sir John removed his shirt, hat and shoes as if nothing was the matter. It was only when he failed to return later that evening that he was reported as being missing by his wife, and the appropriate investigations were started. These unfortunately did not shed any light on his whereabouts.'

Reardon began opening drawers in his desk, and at last emerged with a cast-iron ashtray, onto which he tapped his cigar. With the ash gone, the glowing embers shone as he took another drag. Both men remained silent, as if silence were preordained, as Reardon savoured the smoke in his mouth and then exhaled deeply.

'Sir John's body was washed up on the shore earlier today, not all that far from where he entered the water. I was called by the Bahamian police, who have the body and are conducting an initial investigation into the death. No post-mortem has been done yet. The body was missing for at least half a day before it was washed up. Apparently this is normal — it has something to do with the tides, I'm told.

'Anyway, local law will require an autopsy to be conducted and the police have made clear that they intend to carry out a full investigation into what happened to Sir John. As he was a former High Commissioner, and from what I can gather always enjoyed a good rapport with the Bahamians, this office was formally contacted by the Bahamian authorities. I was talking to a representative of the Bahamian Government when you came in. Of course, I told them that I wanted someone to liaise with them, to provide background to the case, and to help wherever possible. I really wanted to have an investigation carried out by our own people, someone here on the force, or even detectives from Scotland Yard, and I put this to them but, as you may have gathered, the Bahamians didn't agree to this.

'No, they didn't like that idea at all, the Bahamian powers-that-be.' He gestured towards the telephone, as if blaming the inanimate device for the woes it had communicated. 'They're worried about us stepping on their toes, meddling in their high profile cases.

'Anyway, Michael, if you'll allow me to cut to the chase, the point is this: the Bahamian police are investigating the death of my friend Sir John, led by a local man by the name of King, Chester King, and we are permitted' — Reardon spat out the word 'permitted' as if he felt that the High Commission should have an automatic right to do anything it wanted when a British national was involved — 'permitted to provide a liaison officer. I want you to be that liaison, Michael. I want you to talk to this King man, and to help him in any way you can.'

Burton mused over this suggestion. He didn't really know what he had been expecting when he entered Reardon's office, but it certainly wasn't this. He was being offered something outside the normal, run-of-the-mill, routine tasks he had fulfilled since arriving in Jamaica, and that excited him, yet he couldn't understand why he would be singled out for this. He had hardly covered himself in glory during his time at the High Commission, gaining in his own eyes more of a reputation as a lazy wastrel than somebody to whom an extraordinary and, to Reardon at least, important job should be entrusted. Although the opportunity appealed to him, Burton's natural tendency to challenge the views of his superiors kicked in, almost against his wishes.

'Why should we investigate at all? It's an issue for the police. An issue for the Bahamian police. I'm not surprised they feel we're sticking our noses in where we're not wanted. And, then, why me?'

Reardon shrugged his shoulders and paused pensively for several seconds before puffing deeply on his cigar. 'I spoke to Sir John on the telephone early yesterday afternoon, the day on which he disappeared. We talked of his visiting us here at the High Commission at the end of the month. Apparently he was planning to come over on a fishing trip or something. He also invited Felicity and me to spend a few days with him and Melissa in the Bahamas. Said we could go walking on the beach together.

'Sir John had lived years in the Caribbean, first in Jamaica and then in the Bahamas.

Ever since I first met him, he has lived by the sea. He swam every day, twice a day. Loved it. Perhaps not the most technically competent swimmer, but certainly not weak. I find it very hard to believe that he misjudged his stamina, or was swept away. He may have had a heart attack, or a fit, or something, I'm sure the coroner will be able to tell us if that is the case, but I can't believe he simply got it wrong.

'Another alternative is that he committed suicide, but I can't believe this either. Yesterday afternoon, he did not sound anything like a desperate man, and he gave absolutely no indication of a man intending to take his own life that evening. Nor was he a man predisposed to making swift, rash decisions.

'All in all, Michael, I am highly suspicious of his death, but my suspicions mean little to an experienced policeman. He will not investigate on the basis of my feelings. However, we have been asked if we would like to provide a liaison, Sir John being, of course, a prominent British citizen in this part of the world, and I have no intention of passing up this chance. I want to send a liaison officer, and I want him to do as much investigating as he can, subtly of course.

'And, then, why you? Yes, Michael, a good

question. Why you? You, because I think you have a lot of potential but are bored by the mundane tasks we have on offer for you. You because I was pleased to see you had been placed on my staff, but since then you've done nothing to please me. You, because I think you have the ability to do this. And I think that it may just inspire you to get much more out of yourself than you have so far.

'You're what, twenty-seven? Twenty-eight? And, in this office at least, a serial under-achiever. I've seen your personnel report, saw it before I agreed to your appointment, and so far you've not delivered.

'Anyway, Michael, regardless of my reasoning, or lack thereof, I'm offering you this opportunity, and I very much hope you take it.'

As he finished, Reardon's tone softened and Burton could almost discern a hint of an informal, friendly request. Suddenly Burton found the whole situation ridiculous. He had been told to go to Reardon's office by the secretary, who normally sent him up when he'd filed a report in the wrong place, or after he'd been rude to some diplomat's stuck-up wife. Now he was being asked to go and play cops and robbers in another country with some Bahamian detective, without any previous investigative knowledge or even a slight inkling about what he was supposed to be doing. It was probably some scam to ship him out and then have him arrested for perverting the course of justice or some Bahamian equivalent. Nevertheless, he was interested.

'But how exactly am I supposed to start investigating? I won't know what I'm doing. I'll just get in the way of this King bloke and sour relations between ourselves and the Bahamians. It's a guaranteed failure.'

'Michael, Michael. Don't worry about that. The Bahamians are well aware of the fact that we're not sending a policeman. In fact, they prefer that. Then it's clear that they're leading the investigation. You will be there simply as a liaison officer. To liaise. To provide them with background information when they need it. Not to investigate. Well, not officially, anyway.'

Burton knew already that he would do it: the chance to give up paperwork and go and do something interesting was far too good to give up. The whole situation intrigued him. Although it was most likely a simple accident, Burton's mind was already racing with improbable conspiracy theories. And, although he had not known him well, his recollection of Sir John was that he was a good, kindly man, who had seemed interested in Burton and his career; he would accept the assignment if only

21

for that reason. But he also didn't want to look like he was giving in too easily. 'And if I refuse? I mean, I don't recall this kind of unofficial investigative activity being included in the job description.'

'There are others here who will do it. However, you are my first choice, and I would be gravely disappointed if you were to decline.'

'And if something goes wrong? If I get warned off for meddling in the investigation? Will the High Commission deny this conversation ever took place and insist I have exceeded my authority? Disown me?'

Reardon laughed. 'Nothing so dramatic, my boy. We're not sending you on a clandestine mission onto enemy territory. We have a very good relationship with the Bahamians. We don't necessarily see eye-to-eye on every single issue, this being one of them, but in general we get on famously. And this office will back you up whatever happens. Within reason, of course. I'm perfectly sure there won't be any altercations, but if there are then so be it. They will be suitably hushed up and smoothed over in the appropriate diplomatic channels.'

Burton still felt sure he was being stitched up, but couldn't see how. He was also convinced that whatever happened, it would be a lot more challenging that perusing reports of the lost wallets of tourists wandering the markets hunting for bargains, or trying to explain to distraught travellers how they could get home without the passport they had inadvertently taken swimming. And he welcomed a challenge.

'OK. I'll do it. When can I meet this Chester King fellow?'

Reardon smiled briefly, obviously pleased. 'Tomorrow morning. I will telephone the Bahamians and let them know you are coming over. You should be able to catch a flight later this evening. I'll have my secretary book you a seat. She'll also ask the Bahamians to arrange a hotel for you.'

'OK. And I expect you'll want a report of my liaising and, um, investigative duties?'

Reardon looked at him. 'Yes, I would like a report of your work. List all contacts with the Bahamian police and anybody else. Your job is to safeguard British interests in this case. And to find out what the hell happened to Sir John.'

2

It was a few minutes past eight o' clock in the evening when the main wheels of the Air Jamaica Airbus touched down in Nassau. Burton, sitting next to the window, breathed a sigh of relief as the plane's nose wheel settled down onto the runway. He didn't think of himself as a particularly nervous air passenger, but the flight had been simply gruelling. About halfway through the flight, the captain had switched on the seatbelt sign seconds before the plane had plummeted what seemed like fifty feet, and Burton had struggled with shaking hands to fasten himself in. Time seemed to stand still, and then they were on their way again, flying towards ominous black thunderclouds, which seemed to hang above the outline of New Providence Island in front of them.

'Please remain seated until the plane has come to a complete halt,' requested the purser in vain as the plane taxied across towards the apron. As if hearing the starter's gun, the passengers sprang from their seats and competed for a place in the aisle, impatient to leave the plane and continue the waiting process elsewhere. Even the little old lady seated next to him during the flight, who had seemed to Burton to be an almost god-like vessel of patience and calm, unperturbed by the plane's sudden unannounced vertical descent and forgiving of the rushed cabin crew's mistakes when handing round drinks during the small window of opportunity during the flight in which remaining upright whilst not strapped down was physically possible, had suddenly taken on an aggressive and hostile demeanour, and was fighting her way through the crowds. Burton remained seated, content to sit this one out.

After several minutes of taxiing, the plane stopped on the apron. Several minutes passed, during which numerous unidentifiable noises outside and underneath the plane were discernible. Finally, the front doors were opened and the habitual insane rush to exit the confines of the plane started. Burton had long since lost sight of his elderly neighbour, but felt sure he would see her again inside the terminal building. Instead, he watched out of the window as the last vestiges of the orange layers disappeared from the horizon to be replaced with a deep, dark, blue-black. With the plane nearly empty, Burton stood and took the small rucksack he had brought as hand luggage out of the overhead locker. A young man carrying a holdall of epic proportions, the vastness of which made a mockery of the small cages used to gauge hand luggage, let him out into the aisle, and he gratefully hurried from the plane.

On the tarmac outside, he joined a snake of people stretched from the front of the plane to the terminal building. He could hear the soft whirring of the powered down jet engines, and kept well clear of the orange bollard placed in front of the air intake. In the distance, he could hear the roar as another plane started its take-off run.

The air outside the plane was heavy and humid, but with the slight cool edge that follows stormy weather. He breathed deeply and was rewarded with a lungful of night air, only slightly tainted with kerosene. He saw suitcases being unloaded from the hold, catapulted into baggage carts by bored men in blue and yellow coveralls, wondering if his own slightly older case would be crushed by one of the heavy metal-reinforced trunks now being offloaded.

In the terminal building, the snake continued slithering its way towards passport control. Standing in the queue, Burton suddenly felt nervous. Would the Bahamians be wise to Reardon's harebrained scheme of unofficial investigations and suchlike? Would they refuse him entry? Worse still, would they arrest him? He remembered his passport photo and a morbid panic shot through him. His passport was almost ten years old, and the photo didn't resemble him in the slightest. He pulled out the creased document and opened it on the photograph page. The face that looked up at him was that of a youth, with bold, regular features, pale skin, closely-cropped dark hair and penetrating blue eyes, which stared coolly at the camera. Now his hair was much longer, bleached slightly lighter by the sun and pushed back from his forehead, and his skin was deeply tanned after two years in the Caribbean. He had heard from a contact in the UK Border Agency that they looked carefully at eyes for identification, in which case he should be all right. But it would be embarrassing to say the least if he were sent back from his new mission having failed even to gain entry. To his relief, he was waved through after a couple of cursory questions and a throw-away comment about not having been to the hairdressers for some time.

In the arrivals hall, a crowd had gathered by the only available carousel, waiting despondently. The belt remained still for several long minutes, during which tension and irritation mounted by unspoken degrees. Then the belt creaked into life, and people gazed first expectantly, then hopefully, and finally despairingly, at the bags going past. By the time Burton's case made an appearance, he'd almost given up hope and gone looking for the lost luggage office. Exasperated but relieved, he grabbed the case and headed towards the exit.

Chaos reigned supreme in the main hall, but eventually he caught sight of a short, stocky local man wearing a faded pink shirt and khaki shorts and casually displaying a hastily written sign bearing the word 'Burden'. He assumed this was for him, although whether it was a failed attempt to spell his name, or simply a premonition of what he was likely to become for the Bahamian police he did not know.

'I'm Michael Burton,' he addressed himself to the top of the local man's head, as the latter continued to look straight ahead past Burton, who was standing almost directly in front of him. On hearing the words, however, the man looked up and a wide smile slowly spread across his unshaven face, revealing uneven but very white teeth.

'Mr Burton, is nice t' meet yuh, sir. My name is Victor. Come wit' me. We go t' your hotel.' Victor grabbed Burton's heavy suitcase as if it were a child's toy and raced towards the exit, with Burton hurrying along in his wake.

Burton followed Victor outside to a dusty, well-used Ford Focus, which was parked, badly, in the drop off and set down lane of the airport, and waited for him to unlock it. Oblivious to the horn of the irate taxi driver blocked in by the Ford, Victor sauntered around to the boot, opened it without the key and heaved Burton's case in. Burton tried the passenger door, which had been unlocked, and climbed into the car. The grey interior of the Ford was well decorated with papers, maps, cassettes and sweet wrappers. Not exactly arriving in style, thought Burton to himself.

Victor settled into the driver's seat and inserted the key into the ignition. He pumped the throttle a couple of times and then turned the key, and was rewarded with a slight smell of petrol and a dry cough from the engine. He repeated the process several times before the engine fired, and Burton, on hearing the engine catch, gratefully operated the electric control to lower the window and allow the fumes to escape.

The relief gained from the open window was short lived. Burton felt his head pushed back firmly against the headrest as Victor

29

moved off from the kerb, clearly favouring a racing start achieved by holding a few thousand revs and then dropping the clutch immediately. An equally abrupt emergency stop when a crazy pedestrian walked in front of them convinced Burton that the nerve-racking experience on the plane was soon going to pale into insignificance.

Victor certainly concentrated on getting the most from the lightly powered Ford. The engine protested in vain as he shot through the gears, and Burton felt his head shoot forward every time Victor dropped the clutch, sideways when he cornered and backwards when he accelerated. Burton, who had attempted to fasten the seatbelt when they started, only to find that it failed to retract and was fixed loosely enough to fit at least two large people, held firmly onto the hand grip above his head. Victor was equally seatbelt free, but had the steering wheel to hold on to.

As they drove away from the airport, Victor pointed out Lake Killarney, which Burton had seen from the air. In the dusk, it took on a shimmering, silver colour. Not that Burton was able to direct his attention towards the lake; rather, he was scrutinizing the road ahead. They were driving on the left, British style, but the car was a left-hand drive model, probably imported from the States, and Victor swerved dangerously into the middle of the road to assess the situation every time they came up behind another car. The relative lack of vision did not curb Victor's compulsive urge to overtake at any opportunity, and Burton had to warn him a couple of times that there was no room. One near miss had Burton closing his eyes and praying, something he did not remember doing since he was posted to Jamaica two years ago. Just let me get there in one piece, he thought, and I'll turn over a new leaf when I get back to Kingston.

'Tomorrow, yuh go wit' Detective King t' Sir John Little house, eh boss?'

Burton, whose knuckles were white from holding himself upright in the passenger seat, did not consider himself in any great need of a conversation with his tormentor, but leaped at the opportunity in the hope that it would distract him from the road and force him to slow down. In fact, it achieved only the former, which provided scant comfort and convinced Burton that making plans for tomorrow might be both premature and optimistic.

'Yes,' Burton confirmed, although he had not been told of the arrangements that had been made. Reardon's secretary had handed him a printout of an e-ticket for the plane, wished him a 'bon voyage' and told him everything else would be sorted out in Nassau. He began to wonder exactly what she had meant by that.

'The house is that way,' said Victor, pointing to his left as they came to a T-junction. 'We gat' go this way now.'

They turned right after sailing through a stop sign, although in Victor's defence Burton was fairly sure he had detected a slight lift of the throttle on the approach to the junction, and started along what appeared to be a major road. Burton knew that it was about thirty miles to Nassau: he had bought a map and on the flight over had checked the location of both Nassau and Old Fort Bay, where Sir John Little had last been seen. He guessed it would take them about half an hour to get there, although with Victor at the wheel this could be considerably less.

'When will I meet Detective King?' he asked.

'Yuh come t' the police station tomorrow mornin, boss. Detective King, he wait for yuh there. Then y'all go t' the house of Sir John.'

'What time should I be there? At the police station, I mean?'

'Detective King an' de other policemen, they start at nine o' clock.'

32

Burton nodded and sat back in his seat. A nine o' clock start would give him ample time to find his way around. He wondered how much Victor might know about what had happened to Sir John. Plying him for information could hardly work against him, and it might be interesting to see if he could find anything out that may give him a head start in the morning.

'So, Victor, do you know why I am here?'

'Sho' thing, boss. You come t' find out why Sir John dies. I think, eh?'

'Yes, that's right, Victor. And do you know anything about Sir John's death? How he died, for example?'

Victor gave a snort that Burton was unsure whether to interpret as laughter or derision. 'Me, no, sir. I is jes a driver for police here. I is no detective, sir. No, sir.'

'But still, you might know something about what happened. You might have overheard the detectives talking about it. Or as a driver, you may have heard other people talking about it. Who knows, you may even get to hear things that a detective wouldn't.'

'Nah, I don't know nuttin' 'bout it, sir. Nuttin' at all. Mister King, he say that you come here t' find out what happen to Sir John. I don' know nuttin' else. 'Ceptin' that it was chilluns that finded him yesterday. One o' the other drivers, he tell me this morning. Horrid it is, sir. Poor chilluns, them findin' him like that. They mussa bin scared-scared.'

'And they called the police, did they? The children, I mean?'

'I dunno, boss. I guess them did too.'

Victor did not seem to want to expand on the information he had given, and Burton did not want to push him too much. Instead, he settled back as best he could with Victor's driving and watched the scenery changing as they approached the centre of Nassau.

To the right of the main road on which they were approaching Nassau, sporadic settlements gradually gave way to clusters of houses in pastel art-deco colours. A huge flamingo-shaped advertising board implored passers-by to visit the zoo and botanic gardens; and an old fort, which looked remarkably intact, stood proudly atop a small hill. Beneath the fort, a wooden clubhouse, painted white and adorned with advertisements for imported beer, looked out over a deserted cricket pitch, its centre a square patch of roped-off grass slightly less brown than the surrounding turf. Behind the clubhouse, in chain-link nets, small children practised with makeshift bats and tennis balls and upturned crates for stumps. Despite its present emptiness, Burton could easily imagine the ground bustling with enthusiastic cricket fans.

On the left, expanses of beach lined with palm trees flashed past, and in the sea beyond he saw a large, brightly lit cruise ship that was negotiating its way out of Nassau. If they were able to compare experiences later, the passengers would undoubtedly hold a rather different view of Nassau after their brief visit to the busy, tourist-trap laden commercial centres than he would after a somewhat longer stay investigating the death of a diplomat. If a neutral observer were to read his thoughts of the city, and those of the cruise-ship passengers, Burton doubted they would even know that they were writing about the same place.

Burton's reverie was broken by a sharp right turn, followed by a sharp left, and then another left as Victor steered the Ford into the driveway of the hotel.

'British Colonial, boss, very nice,' said Victor, as they pulled up outside the steps of the hotel. Burton grasped the door handle and opened the door, grateful as it was held open by a porter whilst he disentangled himself from the decorative seatbelt and climbed out of the car. He slung his small rucksack over his shoulder and walked around to the boot of the car, where Victor was already handing his suitcase to the porter.

'Thanks, Victor. Perhaps I'll see you tomorrow at the police station.' He handed Victor a few Bahamian dollars.

'Sho' thing, boss.' Victor's face cracked once again into a wide smile, showing his crooked white teeth. As Burton turned to walk into the hotel, he heard tyres protesting in vain as Victor started his journey home.

3

It was already half past nine by the time Burton had found the Bay Street police station and been directed by a surly desk officer to Chester King's office. He went to push open the door, then thought better of it and knocked. He heard a jovial 'Enter!' and walked into the room.

Chester King's office bore little resemblance to Anthony Reardon's, and Chester King bore little resemblance to Anthony Reardon. King sprang up as Burton entered the room, and rushed over to meet him with an outstretched hand. King was a tall native Bahamian, Burton guessed about six foot two, four inches taller than himself, who looked to be in his mid-thirties. His lean frame was smartly covered in a well-cut pale-blue linen suit, starched white shirt and pastel pink tie. His grip was dry and firm, and accompanied by an unexpected but friendly slap on the back. As quickly as he had got up to meet Burton, he retreated behind his desk and picked up a paper document wallet. He then gestured to a small coffee table where two very battered and very different armchairs were positioned.

'Mr Burton, Michael, please have a seat. Did you have a good flight over? I expect you just missed the bad weather?'

It was the standard question, which Burton had expected, but somehow King gave the impression that he genuinely wanted to know the answer. Burton replied non-committally, not wanting to bore King with details of the fact that he had, actually, just caught the bad weather and consequently had been on the receiving end of a rollercoaster ride of a flight over. An almost imperceptible pause halted the conversation momentarily before King replied, and Burton sensed that King was ever so slightly disappointed that he hadn't answered the question properly.

'Would you like coffee, Michael? I can call you Michael, by the way? Or is it Mike? Please, call me Chester.'

'Yes, and yes, Michael is fine.'

King leapt up from the armchair in which he had just sat down and hurried out of the room, leaving the paper document file on the coffee table. Burton sat back and glanced around the office. Behind King's battered, paper-strewn desk was an old office stool, and behind that was a single, large, wooden-framed window, opened as far as possible. Badly fitting slatted wooden blinds covered the window although, as the room was more or less north-facing, there was little direct sunlight, and the slats were wide apart and flat, offering little hindrance to the view outside. The blinds moved gently backwards and forwards with the warm light breeze, and every now and then clunked against the wall. The temperature inside was almost identical to that outside, the air just as hot and just as humid. The police station was close to Nassau harbour, and the interior smelt of the harbour, of sea air and diesel fumes. King's office was on the 'good' side, looking out onto the toll bridge to Paradise Island on Potter's Cay, although that meant that the soundtrack of the busy port was an ever-present character-istic of the room, an unruly cacophony of horns, engines and gulls.

On the wall above the coffee table at which he was sitting was mounted some kind of policing certificate, yellowed by the sun and bounded by a thin black frame. A largish plant, which Burton did not recognize, stood in the corner next to the window. On the opposite wall of the office was a wooden bookshelf, over-flowing with books of all different shapes and sizes. With some surprise Burton recognized the binding of the *All England Law Reports*, a series of which covered three shelves. He stood up and walked over to peruse the shelves in more detail. Two of them contained the Bahamian Statute Law and the complementary Acts and Statutory Instruments, along with editions of explanatory notes, whilst a further two were bursting with English, American and Bahamian text books on criminal law, criminology and forensic science, and a series of newish-looking books on neuro-linguistic programming. Four dog-eared volumes of Blackstone's *Police Manual* and a couple of tomes on civil rights and procedural criminal law completed a collection Burton would have sooner imagined finding in a law professor's study than a detective's.

Seeing a coat stand behind the door, adorned only by several misshapen wire hangers, Burton removed his lightweight sports jacket, inserted one of the hangers and hung it up. It was still early, but the heat was already building up.

Returning to his armchair, Burton opened the paper file that King had left on the coffee table. It was fairly meagre pickings, containing a few pieces of paper and little else. There were three reports containing statements from eye witnesses, and a couple of printouts from a police database. He heard footsteps outside the door, gradually becoming louder, and he quickly inserted the papers back into the wallet and sat back in his chair.

The door opened and King entered, carrying a tray on which two steaming cups of coffee counterbalanced a jug of cream and a bowl of raw sugar. King closed the door deftly with his foot and set the tray on the coffee table. After a few seconds, Burton's nostrils detected the slightly acrid smell of fresh coffee.

'So, Michael, where should we begin? I assume that you already have a reasonable idea about what happened here yesterday — I gather the High Commissioner, Mr Reardon, was fully briefed. However, I think we may have information new to you, so I will summarize what we know thus far.'

King gestured towards one of the cups of coffee and picked up the other one. Burton picked it up, ignoring the cream and sugar and, after blowing gently across the surface, sipped carefully so as not to burn his tongue. The coffee was strong and harsh and sharp. He had been expecting bad coffee in dirty mugs, and was surprised by the obviously freshly brewed coffee, served in matching cups and saucers.

'Sir John's wife, Melissa, reported him missing on Monday evening. There's not all that much we can do when we first receive a missing person notification. Some people aren't missing at all; they've just forgotten to tell their loved ones that they're going to be away. Others leave of their own accord, and want neither to be found nor to return. Others still simply have had a night on the town, and are lying in an alleyway somewhere sleeping it off.

'Anyway, I spoke to Melissa yesterday morning, and learned that Sir John was still missing, so I sent some uniformed officers to the scene to have a look around. They saw several regular beachcombers known to them, and asked them if they had been there the day before. Some had, some hadn't. Anyway, they were able to find three witnesses who were able to positively identify Sir John walking on the beach. Two of them put the time at six o'clock, one at half past. So we can safely assume that it was around that time.

'According to the people who saw him, Sir John was walking calmly and did not appear agitated or flustered in any way. We know that he removed his shirt, sunglasses and sandals before entering the water; one of the witnesses, who happened to be looking out along the beach mentioned this, and one of our officers found them yesterday on the beach where he disappeared. They must have been there all night without anyone disturbing them. They weren't found straight away, though, as the beach was full of people and there were lots of piles of people's clothes and other belongings lying around. When the sun started to set and people started to shift along to the sunny half of the beach, or go home, one of the officers in the area noticed the clothes and, knowing of the missing person, brought them in. The clothes match the description of those Sir John was last seen wearing given to us by the witnesses, and the sunglasses are of the same make as Sir John's, which Melissa confirmed for us by phone. But we will give her a chance to look at all of the items we found, to make sure that they are indeed Sir John's. I didn't want to trouble her when she came in to identify the body.

'Nobody saw Sir John go into the sea — apparently he walked a considerable distance along the shore, where the beach becomes shaded slightly earlier and consequently nobody was sitting, before entering the water. The sun sets completely at around seven o'clock this time of year, so this seems to corroborate the times that the witnesses claim to have seen Sir John.

'His body was found late this morning. It washed up on the shore not far from where we think he entered the water. The body is currently being examined by the coroner, but initial visual reports suggest that there was no trauma of any kind, and we suspect that he drowned.' King looked up at Burton. 'But anyway, we'll have to wait for the coroner's report before we know for certain — '

Burton broke in, 'Who found the body? Victor seemed to think that it was found by some children on the beach.'

'Ah, so you've been discussing the case with Victor? Well, yes, the body was found by children, but not on the beach. They were playing games in one of the rocky enclaves near the beach. One of them nearly tripped over the body. Screamed blue murder until the parents turned up, and they called the police.'

Burton nodded. 'So we don't know when the body washed up? It could have been there all night, like his clothes on the beach?'

'It's possible, I suppose. Generally, the tides tend to bring objects back in at certain times. But the body could have been there for hours; we have no real way of telling. We would have a much better idea had the body washed up on the beach, as it would most likely have been spotted straight away, particularly at this time of year. I don't know how much importance we should attach to this though. The coroner should be able to tell us more about how long the body has been submerged, and we know what time he entered the water.'

'True.'

King continued, 'Anyway, the way I see it, there are really only three possibilities. First: it was a tragic accident. Sir John could have drowned whilst swimming, either because of a misjudgement or a medical condition of some kind, a heart attack or a seizure. It could conceivably also have been contact with a marine animal, although if this were the case we would expect to find some evidence of a bite or sting. He certainly didn't look like he had been mauled by a shark, or bitten by any other large predator. It's more difficult to identify stings from smaller aquatic life, but the coroner will, of course, check for these, although dangerous marine life is not abundant close to these shores, so I think it's unlikely.

'Second: Sir John deliberately drowned himself. There was no note, but we all know that suicides don't always leave notes. Third: he was murdered. What do you think?'

Burton thought for a second. 'How do you think he could have been murdered?'

King sat back and took a long sip of coffee. He looked up at the ceiling for several seconds as if lost in thought. Burton wondered what King's books on neuro-linguistic programming would have made of this reaction — he had read a couple of articles on the subject and knew practitioners read all sorts of meanings into actions and eye movements, but was himself unsure whether to accept it as proven science or not. Finally, King sighed deeply, as if unwilling to seriously consider the possibility that Sir John's death had been murder, and responded.

'Well, there are a couple of possibilities. He could have been held under by a stronger swimmer. Although if this were the case, we would be likely to find bruising on the body. I had a cursory look at the body earlier on, and I have to say that no bruising was immediately apparent. That said, I'm in no way a medical expert, so we'll have to wait for the autopsy to know this for certain. But when we get the results, if there's no sign of physical trauma, we'll at least be in a position to rule this out. And we'll also know if he had any kind of medical condition that we do not already know about.

'It's also conceivable he was given some kind of poison that compromised his ability to swim. It would probably have to be after he entered the water, though, as he managed to walk all the way to the spot where he went in without any problems. I suppose it's possible that he could have been scratched with something containing poison whilst swimming, but again I think it's unlikely.

'Anyway, I've arranged for us to go and visit Melissa late this afternoon. We're expected at around four o'clock. I suggest you get up to speed on the information we have.' He gestured towards the document wallet on the coffee table. 'We have very little in the way of paperwork, which means you won't be too busy. In the meantime, I have to finish typing up a report.'

King picked up his coffee and moved over to his desk, seating himself with another sigh. He didn't strike Burton as the sort of man who would relish paperwork. Burton opened the document wallet and took out the five documents that he had already glimpsed earlier. He looked through them quickly and decided to read the police reports first.

The first police report was on Sir John's wife, Melissa. It was brief, consisting of two pages of A4, stapled together, and contained very little of interest. From the content and layout, Burton suspected it was a report that had been collated by the Foreign Office when Melissa had married Sir John, and had been given to the Bahamian police when she and her husband moved to the Bahamas.

From the report, he was able to glean that Melissa was the product of a mixed marriage between a Spanish man and his English wife, but had lived a good part of her life on the move. Her father had worked for a large hotel group, and had held executive positions in different countries for many years. Throughout this period, Melissa had been educated at various international schools, and had achieved strong grades in almost all subjects in her baccalaureate. Despite having chosen to concentrate on languages and social sciences, she had been awarded high marks in both chemistry and biology. Burton noted with relief that her scores in mathematics and physics were somewhat lower.

Following a year spent travelling around South-East Asia and South America, Melissa had been accepted into Oxford to study law and modern languages. Burton looked across at the stacks of law books on King's shelves and pondered the fact that both he and Melissa seemed to have more than a passing interest in the law. Returning to Melissa's file, he saw that she had been involved in some political debating society, and had played lacrosse for the Ladies 2nd team, probably no mean feat at Oxford. After completing her university studies, she had worked for a multinational company as a press officer. Presumably she had left her job when she met Sir John and decided to join him in the Caribbean. There was little else mentioned.

Burton sat back and considered what he

had read. He was used to reading reports on people before he met them, but normally so that he was able to recognize foreign diplomats at a meeting or a reception. He would see a photograph and some basic information about where they came from and whom they were representing, and perhaps a little cursory information about their interests, political or personal. Now, it was different. He had no photograph, but tried to build up a picture in his mind about what Melissa looked like. His initial guesses had already been proved completely wrong: having met the man, he had imagined that Sir John would have been married to an upper class, public-school educated, stiff but handsome middle-aged Englishwoman. Now he realized that Melissa was from very different stock and, obviously, much younger than Sir John had been; in fact, her age was far closer to Burton's than to her husband's. His original neutral image was now replaced by that of a buxom blonde gold-digger but, given his previous error, he decided to reserve judgement until he met her.

After draining his cup of the remaining now-lukewarm coffee, Burton shifted on his chair to gain a view out of the window onto Paradise Island. He became aware of a monotonous staccato tick from King's keyboard as the detective raced through what

Burton could only imagine would be a novel-length report.

Burton picked up Sir John's file. It was a lot bulkier than Melissa's but still not particularly comprehensive. Burton assumed that the Foreign Office would be in possession of a far more complete file, given that the man had worked for the British Government for a long time. He remembered the interviews he had gone through as part of the vetting process, and could readily imagine that Sir John had also been through his fair share of these. He made a mental note to speak to Reardon about it; it would do no harm to look at a more detailed dossier on the man whose life had so abruptly ended. Whether it would provide any additional clues, Burton did not know.

Apart from Sir John's height and age, Burton learned that he had been educated at Harrow and Cambridge, where he had studied philosophy, politics and economics. Another Oxbridge graduate, he mused to himself. Sir John had clearly been something of a high-flier academically, and had entered the Foreign Office immediately after graduation. There followed a list of his placements, in Europe, Asia and finally the Caribbean. Almost all of the information about Sir John was consistent with the well-bred, refined, serious career diplomat; it was therefore doubly shocking for Burton to read a brief report in which a recent incident was detailed, which concerned Sir John being stopped by two officers in a patrol car for dangerous driving and then being breathalysed on the spot, and subsequently found to be over three times the legal limit. Drink driving was a relatively new offence in the Bahamas and, as yet, was not pursued as diligently as in some other countries. The incident had occurred whilst he was still High Commissioner of Jamaica, just after he had found a house in the Bahamas but before he had retired there permanently, so presumably at that stage Sir John would have still had diplomatic privileges of some kind.

The upshot of the report was that one of the policemen had driven Sir John's car home, and then the two officers had written a report concluding that no action should be taken. The officers' report was folded and stapled into the file. Burton found a passage in the report that interested him:

We explained the situation to High Commissioner Little, and made clear to him that he was in no fit state to continue his journey. I advised the High Commissioner that I would drive him home in his own car, and Sergeant Rice would follow me in the patrol car. Once we started to drive, High Commissioner Little became very emotional and started to cry. He begged me not to say anything as it would destroy his career and his life would not be worth living. He repeated that his reputation would be tarnished and that this was the worst thing that could happen to him. I tried to calm him as best I could, and repeatedly said to him that we were not going to pursue the matter further (we had already told him this several times, but he appeared not to take it in). When he heard this, he would thank me profusely and a few minutes later he would start crying again, and beg me not to say anything. When we arrived at Sir John's house, I spoke to Sergeant Rice as I was concerned that Sir John may try to hurt himself. Although we would have preferred to leave him to enter his house on his own, to spare him any possible embarrassment, we were concerned enough to ring the bell and see if anyone could help him. The door was answered by his wife, and we explained the situation to her. She was very grateful to us, and told us we had done the right thing.

Apart from the drinking incident, there was little information in the report about Sir John that Burton did not already know. He sat back and gazed across the water at the island on the horizon. He wondered about the case, about Sir John's death. Was there really anything untoward about the circumstances of the retired diplomat's death, or was it simply an accident, as it seemed?

Judging from the police report, it was certainly not unthinkable that Sir John had taken his own life. This was, of course, completely contrary to the impression he had been given by Reardon. But the report was written about an inebriated man who had just been caught breaking the law; like a schoolboy busted for flouting the rules, and worried about what his parents would say, he had perhaps overreacted in an effort to get himself off the hook. Burton wondered what Sir John had felt the day afterwards. Had he cowered in shame at his breakdown in front of the officer, or was he happy he had acted with the right amount of contrition under the circumstances? Or maybe he hadn't been able to remember what had happened. In any event, the episode seemed out of character with the picture Reardon had painted. And Reardon had known the man for years, and was, in Burton's experience at least, an astute judge of character.

He tried to imagine Sir John, whom he had met a couple of times, begging a police officer not to arrest him, but was having difficulty doing so. The man he had met at functions had always seemed a boisterous, outgoing man. He had been drinking on these occasions, and the alcohol had only fuelled his extroversion. Burton suspected, however, that Sir John was far quieter and more introverted than he made out. Many of the members of the diplomatic service managed to put on a mask and portray themselves as more open and outgoing than their real persona would suggest. If this was also a trait of Sir John, then he might have used alcohol to help him slip into character: the drink would free him from inhibitions which might otherwise burden him at such a time. He wondered if Sir John had been an alcoholic.

Burton closed the file in front of him and racked his brain in an effort to align all the facts and come to the logical conclusion. But there were too many unknowns, too many facts that might not be facts, too many possibilities that were still mere possibilities.

Burton picked up the three witness statements and sifted through them. All three seemed to corroborate each other, which in itself seemed suspicious to Burton. Quite often, if you ask three people about the same event, which you know all have witnessed, you get three different versions about what happened. Different people tend to notice different things, some accurately retain features or the colour or style of clothes, others actions or character traits. He'd always assumed that this was a consequence of upbringing, interests and profession. A hairdresser would probably notice what hairstyle a person had, whilst a fashion guru would be able to remember the clothes a person was wearing. But these three witnesses remembered almost exactly the same version of events; the only discrepancy was a half hour in one witness's statement. It was almost as if Sir John had taken pains to make sure he was spotted, recognized and remembered. Or perhaps the locals here were particularly observant, he mused.

Burton suddenly became aware that the ticking had stopped. He looked up at King. The detective, who had been watching him, smiled.

'Come on, let's get some lunch. Then we'll head out to Sir John's place.'

4

Sir John's house, located at Old Fort Bay, was a large white Mediterranean-style affair, with shallow arches and terracotta roof and floor tiles. The property was fenced, but the black wrought iron front gates had been left open. In front of the fence was a row of palm trees providing shade to a narrow strip of thick, dark-green, well-watered St Augustine grass. A short drive led up to a small square with enough room to park three or four cars, although at present there was only one — a white convertible Fiat with its roof down, displaying a weathered black leather interior. In the corner of the square was a bright red town bicycle with a shopping basket over the handlebars.

Burton climbed out of King's air-conditioned Ford and was immediately hit by a wave of unrelenting heat. Almost instantaneously, he felt the sweat ready to break on his face and under his arms, and brazenly tried to ignore it. He had been about to grab his jacket from the back seat of the car, but now decided against it. Jacketless, and trying to adjust his tie, feeling on its smooth fabric the griminess of sweat hampering his fingers, he looked across at King, who was slipping his jacket on. He looked composed, cool, untroubled by the wet heat.

There was a steady breeze gently blowing in from the sea, but it did little to mitigate the temperature. Burton could hear a gentle rustling, a constant cadence coming and fading, the sound of the sea breaking gently on the rocks. But the sea was not visible from the driveway; the house was an extended L-shape, one part of which divided them from the beach.

Together they walked towards the front door, a simple but solid chunk of wood emblazoned with black wrought-iron bolts. King ran the bell, which chimed once, loudly, and stood back from the door, hands clasped behind his back. Seconds later, they heard various noises from inside the house, implying that the door was soon to be opened. Burton glanced at his watch; they were slightly early.

A Bahamian woman dressed in jeans and a light floral blouse opened the door. Burton guessed she was about fifty. She had a friendly, open face, topped with grey, curly hair, and a smile which broadened when she saw them.

'Mr King?'

King nodded. 'Yes, ma'am.'

'Please come in. My name is Sarah. Lady Little is outside. Please come through.'

They followed Sarah into the house, entering a tiled hallway, passing a wooden staircase leading upstairs, and going through to a tiled sitting room. The indoor tiles were white, not terracotta, and they gave the interior a cool feel. They headed straight through the sitting room and exited through wooden French windows onto a terracotta-tiled terrace. The terrace looked out over a small fresh-water swimming pool carved into the rocky ground. Sarah gestured along a brick path leading towards the shore, but she remained standing on the terrace.

'Lady Little is on the beach. Please follow the path. The gate should be open.'

They followed the path through a lush garden, carpeted with the same rich St Augustine grass that lined the entrance, which contrasted vividly with the sun-parched landscape that had flashed along on the inland side of the car as they drove from Nassau along the coastal road. Clearly there was no shortage of water inside this gated community. The brick path ended in an open iron gate, which in turn led onto a short wooden staircase descending towards the beach. From the top, they could see an expanse of deserted white sand, in the middle of which lay a figure on a red and white striped beach towel.

As they reached the bottom of the stairs, they were met by Melissa Little, who had donned a white silk kimono with a blue motif over the black bikini Burton had seen from above, and now extended her hand in greeting to the two men. With no shoes on, she stood about three inches shorter than Burton, and she carried herself well, as if taught in a Swiss finishing school to balance a book on her head whilst standing or walking. She had long, dark hair with subtle red-gold highlights, although whether these were induced by the sun or a talented hairdresser, Burton was unable to tell. The visible parts of her skin were dark and tanned and unblemished, and she looked cool and composed, although high on her forehead a few drops of perspiration glistened. He couldn't blame her for that, Burton thought. He himself felt like someone had thrown a bucket of warm water over his back. He could feel drops of sweat running continually down his sides, leaving cool tracks that terminated in wet patches by his waistband. He hoped vainly that there were no wet patches on his shirt under his armpits, but wasn't about to lift his arms and check. He looked across at

King. The detective did not even look warm.

'Good afternoon, gentlemen. I'm Melissa Little, Sir John's wife.'

'Good afternoon, madam,' responded King. 'My name is Chester King and this is Michael Burton. I'm a detective with the Bahamian Police Force, and Mr Burton is a liaison officer from the British High Commission.'

Lady Little looked across at Burton. Her eyes were inscrutable behind retro-fashionable, very large and very dark glasses. 'Did you know my husband well?'

Burton had been afraid of this question. 'No, I'm afraid I didn't have that honour. I did meet Sir John on occasions, though. He seemed a good man.'

'He was.'

King broke the awkward silence that followed. 'I think we may be slightly early, madam. Please accept our apologies for this. I hope we didn't catch you unawares.'

'No, not at all. I didn't know what to do whilst I was waiting for you, so I came out here to lie on the beach. I like to be out here alone sometimes. It's peaceful, and I enjoy just listening to the ocean.' She paused, looking from King to Burton and back again. 'I'm sure I come across as cold and heartless, having just lost my husband, but I don't know what to do. Any form of routine in my life has stopped, and I find myself having to deal with things I never used to handle because John did them, as well as things which now have to be done because of his death.'

There was an undertone of bitterness in her voice.

King responded, 'Of course, madam. I understand.'

'I'm so very upset, but I don't know how to act,' Melissa said, passion suddenly flooding into her voice. 'I have never experienced the loss of someone so close. I feel so empty. So alone.'

She removed the sunglasses awkwardly, exposing big, dark-brown eyes, which were watery and rimmed with red. Without the shades, she squinted against the sun, causing tears to well out of her eyes and cascade downwards, leaving glistening trails down her cheeks.

Burton scrutinized the girl, trying to decide if she was acting or if she was genuinely the grieving widow she seemed. He was unable to make up his mind at this stage, but did get as far as to admit that, if she was acting, she was very good at it. He desperately wanted to comfort the beautiful, hurting woman, but did not really know what to do, or how to do it.

'I'm very sorry, madam.' A tissue magically

appeared in King's hand, and he passed it to her. She accepted it gratefully and dabbed her eyes.

'Thank you. Shall we go back inside?'

Without waiting for an answer, Melissa stood up and picked up her beach bag, a small reed basket, in which a book and a few other small items were placed. Burton offered to carry the bag, but she refused in a dignified yet grateful manner. She led the way up the wooden stairs and back towards the house.

★　★　★

'Would either of you like something to drink?'

They had been shown into the kitchen, a modern minimalist room which Burton couldn't decide whether he liked or not. Huge windows allowed light to flood in, giving the impression of warmth, but, thankfully, the room was cold, chilled by an efficient air-conditioning system. Despite the air-conditioning, a faint smell of coffee lingered in the air. Burton looked around and saw a coffee machine, its glass jug containing the remnants of the morning coffee. In the middle of the kitchen was an island, topped with small ceramic tiles, part of which contained a fridge. Melissa rummaged in it for a second and emerged with a silver bucket of ice. From a cupboard on the wall, she retrieved three glasses and a bottle of Scotch.

'No, thank you, madam,' responded King.

Melissa's questioning gaze settled on Burton. 'Water, please,' he offered tentatively.

Melissa picked up some tongs and deftly threw a couple of ice cubes into two of the glasses. She returned to the fridge and brought out a bottle of mineral water. She filled one glass with a generous helping of Scotch, and then topped them both up with water. She handed the water to Burton, a light frost of condensation already coating the glass.

Burton sipped the icy water. He suddenly felt cold: the cooled liquid in his throat, the air-conditioned room, and his damp shirt, contrived to take him from one extreme to the other. He struggled to suppress an involuntary shiver.

'Come on, let's move to the sitting room,' said Melissa, looking at Burton. 'It's warmer and more comfortable there.'

Burton followed Melissa into the sitting room, with King bringing up the rear. Once they were all seated on a light coloured suite, King cleared his throat and asked Melissa officiously if she would mind if they asked her some questions. At this stage it seemed to

Burton tardy to say the least, but he guessed it was some kind of required procedure. She acquiesced silently.

From the inside pocket of his jacket, King took out a brown paper bag folded flat. He opened it carefully and removed a number of photographs, checking their order quickly before handing them over.

'Lady Little, can you identify the items on these photographs please? We believe that they are your husband's personal effects, but we'd like you to confirm this if possible.'

Melissa looked at the photographs, her eyes resting on each image of an object placed in the middle of a white plastic sheet. At each, she nodded glumly.

'Thank you.' King looked apologetic, as though he did not want to ask more questions, did not want to stay longer, did not want to pry into her life, but was compelled to do so. He took the photographs back from Melissa and, as carefully as he had opened the paper bag, re-inserted the photos and placed it back in his pocket. His hand reappeared with a leather-bound notebook and a silver-coloured fountain pen. 'Can you describe, in a general sense and in your own words, what sort of a man Sir John was?'

'Of course. He was a very committed man. Driven, ambitious and, I think, conscientious.

64

He took his work very seriously, and I believe he was very good at his job. In any event, his career took up a lot of his time. It was difficult for him after he retired. I think he missed his work, the organizing and the responsibilities, greatly. Many of our friends were ex-pats involved in a similar line of work, or who socialized in the same diplomatic circles.' Melissa spoke with sadness in her voice, remembering the man with whom she had shared the last few years.

'I found it interesting to accompany him to functions, or on official trips. There were many: his position as High Commissioner in Kingston, looking after British interests, as he put it, meant that we were always travelling to different places, although almost exclusively in the Caribbean. Obviously, I only accompanied him on certain trips, and he travelled a lot without me. I think that is one reason why his job took up a lot of his time: he was often away, even if only for a day or so, and this meant that we saw each other far less than other couples do. And it's not really the same going to a dinner party with your husband if he's the High Commissioner and expected to entertain foreign dignitaries rather than chat to his wife.' Again, Burton felt he detected a trace of bitterness creeping into her voice.

'He was still very busy towards the end of

his career — when we first moved here, he would travel back to Jamaica for a couple of days at a time. I wouldn't normally accompany him. He always said he liked to work intensively when he was there, and then rest when he returned.'

'And after his retirement?' prompted Burton.

'He retired two years ago, although we moved from Kingston to Nassau almost half a year before that. It was difficult for him, but also good. It gave him time to reduce his activities and prepare for retirement. I don't think he minded the lighter workload. In fact he quite enjoyed it. Not having to spend time on things of lesser importance, and just concentrating on those larger projects in which he had been involved before. And I believe he spent a lot of his time showing his successor the ropes. Your Mr Reardon.' She looked at Burton as she said this, and he nodded.

'Not working at all was, however, a different story. He did not seem to be that excited about the prospect of not having to work, and I was concerned that he would be bored without anything to do. Many people take up part-time consultancy positions when they retire, but John didn't seem interested in doing that. It was almost as if he felt that it was all or nothing, and that a part-time advisory role was little better than nothing. However, he did not seem to be overly depressed, or anything like that. No, I think — 'bored' is the right word. He didn't really know what to do with his time.'

'What were your husband's hobbies, Lady Little?' Burton asked. 'Did he swim often?'

'Yes, fairly often. Since his retirement, he swam more often: normally at least once or twice a day. He would sometimes swim lengths of the pool but, as you've most likely seen, it's fairly small, so more often than not he would swim in the ocean. He never used to go all that far out though — he normally swam along the beach and then walked back. Or other times, he would walk some way down the beach and then swim back. John used to do this quite often in the evenings. He would walk along the beach in the last of the sunshine, and then swim back. The water stays warm long after the sun has set.

'Apart from swimming, my husband used to read a lot, and he played bridge and chess. He used to play bridge with some neighbours of ours in the community, and I would sometimes play as his partner. It wasn't really my game, though. I enjoy cards, but I find the bidding conventions confusing, and John played the game quite seriously. I think he really preferred to play with a more experienced partner, although he was always very nice about playing with me if I wanted to go with him.

'He used to play chess against an old colleague of his in the High Commission — I'm not sure who it was. They used to set up boards at home and send their moves to each other by e-mail, a sort of variant on the old telegraph chess. They have on-line chess games now, where you can play against other people in real time, but I'm afraid John's computer skills weren't up to that, or his colleague's for that matter, so they just sent e-mails.'

'Anything else?'

'Well, he used to listen to opera quite a bit. Normally in his study — he had a hi-fi system there — but sometimes in the sitting room, on the home cinema system. He preferred the study — always maintained that the acoustics were better and that listening to opera in a room with poor acoustics didn't do it justice. Had the speakers positioned to the exact inch and everything. But other than that, he didn't really have any other interests.'

'Thank you. What was Sir John's general health like? Did you notice if he was unwell recently? And did he take any medication?' King asked.

'For his age, his health was very good. He used to visit the doctor every six months for a check-up, but I don't think they found anything wrong. If they did, he didn't tell me about it. He didn't take any medication, although he took lots of vitamin pills and supplements. The bottles are all in the kitchen, if you want to look at them. They're in the cupboard next to the cooker.'

King jotted something down in his notebook. 'And can you think of anybody who might have had a grudge against him? It could be anyone at all. A colleague who didn't like him, a business partner or competitor who felt hard done by, or anybody else with an old score to settle.'

Melissa's face clouded over. She looked confused and angry. 'Why do you ask? Surely you don't think he was murdered. How? Why?'

'I'm sorry, madam. It's merely a standard question in a case like this. We don't yet have any real idea exactly what happened to Sir John, whether he had an attack, or why he drowned. We will know more when we have the results of the autopsy, but I'd like to ask these questions now so we don't have to come back and bother you again. Of course, if the results of the autopsy demonstrate a natural death with no contrary indications, we won't need to pursue any leads you may be able to give us now.'

'Well, all right. I'll answer your question: I don't think anyone was out to hurt him. No, I can't think of anyone at all. We travelled a lot in the area for his job, and he had probably more acquaintances than the average man, but fewer close friends. I had the impression that he was both well liked and well respected by almost everybody we met, both colleagues and representatives of the foreign states he dealt with. And as for business interests, John was definitely a dyed-in-the-wool career civil servant, and had no time for other business dealings.'

'Would you describe him as suicidal? Or, more accurately, would you say that he ever had suicidal tendencies? For example, in periods when he was particularly stressed, or under a lot of pressure,' Burton followed up. Out of the corner of his eye, he noticed a grimace pass over King's face as he said this.

Melissa reacted fiercely. 'What? Now you think he killed himself? How stupid are you people?' She almost screamed, barely in control of herself. All at the same time she managed to look angry, incredulous and patronizing, as if she felt sorry for the poor investigators who had no idea. 'Why would he kill himself? Why?'

'Madam, we are merely exploring all possibilities.' King tried to defuse the situation. 'We must not rule anything out at this stage, not until we know what really happened. I have no doubt that Sir John drowned accidentally, but we are duty-bound to try to confirm this. As your husband was an ex-diplomat, there is a great deal of interest in his death. I apologize for the intrusion in what I know is a very difficult time for you.'

Melissa nodded sadly, calmer now. 'I understand. It's just . . . he . . . he . . . was here the day before yesterday. He didn't seem desperate or crazed. As I said before, he didn't seem depressed at all, only as if he had too much time on his hands. And he seemed to handle stress and pressure very well — I think it was required in his line of work. No, I don't understand why he would have killed himself. Perhaps he didn't want to be with me.'

'I'm sure there's another explanation. We will need to investigate this further. I think it would be a good idea for us to leave you alone now, although we might need to contact you again if we have more questions. May we look around the house? It might be helpful for us to see Sir John's study. You don't have to allow this of course, and you can accompany us if you prefer.'

'No, go ahead. John's study is back through the hall, and the bedroom is upstairs. Ask Sarah if you need any help.' Melissa sounded relieved. She took a long sip of her Scotch and water, which until now had remained untouched.

'Thank you. If I may, just one more question: has anything in Sir John's study been moved or touched? Or is everything the way that he left it?'

'Well, I've not touched anything at all. Again, I think you should check with Sarah, as she may have moved something, but I don't think so.'

'Thank you again. We'll let you know if we find anything.'

King moved towards the door and Burton followed him, leaving Melissa sitting on the sofa clutching her drink.

★ ★ ★

The study had a magnificent view over the ocean. Burton couldn't imagine being able to work there without being constantly distracted by the beautiful seascape framed by the patio doors. Sir John, however, had clearly not had this problem, as he had placed his desk so that he would be facing the window when sitting behind it. There were no curtains, but a quick glance outside confirmed that wooden shutters could be closed to darken the room. The shutters were held open by black, wrought-iron fasteners.

The desk was sparsely furnished with a closed laptop, a lamp, a book, a framed photograph of Melissa and a chessboard. Behind the desk was a comfortable, dark-green leather swivel chair.

Both sides of the study were lined with bookshelves, which were filled with a variety of books, fiction and non-fiction, old and new. Next to the door was a hi-fi system on what looked like a custom-built cabinet, with a couple of shelves of CDs. They were mostly operas, with a couple of what Burton would reluctantly have referred to as 'easy listening' albums.

He walked over to the desk. From the look of it, Sir John had been reading a political satire. A leather bookmark protruded about three-quarters of the way through. The chessboard was in the centre of the desk, and the pieces on the board indicated that a new game had been started not long ago. Sir John appeared to have been a couple of moves in to what looked like an English opening. An unusual opening, Burton thought to himself.

'What are we looking for?' he asked King.

'Well, anything out of the ordinary. But I don't think we're going to find anything here, to be honest. If Sir John had left a note, Melissa would have already found it. She probably would have noticed anything out of place as well.'

'We could have a look at the laptop.'

'We could, but we need a reason to do so, and I don't think we have one at the moment. We could ask Lady Little to give us permission to look at it, and she would probably let us, but we still don't really know whether it was a simple accidental drowning, or not. We can always come back if necessary.'

They walked out of the study and across the hall to the stairs. Upstairs there were three bedrooms and a separate bathroom, none of which contained anything to grab their attention.

Back downstairs, Melissa was sitting where they had left her. The glass in front of her was empty. She stood as the men entered. 'Have you seen enough, gentlemen?'

'Yes, thank you, madam. We've seen all we need to see, and we'll leave you alone now. I can assure you that this case will be our highest priority. As soon as we know more, we will let you know at once. Can we help you with anything before we leave?'

King looked worried, but Melissa waved

his concerns away. 'No, thank you. I just want to be alone right now.'

'Right you are, madam. We'll be in touch.' King gestured for Burton to leave and followed him into the hall, where Sarah showed them to the front door.

5

'Fancy a drink?' King asked as they reached the outskirts of Nassau. Burton immediately thought of Melissa, who had asked the same question. He was about to respond in the affirmative when he noticed that King, without waiting for an answer, had ignored the turning for the police station and was carrying on towards the centre of Nassau. Burton held his tongue, preferring to let King wonder whether he was a willing or unwilling drinking partner. To Burton's unpractised eye, the traffic seemed unusually light for the centre of Nassau, which he had only previously experienced through clouds of exhaust fumes. He caught a brief glimpse of his hotel flashing past on the left as he tried to get his bearings before they passed the New Providence side of the bridge over to Paradise Island. Shortly afterwards, King turned into the harbour area and onto a dusty car-park lined with scrubby borders of yellow-green grass and the occasional boulder.

Alongside the bridge, Burton could see the road leading down towards Potter's Cay which was lined with conch stands and seafood stalls and ramshackle bars crowded with people sitting on rickety bar stools. All along the street, haphazardly placed beer billboards protruded unevenly and fought to grab Burton's attention, which was instead drawn by an out-of-place advertisement for expensive jewellery. From the general direction of the heaving conch joint, from which bustling crowds of people spilled out clutching their paper-wrapped cracked conch, came the lively cacophony of native voices, raised not in anger but in excitement. The typical lingering dock smell was losing a valiant battle against the pungent scent of fresh fish as it was being sold, prepared and eaten. At the near end of the street, two men were sitting on overturned crates, beer bottles in their hands, concentrating on a chequer board as a small group gathered to watch.

Burton followed King into a nautical-themed restaurant, dominated by a blue and white motif, and then up a flight of stairs to a balcony overlooking the strait between New Providence and Paradise Island. The balcony was packed with an eclectic mix of chattering folk. Burton was surprised at the number of locals in the restaurant, which he took to be a good sign as he had initially taken the restaurant, with its unsubtle bold colours and copious lengths of decorative rope, for an undisguised tourist trap. Burton followed in King's wake as he carved a path through the crowded tables towards an empty spot near the back of the terrace.

They both elected to sit with their backs towards the interior of the restaurant looking out over the harbour. Before them were boats of all sizes and descriptions, from dinghies to huge ocean-going tugs. Burton saw the big yellow and blue post boat, which also functioned as a ferry for those looking for a cheap way to island hop, heading in towards Potter's Cay from the east, probably returning from Eleuthera, dark clouds billowing from its funnels. In the distance, a small speedboat stopped to refuel at an Esso fuel pump, a surprisingly close replica of those visible by the roadside, whilst in front of the restaurant the pontoons rocked as a motor boat disgorged its cargo of sunburned tourists clutching snorkels and fins. Across the water, Burton could see a private beach backing on to a hotel. It was now early afternoon, the harsh bright light glaring angrily off reflective surfaces; only the truly committed were out on the sands soaking up the radiance of the sun, tanned figures that periodically darted in or out of the light green water which separated Paradise Island from New Providence.

'What will you have?' King asked, as a young, pretty waitress finally spotted them and ambled over. Her broad hips swung from side to side as she approached their table, dodging deftly around other customers on the way.

'A beer, please,' ordered Burton, as the girl looked questioningly at him. He hoped that no rules on drinking whilst on duty applied to liaison officers.

The girl slowly transferred her gaze to King, looking at him mutely. King said, 'Tea, please.'

The girl finally broke her silence in a colourful native lilt. 'Yessir. Coming right up.'

Burton watched the girl heading back inside the restaurant towards the bar, a well-appointed mahogany affair with wooden bar chairs with seat backs. Overhead were a number of blue-painted oars and framed certificates mounted on the wall; the bar area resembled to him the interior of a golf club, and Burton wondered if some of the local ex-pat sailors had made some kind of unofficial retreat there.

The waitress moved in a languid, unhurried gait that so many Bahamians seemed to adopt. Burton was still not completely used to the slow pace of life here, although he could understand that the heat tended to make people lethargic. He had noticed that people would often say things like 'right away' or 'immediately' whilst meaning 'when I'm ready' or 'sometime today'. He liked it.

'So, what do you think of our case so far?' asked King, once the waitress was out of earshot.

Burton cleared his throat. 'Well, obviously we'll be in a better position to say whether there was any foul play involved after we have received the autopsy results. I don't know a lot about drowning somebody, but I think it's highly unlikely that somebody managed to forcibly hold him under the water without leaving any visible marks. He may have been tanked up and drowned through a silly mistake, but I don't have him down for that sort of guy, despite the police report. What did you think of that report, by the way? To me, it seems to suggest two things: one, that Sir John may have had a drinking problem; and two, that on one occasion at least he aroused suspicion that he might want to do himself an injury. And this was the opinion of a cop, not just any person on the street.'

King nodded. 'Yes, that's right. I was quite surprised when I saw the report for the first time — I hadn't heard about the incident before. But my guess is that almost everybody is going to have one or two incidents in their

80

past that they are less than proud of — I'm not sure we should read too much into it.'

'I agree, but then, what is too much? And what did you think of our grieving widow Melissa? I'm not all that certain that she didn't have something to do with Sir John's death. She didn't come across as one hundred per cent trustworthy to me. On the other hand, though, I don't really see what she could have done. Nobody mentioned seeing Melissa there, and she's not the type one would easily miss. All we have is a lot of witnesses saying Sir John simply walked down the beach and went for a swim.'

'And you believe them?' asked King softly.

Burton thought for a while. It was an interesting question, and yet one he had not really considered. It had all seemed so irrefutable, and yet the only reason they knew that Sir John had voluntarily gone swimming was that they were told this by several witnesses. Was that proof enough? If they had lied, if they were conspirators, perhaps it was they who had drowned Sir John.

'I think we would be right not to take their stories as gospel, and to challenge them if necessary, but my feeling is that they are more or less reliable. After all, from what you say, it was the police who approached these witnesses — they didn't put themselves

81

forward. And the police only asked regulars on the beach. If we actually went further and took steps to find out if other people noticed him, we could try to corroborate their stories. But in my view that would be a poor use of resources — we have three people who claim to have witnessed the events of that evening. They can't all be involved in a plot to rid the world of a retired British diplomat.'

The waitress came back with their drinks. She was wearing a light, wrap-around dress in a floral print, which was fairly low-cut at the front, emphasizing her voluptuous figure. Burton was treated to a generous view of her ample bosom as she bent over the table to place his beer in front of him. Burton could see no suggestion of a bra, and he suddenly felt a flush of desire for her. He watched her as she put a glass cup, a pot of hot water and a small wooden chest of tea bags in front of King, and then as she walked away, her wide hips again swinging from side to side.

King filled his cup carefully with boiling water from the pot. Then he lifted the lid of the box and, after careful consideration, selected an Earl Grey blend, unwrapped it and placed it into his cup. King seemed intent on watching the strands of brown dispersing through the water in his cup. After a while, he lifted the tea bag out, placed it against his spoon, and wrapped the string to which the label was attached around the tea bag, squeezing out the trapped tea. Then he carefully unwrapped the string and placed the almost dry bag on his saucer, the finale to a performance of infinite care.

King said, 'I'm curious as to the results of the post-mortem too. We are assuming that drowning is the cause of death. Perhaps he had a heart attack, or cramp, or something. Even if he did drown, it will be interesting to see if there are any drugs or alcohol in his blood.'

'Then you don't believe it was an accident either?' asked Burton.

King was silent for a second, and then he pursed his lips. 'I don't know whether it was an accident or not, but I have my suspicions. We will know more once the coroner has done his stuff. Even if nothing further is discovered, we will know more, as we can rule out certain theories which at present we cannot. For example, if no traces of alcohol or drugs are found, we can discount these as having had anything to do with his death. If there are indeed no signs of a struggle, we can be reasonably certain that he was not forcibly drowned.'

'When will we receive the report?'

'It depends how busy they are in the

coroner's office, but I'd expect to receive the report tomorrow. I'll let you know as soon as I have it.'

'Thanks.' Burton glanced around to see if anyone was following their conversation. The people at the tables closest to theirs were all involved in highly animated discussions, and looked totally uninterested in the two gentlemen sitting at the table at the back of the terrace.

Burton's gaze was drawn to a girl walking along the dock. She was tall, dark and tanned, and at first he thought it was Melissa. As she came closer, though, he saw that it was not her.

'What about the girl, Melissa?' asked Burton. 'What was your impression of her?'

King smiled. 'Enigmatic. Very difficult to read. She certainly seemed to be shaken up by Sir John's death. It's difficult to tell, though. She's just gone through the traumatic experience of losing her husband. People can react differently in stressful times. She certainly didn't seem to me to be obviously lying or holding something back. We may have to talk to her again, though.'

'What about a motive? If someone murdered Sir John, they would have to have a motive. He was high up in the diplomatic service, very high up in fact. Or, at least, he was until he retired. I assume he was a very rich man.'

King nodded. 'Yes, he was. He held the highest post, British High Commissioner in Kingston, responsible for the whole region. I think he would have earned a fairly hefty salary. His real wealth was inherited though. His family is very rich, and I suspect Sir John could have lived a life of luxury without having to do a day's work had he wished to do so. My guess is that his estate will be worth many millions.'

Burton whistled through his teeth. 'And Melissa is his first wife? Or has he already been married?'

'No, Melissa is his first wife. As far as I know, he has no children. I assume he left everything to her, but I don't know. We will have to check.' King scrawled something illegibly with his left hand in a small notebook he had fished out of his suit jacket.

'And now we need to cover some ground rules. When we interview people, I will lead the questioning. I am happy for you to ask questions as we go along, but these questions should be relevant and not change the line of questioning. I may want to take a roundabout route to a certain query that I believe the person being questioned may not wish to answer directly, or I may want to lead a person to a thought that they will then think they had themselves. I don't want you to disrupt this process. Is this clear?'

Burton nodded silently.

King resumed. 'I also do not wish to have you introduce your private theories to people we are talking to. For example, your questions to Melissa about Sir John's state of mind and whether he was capable of killing himself. At the moment, we have little to suggest that he committed suicide, and it is therefore not appropriate to ask this now. If you do have these visions of yours, do me a favour and discuss it with me first. Then, and only then, and only if I'm convinced you're not on totally the wrong path, can we introduce the subject at the right time in the right way. OK?

Burton smiled faintly. 'Yeah, OK.'

'And lastly,' King continued, 'I don't want you to go off gallivanting around on your own. This is for two reasons. One, I don't want you messing up my investigation. I'm a trained police officer with experience in these kinds of affairs. You are not. You might alert a criminal to our proximity and cause him to flee, or, much worse, commit further crimes in his panic. Secondly, this work can be dangerous. We have a good relationship with the British contingent here, and I intend to keep it that way. I don't fancy trying to explain why their golden boy ended up with a bullet in him when he should have been a mere observer.'

Burton listened impatiently. King had until now been a quiet, modest man who hardly opened his mouth, but now he seemed intent on emulating a garrulous sergeant ordering his minions about. The act didn't quite work though: Burton could sense that King was as uncomfortable dishing out orders as Burton was taking them, if not more so. He smiled inwardly at the description of himself as the golden boy of the British contingent in the Bahamas, and wondered where on earth King had got that idea from.

'Are you clear about what I have just said? Do you agree with me? Or do you have other ideas about your role as a liaison officer?' King looked at Burton, who seemed to feel King's eyes boring into him.

'No, I agree with you.' Burton could see that argument was useless at this point.

'Good. I'm going to head off now. Can you make your own way back to the hotel? It's not far. If not, I'll give you a lift. Or you can get a cab.'

'No, I'll walk. It's a pleasant afternoon.'

King stood up and reached into his jacket. From a slim wallet he pulled a couple of notes and left them on the table although

Burton waved his hand to signify that he would pay. King pushed his chair carefully, almost meticulously, under the table and walked towards the pavement. Burton watched as the detective smiled and waved a greeting to a group sitting on one of the tables on the way out. He followed King's figure as he walked with long, slow paces along the beach road.

Burton was glad the preaching was over. It wasn't as bad as he had been prepared for. He had expected that a policeman would not be overjoyed at the thought of an observer following him around, but King did not seem to mind too much as long as he didn't mess things up. Burton liked the detective; he seemed totally unflappable, impeccably logical and not without a sense of humour. He had also seemed to recognize some ability in his young charge. Burton smiled at this last thought; King was not much older than he was.

Burton looked around to see where the waitress was. He caught her eye almost immediately and, smiling broadly, she sauntered over. Burton grinned and her and indicated his empty beer bottle. 'Could I have another beer, please?'

'Certainly, sir.' The girl stressed the word 'sir' and, with her Bahamian accent the word came out as 'surruh'. It sounded lightly comical.

Burton watched the girl as she walked inside, studying her well-rounded legs. She was wearing flip-flops and her toes were brightly painted.

Burton sat back and stretched his neck backwards, staring for several seconds at the canopy above his head. Then he looked back at the unchanged scene on the terrace. He was still surrounded by groups of laughing people and, although the composition of the groups may have changed and many people may have come and gone, he had the impression that time stood still whilst he sat there.

The girl came back with his beer. He smiled and thanked her, and once again was rewarded with a flash of white teeth as she smiled back at him.

Burton sipped the cold beer, savouring the taste and then the feel of the cool liquid in the back of his throat. It could be worse, he thought: sent to the Bahamas on some wild goose chase, to investigate the death of a diplomat, a task for which he was completely unqualified. But it would be fun.

6

On the patio outside the hotel restaurant the morning was cool despite the rising sun. Michael Burton sat on a wooden chair at a table close to the corner of the hotel patio. The area was slightly elevated, so that the view out over the bay was undisturbed. There was a gentle northerly sea breeze, and the turquoise sea was striped with soft breakers moving slowly towards the shore and crashing against the rocks below. The shrill cries of children playing were audible high above the constant, rustling noise of the breaking waves. The air coming off the sea brought with it a heavy salty smell, augmented by traces of the cooked breakfasts being served by hasty, rushed waiters, and cut with an acrid tang of stale coffee.

The small patio was full, the majority of the guests in the hotel having chosen to take their breakfast outside. The small enclosed space enjoyed a degree of atmosphere that would not have been present without the groups of chattering people. He had debated calling for breakfast in his room, but now he was glad he had come down, if only to view the hustle and bustle of tourist life in the Bahamas.

Burton nursed a strong, bitter double espresso brought to him by a surly waiter, whose mood had not been improved by Burton's refusal of the percolator coffee that had been standing there since the crack of dawn. The waiter, cursing under his breath, had ambled off moodily to make the espresso, leaving Burton to wonder why more guests didn't insist on a decent cup of coffee in the morning.

Burton envisaged the day before him: he was to go to the police station to meet Chester King. The detective had left a message at the reception, which Burton had received when he had arrived back the evening before. The text of the message had been brief: *Meet me at the police station tomorrow at 0900.* Burton could imagine the detective dictating in his precise, efficient, quasi-military style ('o-nine-hundred'), which the receptionist had amazingly managed to capture in her bold, rounded, no-nonsense handwriting.

King had told him nothing about what they were going to do, but he imagined that the result of the autopsy would be available soon. Of course, it was difficult to know if that would shed any new light on the situation. Burton couldn't believe that Sir John had been forcibly drowned, but it would be interesting to know if he had been drunk, or if he had had some kind of seizure, a heart attack or something.

He would no doubt have time to ponder the results later that day. Although King seemed to be giving this case a good deal of his attention, Burton was certain that this wouldn't be the only thing he was currently involved with, and that he would have to spend some time looking after his other tasks. Despite King's speech the day before, Burton decided to run some thoughts past King to see if he could pursue a few ideas of his own.

Burton's train of thought was disturbed as two parties of tourists came out onto the balcony. One appeared to be the members of a large family, complete with grandma, grandpa and several grandchildren. The corpulent lady he assumed to be the mother of the small children had apparently already inherited the title of matriarch, and she controlled her minions with aplomb. The other group was made up of two couples, the male members of whom sported almost identically bloodshot eyes, the vestiges of an overly alcoholic night, set in pale, unshaven faces. Their young girlfriends, dressed snappily in short, revealing dresses, looked irritated and impatient, glaring around for an empty table. One of the waiters scurried up to them, clearly anxious to please, but was interrupted mid-stride by a sharp bark from the matriarch. Burton hadn't been able to distinguish what she had said, but the waiter obviously had as he subtly changed course and presented himself obsequiously before her.

Burton finished his coffee and stood up to leave. He saw immediately that his departure had ignited an impassioned assault by the two opposing groups on his now-empty table. One of the young ladies strode purposefully towards the table, but was cut off by the matriarch's bulk.

Shaking his head, Burton took a long route to the patio doors, avoiding the ensuing race for his vacated table.

★   ★   ★

The autopsy was carried out in a dark, dank, cellar-like mortuary somewhere in the hospital. A police driver had brought King and Burton swiftly and unobtrusively to the hospital, making steady progress in what passed here as the morning rush-hour. Burton now knew that busy roads were the exception rather than the rule, and the few drivers on the road didn't appear to be in much of a hurry to get anywhere. Burton reflected on the relaxed approach to life, and above all work, in the Caribbean. The Bahamians didn't seem to suffer from the European and American disease of punctuality, which afflicted many who thought themselves 'civilized', whose lives were ruled not by instinct or feeling but by meetings and clocks. Even King, for whom punctuality was important, was not overly concerned when others around him were late. Burton preferred the Caribbean way.

Burton did not have any idea exactly where he was in the hospital — he and King had presented themselves to the receptionist and, after waiting for about five minutes for the coroner's assistant to arrive, had each been given a plastic coverall and been asked to follow the assistant through a labyrinth of corridors, each one lit by a row of alternating red emergency lights and dull yellow lamps which seemed to emit more noise than light. The hospital was surprisingly clean and modern, no doubt in part owing to the contributions of the moneyed inhabitants of the island group, many of whom had undoubtedly moved there to protect to some extent their vast fortunes from the tax authorities of their previous domiciles.

When, after reaching the end of several

darkened corridors, they reached the post-mortem room, they had been met almost too enthusiastically by the pathologist, a short, rotund and jovial native man peering out at the world through squinting eyes behind gold-rimmed half-moon spectacles. He offered each of them in turn a pudgy hand whose grip was surprisingly dry and firm. Burton guessed that his obvious enthusiasm came from having few visitors to his domain for most of his working life, and those who did come were probably nearly all policemen investigating homicides. Not much difference there, he thought.

The pathologist was wearing green coveralls not dissimilar to those King and Burton had been provided with, the unzipped top of which displayed the collar of a tweed jacket and shirt, and a knitted wool tie with a striped motif. Given the heat, Burton was astounded that he should dress in this fashion for his kind of work, although he speculated that he may have dressed knowing he had visitors that day. On the other hand, the general impression he had of the pathologist was of an extroverted, colourful character, who may well dress like this every day. Burton found himself picturing the man with a floppy, colourful bow tie and a matching handkerchief fanned out of his breast pocket.

On top of his fleshy neck was perched an intelligent face, speckled on the cheeks with a light sprinkling of stubble and topped with an unruly mop of greying black hair. The half-moon glasses, with a cord hanging down behind his neck, increased the air of intelligence.

The room itself was square with green tiled walls lit with cold, bright fluorescent lamps set into the ceiling. The floor was tiled in white with an abundance of drains. Forming the gristly centre-piece of the room were three stainless-steel tables, each one equipped with some kind of drainage system and, at one end, a sink. Around the edges of the room were a series of work surfaces decorated with an array of gadgets whose function was not known to Burton. And he wasn't sure he wanted to know. Although ventilators could be heard whirring away somewhere behind the metal grilles in the ceiling, the air in the room smelt musty. However, the overpowering smell of decomposing flesh Burton had been expecting was conspicuous by its absence.

'Come on, it's over here.' The pathologist, who had introduced himself as Delon Friday, led them past the first table and stopped by the second, on which a human form was apparent under a plastic sheet. Friday spoke with a curiously British accent, no doubt a by-product of having studied in the UK. He drew back the sheet slightly to reveal only the head of Sir John Little, whose eyes stared up at the ceiling, as if concentrating on the light fittings. Although puffy and, in patches, a livid, bright purple, the man's face looked strangely serene. Having not seen a human corpse before, and certainly not under these conditions, Burton didn't know exactly what he had been expecting, but he certainly wouldn't have been surprised if the mouth of the cadaver had been snarled upwards in a rictus of death, or if the pain and fear of the vain struggle against the omnipotent sea had been there to read in his eyes and on the features of his face. Of this, however, there was no sign.

Friday picked up a clipboard, which had been attached to the end of the table, by the head of the corpse. 'Well, gentlemen, I can already tell you a little about how your man died. As I've been conducting the autopsy, I've been dictating notes.' At this point, Friday pulled from one of the deep pockets on the front of his coveralls an old dictaphone. 'I will, of course, produce a full report, based on my recorded notes, which will no doubt go into your files and which may be used as evidence in any future court proceedings related to this death, but I can go through my findings and give you the important details now.'

He glanced at the notes on the clipboard, his small brown eyes darting left and right as he scanned through the details. Burton wondered how much this was a gesture rather than a reminder. He couldn't have done the autopsy more than twelve hours ago and almost certainly could have covered the main points without referring to any notes.

Friday cleared his throat. 'First of all, some background information about your victim. He appears to have been in his late sixties and in reasonably good health. I should say that he did a fair amount of exercise, most likely daily. He was a non-smoker, but a moderate to heavy drinker.

'We suspect the cause of death to be drowning. Drowning is typically defined as suffocation due to immersion of nostrils and mouth in a liquid. This leads to asphyxiation and sometimes, as we believe in this case, to cardiac arrest.'

He moved the sheet further down the body, folding it over just above Sir John Little's hips. The skin on the corpse's shoulders, neck and head was mottled and discoloured, showing purple blotches on the otherwise pale, wrinkled skin. Two diagonal lines crossed with heavy stitches tapered from the shoulders in to the breastbone, and then a single line headed down towards the victim's genitalia, leaving the body marked with an ugly 'Y' shape. Burton thought that he probably should feel nauseous at this sight, but he felt only a faint twinge of disgust. Ironically, when the body had arrived, without the incisions from the autopsy, it had probably looked much better.

'It is often difficult to confirm death by drowning with absolutely no room for error, no margin for doubt. This is no exception. As I said before, we are of the opinion that death was due to drowning. A great deal of salt water was found in the lungs, indicating that he was almost certainly still alive when he entered the sea. And when I say a great deal, I mean a great deal. But, curiously, very little in his stomach. This absence of water in the stomach would normally indicate death prior to submersion, but it can also indicate rapid death by drowning, which I believe to be the most likely explanation here. Let me explain.'

Burton settled in for a long lecture. It was clearly not going to be a quick summary of cause and time of death, which he regularly watched on the American cop shows, but an elaborate presentation of Sir John's demise.

'Usually, when a person drowns, they hold

their breath for as long as possible before finally trying to inhale. As they hold their breath, their body uses up the oxygen in that breath, and it is replaced by carbon dioxide, which is the human body's by-product of breathing and, of course, what we normally exhale. The body, which is used to regular breaths, sends out an alert when it notices a rising carbon dioxide level in the blood-stream, rather than a falling oxygen level. A person who is underwater and conscious will either succumb to the urge to breathe and start inhaling water, or will fight against the body's urge, overriding it until lack of oxygen, or hypoxia, leads to unconsciousness. At this point, the body will try to gasp for air, and will gasp water instead, but oxygen levels are already depleted and the amount of water entering the lungs will be minimal. In either a conscious or unconscious person, water in the airway will almost always cause laryn-gospasm, a contraction of the larynx or vocal chords in the throat, which prevents water from entering the lungs and means that water enters the stomach instead. So, in the initial phase of drowning, typically we have water in the stomach but not in the lungs.'

Burton listened carefully, trying to picture these events occurring to the man on the table, whom he had met and whom he had found to be gentle and kind.

'Some time after unconsciousness, in most but not all victims the laryngospasm relaxes, and this allows more water to enter the lungs. This is what we call a wet drowning. In a dry drowning, the laryngospasm is not relaxed and very little water enters the lungs. However, in both cases, water is present in the stomach. Continued hypoxia will lead to brain death, but in most victims cardiac arrest occurs before this is complete.

'There are many other indicators that we can use in order to try to confirm the cause of death. Foaming at the mouth, for example, which was present with our friend here, although much of the foam was washed away whilst he was submerged. Another indication is the excessively voluminous nature of the lungs, and their marbled and discoloured appearance.' As he talked about the lungs, Friday strolled over to one of the work surfaces at the back of the room and indicated a large glass jar with what looked like a squishy sack of multicoloured potatoes. Burton felt the bile rise in his throat but he swallowed bravely and moved his gaze back to the little pathologist, who was now approaching the dissection table again.

Friday smiled slightly, although Burton wasn't sure whether it was because the pathologist had noticed him holding down his vomit. 'We also carry out a variety of tests that will either support or contradict the finding of death by drowning. Myself, I prefer to use a diatom test, which is widely used in the UK. Diatoms are microscopic algae present in water. In this test, we analyse the diatom content of the organs, such as the liver and brain, using the theory that it is impossible for these diatoms to enter these organs other than by systemic circulation via the lungs.

'We found a high concentration of diatoms in your man's organs. I already have samples of all of the areas of water around these parts, and I compared the diatoms I found during the autopsy with those known to be present in the waters where the body was found. They are the same, which strongly supports the theory that our man drowned there.'

Friday glanced back at the clipboard, as if he had lost his train of thought. For a second the strain of the job showed on the man's face, a sudden flash of doubt and exhaustion over his otherwise relaxed features. As quickly as it came, it passed. He sniffed almost indiscernibly and continued.

'So, in this man's stomach is only a little water, but all other evidence indicates that he drowned. This seems to me to indicate that he drowned very quickly, and I would even postulate the theory that he purposely inhaled the water to drown himself but, of course, I can't be sure of this. If he did, it's amazing that he was able to control the body's natural reaction to water in the windpipe and counter the laryngospasm. What I can tell you is that the warmth and relative passivity of water in the Bahamas in general, and where this man was last seen swimming in particular, makes accidental drowning fairly rare, particularly when the victim is not inebriated.'

This will be interesting, thought Burton. He already had a suspicion that alcohol may have played a part in Sir John's death, although he admitted that he had no evidence for this apart from the police report suggesting a possible melancholic drunk.

'All of which brings me on to the tox screen,' continued Friday, as if reading Burton's mind. 'I tested for alcohol, of course, and for a variety of other drugs as well. Many drowning victims, particularly adult males, drown because they are drunk. But I don't think this was the case here. Your man had had a drink, but I would say he was definitely not intoxicated to the stage that he would have been unable to co-ordinate his movements enough to stay afloat and as a result drowned. My best estimate, based on stomach contents and blood alcohol level, is that he drank one or two small tumblers of single malt Scotch. The alcohol had only started to be absorbed into the bloodstream, so I would say that he consumed this amount of alcohol very quickly and not long before he entered the water. Some people may show some level of inebriation after this amount of alcohol drunk very quickly, but our friend here had quite a high tolerance for the stuff, I should say. His liver seems to have experienced a fair deal of it, at any rate.'

Friday started on another excursion towards the work surface at the back of the room, but stopped at the halfway point and pointed at a metal bowl, which was covered in a white cloth with a red stain. An object about the size of a small football was visible under the cloth.

'The rest of the tox screen was negative. I tested for all the usual suspects, recreational drugs known to have an intoxicating or hypnotic effect, but I found nothing. The test is not exhaustive, but it is a good indication that your man was in control when he entered the water. I don't have him down for a drug user anyway. No needle marks on his arms, nothing like that.

'So, what else can I tell you? Very little, I'm afraid, gentlemen. I checked the contents of the stomach. Not much there. Apart from a little sea water, it was clear that our man had some food, I'd say some kind of seafood salad, a couple of hours before he decided to go swimming.'

Burton decided to hazard a question, one which would probably demonstrate his lack of knowledge. 'You mentioned that Sir John had a cardiac arrest caused by drowning. Can you say definitely whether Sir John had a seizure, or even the cardiac arrest, before he drowned?'

Friday's kindly eyes peered at Burton. 'Yes, a good question. And no, we can't say for certain. But we can say that *in all probability* he did not have a heart attack before he drowned. You see, the state of his body is more or less an example of all the classic drowning symptoms. If his cause of death was in fact a heart attack whilst he was in the water, I'd have expected him to have inhaled less water than he did. The evidence points to heart attack caused by lack of oxygen due to drowning.

'Our man could conceivably have fainted, but again I doubt it. A syncope is a loss of consciousness caused by insufficient oxygen supply to the brain through hypoxia. However, it is usually a reaction of the body to a lack of oxygen to the brain when standing up — the legs go weak and the

105

victim sits or falls, thus allowing the blood to flow more easily to the brain. It is unusual for someone already in a horizontal position to faint, unless the syncope is due to other causes, such as low blood pressure, which our man did not have.

'I'm afraid it is also difficult to discount a seizure with any degree of certainty. Often, a person who suffers a seizure will bite their tongue. Our man didn't bite his. I've also looked at his muscles, but there are no obvious signs that they weren't fully under his control. This is obviously a fairly rudimentary indication. Furthermore, it's possible that he had cramp, which could have led to his drowning.'

King interjected quickly, not giving Friday the chance to elaborate, 'What about time of death? We already have a window of time during which we believe Sir John's death occurred, but I'd like to have your views on it.'

'Of course. Well, I should say between three and five days ago. Rigor mortis has been and gone, which tells us that your man has been dead for more than twenty-four hours at least. Decomposition, which slows when the victim is submerged, also corroborates the time.

'The body was immersed in water for

several hours. When a person has drowned, the body tends to sink until such time as putrefactive gas formation increases the buoyancy and allows it to resurface. This occurs far more quickly in the warm waters here than it would in cold waters, despite the salt content of the water, which tends to slow the process down. Once it resurfaces, a floating body tends to assume a head down position. This leads to pooling of blood in the head.' Friday pointed at the purple blotches in the corpse's upper body. 'In this case, I believe he was in this position for the best part of twelve hours. Also, you can see maceration of the skin, where it has started to come off the extremities, which tends to happen when it is immersed for a long time. Apart from this, though, skin damage is light.

'Temperature of the body is approximately the same as that of the water where he was found. This is fairly normal: the water here is warm, not a lot colder than the human body when it's functioning normally. A body will cool in water at a rate of approximately five degrees Fahrenheit for every hour it is immersed until it reaches the ambient temperature.

'I don't know if this coincides with your suspicions about time of death.' Friday looked for confirmation from King, who nodded his head slowly.

'Good. Now, if we accept that our man drowned, we have to assess the possible reasons for this. Homicidal drowning is rare, and almost always involves a significant imbalance between the relative strengths of the killer and the victim, or a sick and weakened victim. Although he was well over sixty years old, Sir John's body does not appear to have been sick or weakened to the extent that he would be unable to struggle, which leaves the possibility that he was drowned by an assailant whose physical strength was far in excess of his. Again, however, I think we can discount this. There are no signs of a struggle on our man's body, which is almost inconceivable unless he willingly let himself be drowned by another man. And even then, I'd expect to find bruising where the assailant held him under.

'Accidental drowning is difficult to rule out. As you asked,' Friday looked at Burton, 'we cannot discount the possibility that our man had cramp or a seizure. It is also very difficult to rule out a syncope.

'So to conclude, the cause of death is almost certainly rapid drowning. Manner of death is more difficult. My best guess, though, based solely on the medical evidence, is that he drowned himself by purposefully inhaling water. Any further questions?'

Friday looked at Burton and then at King. Both men shook their heads slowly.

'Well, then, gentlemen, there you have it. As I said, you will receive a formal report detailing all this, in which I will conclude that the balance of evidence supports the hypothesis that Sir John Little died from cardiac arrest caused by drowning. Thank you, gentlemen, I wish you the best of luck with your investigation. Sir John was a good man.'

It was the first time Friday had referred to the victim by name, rather than calling him 'your man' or 'our friend' or something similar.

Friday offered his hand to King and Burton, before calling the assistant over. 'Saunders will show you back to the reception, gentlemen. If there's anything else you need, please don't hesitate to give me a call.'

The journey back to the reception seemed to go a lot more quickly than the journey to the post-mortem room. Burton's mind was digesting the information they had been given by the pathologist, trying to find a pattern hidden in the evidence. He barely registered being asked to remove the plastic coverall until King jogged him out of his reverie. He handed over the green uniform, thanked the assistant, and followed King outside into the sunlight.

* * *

A taxi brought them back to the police station. The rear windows of the taxi appeared to be stuck in the closed position, and the interior felt like a sauna. Burton had loosened his collar and tie, and on glancing across at King, was unsurprised to see that the detective looked unperturbed by the heat. He was, though, surprised that King also seemed unperturbed by the driver's driving style, which in Burton's view was bordering on lunacy.

'Well, there were no real surprises there. What next?'

King looked pensive. 'At the moment, we have no evidence that a crime has been committed, no motive and no suspect. In the interests of trying to make some progress on these unknowns, I think our next step should be to check with Sir John's lawyer. After all, Sir John must have left a tidy sum behind, and whoever inherits this would obviously benefit from Sir John's death financially. That would give us *possible* suspects and *possible* motive.'

7

The waiting room of Sir John Little's lawyer was, as opposed to most other places Burton had experienced recently, dark and cool. They were seated in comfortable leather chairs arranged around a circular glass table on which the obligatory magazines, women's weeklies for her, cars and yachts for him, had been placed. The modern furniture and fittings contrasted pleasingly with the old white-washed colonial building in which they were housed. The receptionist, a tall but slight girl smartly dressed in a stern grey two-piece suit and pale blue blouse, had risen from her chair behind an antique dark oak desk and greeted them warmly. She looked to Burton as if she had arrived in the Bahamas a couple of years ago by accident and had never got round to leaving. Her accent was broad American, most likely West Coast. The efficiency suggested by the brand-new looking computer and neatly positioned, nearly empty in- and out-boxes on her desk was emphasiszd by the scraping back of her tousled, sun-dyed blonde hair into a small pony-tail. But there was something about her

111

which made Burton think it was forced. He could imagine her arriving home, replacing the suit with an old pair of cut-off jeans and a T-shirt and removing the hair band, allowing her hair to explode into a mass of unruly curls, and then she would once again be rid of the daily encroachment onto her freedom.

Burton took a sip of the water the girl had fetched for him. Both he and King had refused a cup of tea, which had so nearly been forced upon them. Indeed, the girl had protested so vehemently when they declined her offer that he felt she must have some ulterior motive for offering to brew tea; perhaps she wanted some herself, or wanted merely the chance to get away from her desk and to do something different. After this outburst he had somewhat meekly requested some water, and was rewarded with a broad smile from the girl, who seemed pleased that they had after all accepted something.

The meeting with Sir John's legal representative, Agatha Wells, had been planned the day before. At first, when one of the secretaries at the police station had called to make an appointment, Mrs Wells had seemed reluctant to talk to the police about her client's affairs, particularly the details of the will, for which, she said, they would have to wait until probate had been completed. At this point, King had been concerned that they might have to issue a subpoena compelling her to provide the information. He disliked issuing such documents to anybody, but trying to subpoena a lawyer unwilling to talk was not his idea of fun. King himself had called her up later that day and explained the situation and the ongoing investigation into Sir John's death. He had been very cautious about saying too much about the case, but he had subtly hinted that there may have been foul play and, if this was so, the investigation would be helped immensely by the knowledge of the contents of Sir John's will. Mrs Wells, who had liked Sir John and certainly wanted any potential investigation to proceed without hindrance, had given in and asked King to drop in the following afternoon.

Burton looked across at King, who seemed engrossed in an American magazine about golf. Burton shook his head, amazed that King would be interested in golf. Try as he might, he just couldn't imagine the tall, serious Bahamian on a golf course wearing plus fours and debating with an ageing caddy about which iron to take for his approach shot. The girl's voice interrupted his reverie.

'Mrs Wells will see you now. Please come this way.'

Burton stood up and waited for King to

113

reluctantly close the magazine and climb to his feet. They followed in the wake of the girl as she led them down a corridor and indicated an open door.

'Do come in, please.'

Agatha Wells's voice boomed across the room and the person from whom it emanated was a large, friendly-looking native lady of about fifty, whose thick black hair showed no signs of grey above her heavy horn-rimmed glasses. Mrs Wells was ensconced behind a large, dark-stained walnut desk which was empty save for a single legal pad, one slim folder and a gold fountain pen. She gestured towards two comfortable leather chairs arranged on the other side of the desk.

'Please, do sit down. Would you like Stephanie to get you something?'

'Er, no thank you,' Burton managed to mumble. He wasn't sure how the young girl, or the lawyer, would take it but he really couldn't face any further drinks.

'Now, what can I do for you, gentlemen?'

King cleared his throat. 'We're looking for information about a client of yours, Sir John Little. As I'm sure you're aware, Sir John was drowned three days ago and we are currently investigating his death. We are trying to find information which may shed some light on Sir John's actions, his disappearance and his death. Specifically, we are interested in the provisions of Sir John's will.'

'And why do you want to know the provisions of Sir John's will?' Despite her friendly appearance, there was a business-like edge to her question, reminding Burton immediately that, as the chosen legal adviser of Sir John Little, she was almost certainly the consummate professional counsel.

'Well, we need to know who benefits from Sir John's death. This may help us to eliminate possible suspects who would not have had a motive for the killing, or it may provide us with grounds for looking further in a particular direction. You should understand, we are still not certain whether a crime has been committed or not; at the moment it is merely a question of gathering as much information as possible so that, when the time comes, we are in the best possible position to draw our conclusions.'

Burton was surprised by the detective's use of language, which did not in the slightest resemble the gruff, no-nonsense snippets from serving police officers in the UK and US that he had often seen on the television. His tone seemed subtly tailored for his audience, playing the intellectual problem solver assessing all the information rather than jumping to early conclusions. Burton noted immediately that the kindly lawyer's face softened appreciably as King continued. He smiled inwardly to himself.

'Of course, I understand that probate has not as yet been completed. And I should advise you right now that we do not, at the present moment, have a warrant to compel disclosure of any information concerning Sir John's estate or his affairs. Now, we could obtain a warrant, or we could wait until probate is completed, but we were really hoping that you would be able to provide us with the details of Sir John's will. In full confidence, of course.'

Burton listened, bemused. He could not envisage any lawyer giving King the details he had asked for in any circumstances short of a bona fide warrant signed by the head of the judiciary. He awaited the response with gleeful anticipation.

'So what you are asking me, Mr King, is that I voluntarily disclose the contents of Sir John Little's will to you without the consent of Sir John's executors, of which I am one? Is this correct?'

'Yes, it is.'

'I can't do that, Mr King. You know that as well as I do. What I can do though is expedite probate so that you and your colleague can obtain the information you require later today. As I mentioned before, I am one of the executors of Sir John's will. His wife is the other. I have actually been in contact with Melissa Little recently, and she is planning to visit my offices after lunch. I will call her now and ask her if she any objection to your presence when I read the will. Would you care to wait outside?'

Burton looked across at King. The detective's face was impassive, unaffected by the rebuttal of his proposal. King stood up to leave. 'Of course.'

The two men walked back out of the office and headed back towards to the waiting room. They had barely reached the hallway when the lawyer's door opened again.

Burton heard the call 'Detectives!' and they turned to see Agatha Wells walking towards them rapidly brandishing a sheaf of papers tied together with a red ribbon. 'Lady Little is happy for you to join us at two o' clock. We shall meet with her in the conference room. Now, would you both care to join me for some lunch?'

★   ★   ★

The conference room was a narrow rectangle whose sides were well over twice the length of its ends. A long highly polished table filled up most of the available space, leaving a small three foot gap along either side. Burton sat wedged into a seat in the middle of the table opposite a long row of windows set in unpainted wooden frames looking out onto a small grassy courtyard. King sat next to him with even less space, sprawled low in his chair. Agatha Wells sat opposite the two men, silhouetted against the window, the blinds of which had not been drawn. Despite the brightness, Burton preferred the natural light and had demurred when the lawyer had asked him if she should close the blinds. He couldn't understand people who closed out the sunlight to sit in a darkened room staring at presentations and peering at documents poorly illuminated by the dirty, warm glow of fluorescent lamps. In front of each of them, and in front of an empty space next to the lawyer, was a pad of paper, a pencil and a glass. In the centre of the table were two bottles of still water and two of sparkling — the receptionist had obviously been busy preparing the room whilst they had been at lunch.

Burton glanced at his watch. It was already ten past two, and there was still no sign of Melissa Little. He wasn't surprised: Melissa didn't strike him as the sort of person who would rate punctuality very highly on her list of priorities. She would turn up when she turned up, and would probably be fairly unsympathetic to any complaints about her tardiness. Still, he mused, they were only here because she had consented to their presence, so one couldn't be too hard on her, but they had reached the point where all the forced small talk had dried up and they desperately needed to get down to business before tempers started to fray.

Agatha Wells seemed to sense Burton's impatience. 'I can give Lady Little a call, if you like?'

'Well, perhaps, if you could . . . '

As the lawyer pulled her mobile phone towards her, a banging of doors from down the hall became audible. 'That's probably her now,' she said, and extricated herself with surprising dexterity from the narrow space and headed towards the door. Before she could reach it, the door flew open and Melissa entered the room, striding confidently despite looking somewhat flushed.

'Good afternoon. Sorry I'm late,' she said, looking anything but sorry. Her face seemed to reflect a certain amount of boredom, and the tension that was there when they had met her before seemed to have disappeared. Burton was unsure what to read into this, though, as he knew that people who were affected by strong emotions, be it grief or stress or anything else, tended to behave abnormally, and what could be seen as rude or obnoxious in one person could be a natural response to an emotional blow in another.

Melissa and the lawyer took their seats opposite the two men. Melissa accepted a glass of still water from King, who stood as she came to the table and offered her the two bottles. Agatha Wells cleared her throat gently and began.

'We're here to look at Sir John Little's last will and testament, as evidenced here in writing.' She indicated the buff manila folder in front of her, from which protruded an envelope with a waxed seal. 'Sir John deposited this envelope with me almost six months ago and, as is normal in these cases, I am not familiar with the contents.'

Agatha Wells picked up a letter opener with a slim blade and a heavy embossed handle and slid it smoothly under the flap of the envelope, using a quick, practised movement to break the seal. Putting down the opener, she reached inside and withdrew the contents of the envelope, which appeared to be little more than two or three sheets of paper that she placed on the table in front of her.

'As Sir John's will is fairly short, I will

quickly read through it and summarize the contents, unless you would prefer if I read the whole thing word for word?'

The question was directed at Melissa, who smiled and shook her head slowly.

'Good, that will save us some time.' The lawyer stopped talking for a few moments as she scanned the provisions of the will.

'Right, it's all fairly straightforward, if a little unusual. The will was drawn up on the 7 January of this year, and was witnessed by Herbert and Edie Redford, neighbours of Sir John. I have no idea whether it was drawn up in the presence of Lady Little.'

The lawyer glanced casually at Melissa as if requesting confirmation, but at the same time intimating that if she didn't want to answer she didn't have to. Melissa caught her glance, nodded and said quietly, 'Yes, I was there. But I couldn't act as a witness because I am a beneficiary under the will.'

'Yes, of course, very true. Anyway, going on to the contents of the will, first of all, as you already know, Sir John appoints Melissa and myself as executors. Sir John has left certain valuable items and a cash sum of one million dollars to a Mr Aqmar Kalifi of fixed abode in Fernandez Street, New Bight. There is an alternative address for Mr Kalifi in Arthur's Town, but no other information about him.

Sir John's housekeeper, Dolores, has been left a mahogany table and a cash sum of twenty thousand dollars. Sir John's gardener has been left a cash sum of ten thousand dollars. Then we have a cash sum of two hundred thousand dollars to be divided amongst Sir John's living relatives apart from his wife, Melissa. Finally, Sir John leaves his residual estate to Melissa.'

Agatha Wells looked up and glanced in turn at all three of the other people sitting round the table. 'Lady Little, gentlemen, that's it.'

★ ★ ★

Outside the office, the early afternoon sun was high and fierce and the pavements glared brightly. Burton hugged the buildings along the road to stay in the shade. King walked next to him, unfazed and comfortable. Burton could feel sweat seeping from his brow, and saw a drip run down the inside of the lens of his sunglasses. He blinked involuntarily as he felt another bead run past his eyebrow.

'Bit of a surprise, the million dollars to someone on Cat Island, wasn't it? Did you recognize the name?' he asked King.

'Not immediately, no. But then I thought about it and I fancy that I do know who he is, although I will need to check. I believe that he is an Obeahman, one of the practitioners of the obeah faith, religion, magic, sorcery, call it what you will. Now, quite why he features in the will of a respected British subject like Sir John Little, I have no idea. Perhaps Sir John visited him for some reason; who knows?'

'If we assume that there is no possibility of the will being faked.'

'I thought about that, too. But Agatha Wells claims that Sir John deposited the will himself in the sealed envelope and that it was kept in a locked cabinet and could not have been tampered with since. Melissa also knew the contents of the will, so I'm sure she would have said something if the one million dollars for Mr Kalifi had been added since the original writing. From her reaction we can assume that nothing had changed in the will unless, of course, she changed it herself. We can ask Mrs Wells for the will, and we can have it checked by our forensic teams, but I'm not convinced that they will actually find anything.'

'What about a handwriting expert? Couldn't they tell if Sir John had been compelled to write the will under duress?'

'Possibly, but remember that the will was signed by two witnesses. We would be better off asking them about drafting of the will and their signatures. We know who they are, and it would be relatively easily to ask them about the signing of the will. Personally, I don't imagine there is anything wrong with it. There is no suggestion that Sir John was not in sound mind when he wrote the will, it was properly drafted in the presence of his wife and two witnesses, who then signed it. But we will check it nonetheless.'

They paused at the corner of the main road leading up the hill to the police station. They had just missed the lights and a stream of cars hurtled past. Burton looked around to see if anyone was in earshot and then said above the din, 'What about the whole obeah connection? What is obeah, and why would Sir John Little be involved in it?'

'Good question. I don't know the answer to the second, but I can tell you a little bit about obeah. It is similar to voodoo as practised in Haiti or shango as practised in Trinidad. Obeah itself is practised in Jamaica and, to a lesser extent, here in the Bahamas, particularly on Cat Island, where our man lives.

'Obeah is usually regarded as a kind of religion or belief. It includes elements of what one would call sorcery or witchcraft, and practitioners, or obeahmen as they are called, will cast spells on people for a variety of purposes, both good and evil.

'The origins of obeah are generally accepted to lie with the tribal peoples of the Gold Coast of Africa. Obeah was brought to the Caribbean by slaves imported to Jamaica. The slaves were poorly treated by the colonists and looked to the obeahmen, who helped them to develop their own form of resistance and power, which could be loosely described as the belief that they could harness the power of the supernatural to help them, and to harm others. Those who practised obeah quickly gained the trust, respect and fear of other slaves, using herbs and poisons to cure friends and dispose of enemies.

'The lack of development and barbaric bloodletting practices of European medicine at the time meant that an obeahman was probably just as likely to be able to cure a sick person as a western doctor, which added to their power and social place.

'Obeahmen exploited their power well. They would offer their services for a consideration, which could be payment in cash or something else they needed, but could also be simply the obligation to repay the favour at a later stage. An efficient obeahman could have had a network of people who owed him a favour, meaning that he could call in these favours whenever he needed to in order to perform dangerous tasks or further his development in some other way.

'With the power they held in the community, they quickly became instrumental in slave uprisings and rebellions, and were regarded with fear by the plantation owners, who passed legislation outlawing the practice of obeah and imposing harsh penalties on people found in possession of items used by obeahmen or suspected of practising obeah.'

The steady stream of traffic suddenly dried up as the lights changed. They walked across the road and started up the hill past the Bahamas Supreme Court.

'Do you have plans for the weekend?' King asked. 'I have some other cases to work on for the rest of the afternoon, so I suggest we knock off now and meet again on Monday morning. Let's say nine-thirty. I will ask my secretary to arrange a meeting with Sir John's neighbours, and we can investigate the signing of the will.'

'Yes, OK, sounds good. I thought I might go and have a good look at the beach where Sir John disappeared. I don't imagine I'll find anything else there, but I'd like to check that I haven't missed anything.'

'Working at the weekend? Why not? Anyway, I'm heading up to the police station.

If you want, you can go back to your hotel. There's not much more we can do now.'

'OK. See you Monday.' Burton turned around and walked towards the hotel. Once King was out of sight, Burton turned back up the hill and headed for the library.

★ ★ ★

The number of books on obeah was very thin. Burton found little in the way of academic literature and equally few books containing more than what he had already learned from King. It appeared indeed to be a mystic art. In the corner of the main room were four vintage desktop computers, and Burton spent a couple of hours searching on the Internet for information. He located quite a lot of generic articles, and even some covering Cat Island, but nothing really specific. He tried searching on the name of the man mentioned in Sir John's will, but this also turned up nothing.

Some time later, Burton gave up and headed back to his hotel. He was hot and tired, but felt that there was some importance in the mystical obeahman to whom Sir John had chosen to leave a small fortune.

8

From the driver's seat of his rental car, parked close to the beach, Michael Burton gazed out through the palm trees at the low sun rising slowly into the sky. He had picked up the car that morning before continuing on to a scuba-diving school to hire a couple of filled tanks and full diving equipment. The soft rolling suspension of the small, nondescript car had given immediately when he had put the weighty equipment in the boot and whilst he was driving, he had the curious sensation that he was continually going uphill.

He had parked up to the west of Cable Beach, still some distance east of Old Fort Beach, where Sir John had disappeared. Old Fort Beach was dominated by residential areas, and he was reluctant to draw attention to himself by arriving at an essentially residents only beach with a carful of scuba-diving kit.

Burton was glad that he had brought his diving certification, and that they had asked few questions about where and with whom he intended to dive. He had dismissed his initial plan of hiring two complete sets of equipment, one for him and one for his imaginary 'buddy', as being just a little bit too paranoid, but he had nevertheless a well-prepared story about diving with a local who had his own equipment. Realizing that such a story would almost certainly fall down under any form of close scrutiny, he was hugely relieved when the girl behind the counter glanced only cursorily at his certification and took his deposit.

He had not been entirely truthful to King when he had said he merely wished to check out the beach where Sir John disappeared. Even though he did not know what he expected to find diving from the beach, he didn't want to risk King disapproving the idea, or even attempting to prevent him from doing it.

It was early on a Saturday morning and there were few people about, apart from a few locals here and there. Burton guessed that most tourists were probably in bed sleeping off the heady parties of the night before.

After leaving Cable Beach, he had driven along slowly and parked where the beach had looked deserted. He had waited a few minutes and seen nobody walk past. He wasn't too worried about people seeing him anyway — after all, he wasn't doing anything wrong — but he just didn't want the attention a lone diver entering the water from the shore was likely to attract. Between the road and the beach was a concrete causeway lined on the roadside by trees. He opened the boot of the hire car and removed the wetsuit he had hired. He hadn't tried it on at the dive shop as he wanted to get away quickly, so it was a pleasant surprise when it fitted well. The water was warm anyway, so he could probably have dived without one, but he wanted to have the flexibility of staying down for a reasonable length of time if he needed to.

Burton assembled and checked the diving gear until he was satisfied that it was all in good working order. He put on the weight belt, which contained about ten pounds of lead. Then he brought the tank in a standing position to the edge of the boot of the car, turned and backed into it, slipping his arms into the buoyancy jacket and lifting it onto his back. He fitted and tightened the straps and moved his shoulders slightly to check that it was firmly in place. Finally, he picked up his mask, snorkel and fins and closed the boot of the car.

Burton locked the car door and placed the keys on top of a small ledge in the front nearside wheel arch — he didn't want to take the modern, electronic key into the water and risk damaging or losing it. Then he started walking towards the sea, first on a bed of twigs, then a cool concrete strip and finally on the soft, fine sand of the beach.

The water close to the beach was a clear turquoise colour with white horses here and there, giving testament to the light wind that was blowing in from the north, turning a deep dark blue further out. The wind had brought in some seaweed and Burton could see patches of brown where the surface was covered in a diverse collection of it. The beach itself sloped down fairly steeply towards the sea, and the last part dropped off almost vertically, a consequence of the constant battering the sandy beach had taken from the larger waves created by the harsh weather that the islands, and he himself whilst flying there, had experienced a few days before.

It was still early and, as the land had yet to be warmed by the sun, the sea felt relatively warm as he stepped into it. He took a few steps and felt the bottom fall away sharply. With a few more paces he was already up to his waist and could feel the weight of the tank being shared by the water. He spat in his mask, and then rinsed it in the sea water. Then he put the mask on, inflated his buoyancy jacket slightly, gripped the mouth-piece of the snorkel between his teeth and let himself fall forward, floating under the buoyancy of the jacket. He started to swim away from the shore using long, slow kicks.

After the stormy weather, the sea was turbid and visibility was down to several metres at best. There was anyway very little to see: the sandy bottom was devoid of any reefs or other objects of interest, and Burton had few visible objects to head towards. He could just make out what looked like an old anchor weight, a concrete lump with an iron ring set in it, adorned by an old piece of rope, which he judged to be little more than ten metres away. He looked at his watch and swam for two minutes, passing over the anchor weight and heading further out to sea. He was not in a marked swimming area, so he did not have to worry about buoys and lines, but equally he could not be sure that no boats would be about. However, he had not been able to see any when he started swimming and, as sound travels well through water, he was fairly confident that he would hear any approaching boats long before they became a risk.

When the two minutes was up, Burton stopped swimming and looked back towards the shore. He was now a reasonable distance out, and slightly to the east of where he had started, which was in line with the parked car. This meant that there was a gentle current, which would hinder his swim to Old Fort Beach, but would help him on the way back. On balance, he was happy with this as he would be able to expend his energy during the dive knowing that he would not have to struggle back against the current.

He once again submerged his head, registered the time and continued to swim to the east. He was glad that the depth gauge he had chosen had a compass fitted — he had had to specifically request one, as the majority of consoles at the dive shop had simply sported an empty hole where the compass normally sat, and for a while it had looked as if they had none. For a further two minutes he swam due east and then stopped and checked his position in relation to the beach. He had drifted slightly inward with the current, and he calculated that it was coming from approximately west-north-west. He changed his heading accordingly, and was pleased to note that he appeared to be on course. He then swam for another ten minutes on the same bearing, checking his position and progress every now and then.

When he was approximately at the edge of Old Fort Beach, he scanned the horizon briefly and identified Sir John's house. He ran the descriptions of the three eye witnesses they had spoken to in his mind, and tried to picture Sir John's last movements. Satisfied that he was in approximately the right area to search, he replaced the snorkel mouthpiece with that of the regulator and took a long breath, whilst checking the pressure gauge, to verify that it was still working. Then he dumped the air in his buoyancy jacket, breathed out and waited as he slid slowly beneath the water.

Burton fancied that he caught a glimpse of a reflection from the shore close to Sir John's house just as his line of vision was curtailed by the internal mirror of the sea. He kicked his feet, breathed in and surfaced again, but was unable to see anything more, so he once again emptied his lungs and made the transition to the underwater world.

Burton descended all the way to the bottom, which according to his depth gauge was seventeen metres. He allowed his knees to rest in the sand and took on a kneeling position. He looked at the dive table he had brought with him and saw that, at eighteen metres he would have a maximum of sixty minutes bottom time. As this would be the deepest point of the dive, he would be diving at much less than eighteen metres, so he could probably stretch it a bit, but as he had no buddy to rely on in case of trouble, he decided on a maximum of fifty minutes bottom time, and vowed to check continually his depth gauge so that he didn't keep hugging the bottom and not notice if it became deeper.

Burton looked around to see if he could see any kind of landmark at all, but he could see almost nothing. There were several small rocks scattered about and he collected these and made a small pile of them. As visibility was not good, he'd have to be virtually on top of the pile before he could see it, but if he planned and swam his search pattern correctly, he should come close enough to see them and, if so, it would provide a useful marker.

He wanted to search an area from shallow to deep, even though this would mean his dive profile would not be ideal, as if swimmers were to come out later they would be more likely to swim closer to the beach. He took a roll of lightweight fluorescent-yellow nylon rope from his pocket and headed towards the beach. The rope stretched thirty metres and, by the time he had reached the end, the depth was only seven metres. He took some of the rocks he had brought with him and made another pile around which he tied the string. He would swim a uniform search grid, but with the errors that would be caused by the current, the rope would enable him to know when he was back in line with his starting point.

Working on the initial assumption that the current at this depth would be similar to the current on the surface, Burton began swimming on the bearing he'd used before, looking carefully at the bottom on both sides. He saw little in the way of interesting objects on the sea bottom and was surprised that this area of the shore was so devoid of reef life or activity. After five minutes, Burton turned and calculated his route back. He estimated the bearing and time that would bring him back where he started and set off.

Looking from side to side, peering through the murky water, Burton again saw little of interest. After three minutes he saw the rocks to his right and the rope in front of him, and was pleased to note that he appeared to have calculated the current correctly. He then turned and repeated the process, moving gradually deeper every time he turned.

When he was almost at the far end of his search grid, Burton noticed in the distance what looked like an old anchor and chain. Swimming over to the anchor, he followed the chain a little way and came across a rusted plate of metal, possibly part of a small ship or boat that had been ripped off in a storm when the boat had been anchored. Most of its brown, rusty colour was camouflaged by a layer of coral encrusted on it. Here Burton saw his first fish of the dive, a French angelfish that darted away when he approached. He watched the shimmering, colourful flash disappear into the murky distance.

Burton looked carefully at the remains on the sea bed. He didn't really know what to expect or whether it could have any bearing on the disappearance of Sir John — it would have been almost impossible for him to get stuck on anything at this depth unless he had swum down and purposefully tried to get caught. Also, no marks had been found on Sir John's body to suggest that he had been wedged in anywhere, or that he had struggled to free himself. Contact with an object such as an anchor or chain covered in coral would almost certainly leave lacerations on the skin. Swimming over the remains, Burton found more fish. Apparently, they congregated around the only alien object on the otherwise barren sea bottom. A spiny lobster, disturbed by the large fish that swam overhead, moved in an arachnid fashion under its armoured shelter. Seeing little else, and expecting to find little else, Burton turned to swim back.

As he turned, he saw a shark swimming in his direction, watching him warily out of its bland, almost catlike eye. His heart thumped at the appearance of the unexpected; Burton was flabbergasted that a shark would venture so close to the shore. It was about two metres long, a sleek torpedo of gunmetal grey and white, which Burton identified as a Caribbean Reef Shark. As always with sharks, the beast was characterized by its ugly, perpetually dangerous-looking mouth. Although he knew the shark was highly unlikely to attack him, he felt a flush of fear go through him. It always seemed simple when you were told that a shark wouldn't attack you, but it was very different when you were alone with one. He struggled to master his fear quickly, determined not to panic. Remembering the advice he had been given about sharks, he continued to swim in the same direction, obliquely away from the shark, with slow, bold kicks of his legs. He folded his hands in front of him and kept them there, so that the shark wouldn't see the fluttering white expanse of skin, mistake it for a fish and pounce.

He concentrated on swimming in a smooth, rhythmic fashion, letting the shark know that he was not injured and would be a difficult target. Why was the shark here? It was highly unusual for sharks to venture in this close to the coast and, given the scarcity of fish, it couldn't be a very good hunting ground. Perhaps the stormy weather had produced currents which had brought the shark in, or persuaded it for some other reason to move away from its normal haunts. Anyway, another good question was why he was here. This had turned out to be a complete waste of time. He had found nothing, and he was now swimming away from his search site being shadowed by a shark.

As he swam along, he glanced periodically and subtly at the shark, which continued to swim along with him. He knew he was heading away from the shore, and engineered an opportunity to reach the compass and direct its face towards him without disturbing his rhythm. He confirmed he was heading in a northerly direction, with nothing to do but bide his time until he had a chance to return.

After several minutes, Burton made his routine glance for the shark and saw nothing. To be safe, he continued swimming in the same direction and looked more carefully around. Satisfied the shark was gone, he then settled onto his knees on the sandy bottom. Having left his search pattern, Burton was disorientated for a few moments. He tried to mentally picture his route back and swam slowly off in the direction he had come. When he estimated that he was approximately back into his search grid, he swam back on the same bearing he had used on the first return run, checking the time before he started. After three minutes he looked around, but was unable to see either the pile of rocks or the brightly coloured nylon rope. Once again, he settled onto the bottom to try to get his bearings.

He looked carefully in both directions, but was unable to see anything. He realized that he must have gone off-course. Too late, he looked at his depth gauge and saw that he was now at twenty-two metres. He cursed to himself and almost started to swim immediately for the surface, but stopped himself in time. He forced himself to wait and take stock, reaching for the dive table. He concentrated first on breathing slowly and then on the figures in front of him. His bottom time at twenty-two metres had reduced to fifty minutes, and he had been down almost that long. Again trying to stop his rising panic in its tracks, he told himself that he had not been at that depth for very long, so he was well within the no-stop dive time. However, he decided to surface slowly anyway. He had lost his search grid, which he had fortunately almost finished, so there was little value in remaining on the bottom.

Burton kicked up towards the surface, periodically dumping air from his buoyancy jacket to prevent a fast ascent. He approached the surface very slowly whilst watching his depth gauge, and stopped at five metres to make a long, conservative safety stop.

When his head broke the surface, Burton looked around for the beach. He was shocked to find that he was a considerable distance from the shore. Although the current would aid him, he had no wish to stay out longer than he had to, and decided to head straight for the shore, and let the current push him some way towards where he started from, rather than swimming back to the area he had left the car.

Burton inflated the buoyancy jacket and started to swim towards the shore. He kept the mask on and used the snorkel to breathe, keeping a wary eye out for the shark. He knew that sharks rarely attacked divers, but they were known to attack swimmers or surfers who were at the surface, most likely mistaking their kicking white feet for some kind of small fish. Burton was thankful for the black fins, which would make his feet less conspicuous.

He swam strongly towards the shore,

mustering up all his energy to get there as quickly as possible. He considered dropping his weights to speed things up, but didn't really want to have to explain their absence to the dive shop when he returned the equipment. Besides, he didn't really know how much difference it would make. Without the weights, he could use less air in the buoyancy jacket to maintain positive buoyancy, which would in turn mean less volume and therefore less drag, but he couldn't help feeling that this would probably be an academic exercise that would make little difference in practice.

Burton kept looking regularly past his feet for any tell-tale warning signs of the shark returning, but he could see almost nothing in the murky water, so he gave up and concentrated on swimming. This seemed to take much longer than he thought it would. Every now and then he raised his head to check his progress, but he didn't seem to be making much headway at all, especially considering that he should be aided by the current. He wondered if the current had now become unfavourable.

The wind was picking up and the waves were becoming progressively bigger. A few times, Burton's snorkel was swamped, and he was forced to exhale violently to clear it. This would not normally be a problem but, now that he was exhausted, each time he was forced to muster his reserves to blow out hard, his heart sank, knowing his energy reserves were slowly being sapped.

When he felt he could not carry on any further, he turned onto his back, spat out the snorkel and lay motionless to restore his energy. Thank God for the buoyancy jacket, he thought. He knew that without it, he would not be able to get back. He started to kick his legs, ignoring the pain creeping into his thighs and trying to maintain his momentum. He decided to continue in this fashion for a while, as he would be able to conserve more energy. He kept scanning the water, looking for the grey triangular fin of the shark, but saw nothing.

Finally, Burton saw that he was getting close to the shore. A wave of relief spread through his body, but he forced himself to keep going as fast as he could — he knew he would only be safe when he was out of the water. He kept swimming on his back, throwing an occasional glance over his shoulder until he was almost beached. Then he pulled off his fins and turned onto his front, grinning happily as he felt his knees bury themselves into the sand. He managed to stand and staggered the last few metres onto the beach, where he threw the fins down and took off the buoyancy jacket and tank, dropping it down next to the fins. Then he collapsed.

He lay on his back for several minutes, concentrating on breathing deeply and trying to recover. The sky above him promised fickle weather. Large areas of clear blue sky were broken up by fluffy white cumulus clouds with angry grey streaks. Out to sea, a number of the fluffy clouds were piling up into the familiar anvil shape that preceded a thunderstorm. A flock of birds flew over the beach from somewhere inland, busy black beings darting across the sky, heading out to sea.

Burton stretched his neck back and looked to see where the birds had come from. He was surprised to see that he was almost in front of Sir John Little's house. He was even more surprised to see a figure silhouetted against the horizon, standing close to it. He rolled onto his front, summoning the energy to get up onto his knees, but when he did so, he could see no sign at all of the man.

Burton struggled to his feet and walked over towards Sir John's house. He saw now that he was very close to the spot where he had first met Melissa. The gate at the top of the wooden stairs was closed but not locked. Burton looked at the house for a bit but could see no movement at all. He walked over to the gate, but decided not to enter. There were many footsteps in front of the gate, leading in all directions, but then it was a public beach. Exhausted, and none the wiser after his energetic morning, Burton headed back, picked up his equipment and started the long walk back to his car.

9

Michael Burton sat at the highly polished mahogany bar in Blackbeard's Cove, the hotel watering hole, nursing a cold Kalik beer. He was perched comfortably on a high stool, having found the ideal position to rest his weary muscles in a semi-extended state. In front of him was a fresh-smelling shock of bright yellow flowers, which was reflected prettily in the gleaming veneer of the bar, and he was overwhelmed by a comforting feeling of homeliness and safety in the company of the exuberant barman. The dimly lit bar looked out onto a small terrace adorned with iron tables, which itself gave way to the gardens of the hotel and, eventually, the strait of sea separating New Providence from Paradise Island. A steady stream of hotel guests and travellers enticed in from the warm streets outside entered the bar, most opting to sit outside in the balmy shade of the gardens but a few sitting at the tables close to the windows, providing a low background noise of friendly chatter that added to Burton's feeling of security.

He had arrived back at the hotel an hour or

so ago after returning both the car and the diving equipment in a zombie-like state of exhaustion. Relieved that he had managed to complete both challenges without too much fuss, he had quickly cleaned up and headed down for a well-deserved lunch, washed down with a cool beer. In spite of his recent exertions, he still wanted to go back and have another look at the beach house, but this time not burdened with heavy scuba gear. He drained the beer and looked up at the barman, a short, heavy-set Bahamian with an impeccable white shirt, black bow tie and a patterned waistcoat that seemed to match the wallpaper. The gold badge on his waistcoat informed Burton that his name was Sam.

'Another Kalik, please, Sam.'

The waiter's round face was immediately split by a wide grin, showing even teeth that gleamed white against his dark skin. 'Sure thing, sirruh. Gold or reg'lar?'

Burton looked at the bottle in front of him. The label proclaimed that it was regular. He was about to ask for the same again when the barman broke in.

'Yuh should try the Kalik Gold, sir. In the old days, they used to brew Kalik Gold only around the time o' the Junkanoo. In the winter. Round Christmas an' New year. It's stronger an' tastes good. Very good. 'When it's cold, it's got t' be Gold', we used to say. Now, everybodys liked that beer, sirruh, everybodys liked it so good. So they decided to make it all year round. So now yuh can always have yuh a Kalik Gold when yuh want. Oh, yes. When it's cold, it's got t' be Gold.'

'Of course, Sam, I'll have a Kalik Gold then.'

The waiter opened the bottle of beer. It made a loud popping sound, reminiscent of a champagne cork popping out of a bottle. A couple just entering the bar looked around sharply at the noise. Sam grinned broadly.

'I remember one time, sir, round New Year it was. I was working 'ere in the bar and nobody was drinking champagne, I don't know why. Now, obviously, we like people to drink champagne. Good for the atmosphere. And' — he grinned and winked — 'for the pocket. More fellas drink, bigger the check, the bigger de tip. So, anyways, nobody's drinking champagne, and so I opens a bottle of Kalik Gold, like this, under the bar. And the people, yes, they heard the noise and they think that means ordering champagne, and so they comin' to me and they're ordering champagne as well. And, pretty soon, everybody's drinking champagne. And the tips are mounting up.'

Sam broke into peals of contagious

laughter, joined by Burton, who offered to buy the barman a drink.

'No, thank you, sirruh. I jes' start my shift. If I starts drinking now, I not last till the end!'

Burton smiled and left Sam at the bar, looking for a table outside. Finding one, he ordered lunch from the waitress who appeared as if by magic soon after he sat down. Burton could only assume that she had been following his conversation with Sam, as normally in the Bahamas one had to wait quite a long time before being served.

Although the table was in the shade, it was warm and humid, as if the heat was hanging in the air. In the shelter of the hotel there did not appear to be any breeze, although the smell of the sea was readily discernible. A couple on the table next to him were conversing in German. Burton, who had studied German at school but afterwards had done very little with it, gave up trying to follow their conversation after a few minutes.

He sat back in his chair and ran through the events of the morning in his mind. Although he had found nothing during his dive, he was convinced that somebody had been watching him. It was all too much of a coincidence: first he had spotted the flash of light before he had dived, which he was fairly certain was the sun glinting off a pair of binoculars, and secondly, he had seen the figure watching him from near Sir John's house. Again, he wasn't sure how seriously to take it; he could hardly talk to Chester King about these two 'incidents'. Together they amounted to little more than the sowing of the seed of suspicion that things were not all they seemed.

The waitress arrived with a substantial steak sandwich with chips and salad, which Burton wolfed down hungrily. As he finished off his beer, he was convinced he needed to return to Sir John's house, and he needed to do so soon — he wanted to see if he could find any trace of the figure he had seen before, and look for more clues about Sir John's disappearance. Chester King would probably return next week anyway, but that needn't stop Burton having a look beforehand.

Burton placed his empty beer bottle on the table and sat back, taking in the view of Paradise Island the other side of the water, framed by the palm trees bordering the hotel garden. After several moments of quiet contemplation, he stood up and headed towards the lobby.

★   ★   ★

The taxi dropped him off in a cleared sandy area at Old Fort Beach, close to the marina. Burton walked over the thin layer of sand, which covered crumbly, cracked ground. As he reached the beach, Burton removed his sandals and walked along the shore close to the water.

Old Fort Beach was undeniably beautiful, far less developed than its neighbours and frequented by many locals. It was also quite far afield for most holidaymakers, being a fifteen minute drive from the airport in the other direction to Nassau or Paradise Island, where most visitors to the island stayed. There were a couple of golf courses and a dive centre in the nearby Lyford Cay to the west, but the majority of tourists probably wouldn't come anywhere near it. In fact, Burton thought to himself, if it wasn't for Sir John Little's disappearance, he wouldn't have come anywhere near it either.

As he strolled along the water's edge, he looked up at the houses, quickly spotting Sir John Little's. There were a few people along the beach, sporadically placed here and there soaking up the sun, but most people had clearly stayed at home to avoid the wind, which was a fierce, gusting northerly.

Burton couldn't see anyone outside the house, but was unwilling to make it too

151

obvious that he was watching the place, so periodically he looked around and gazed out to sea. He knew that if someone were watching him from inside the house, he would not be able to see them: it was far brighter outside than in and the windows appeared dark and featureless. Anyway, his suspicion was not that someone was watching him from inside the house; he had seen a reflection and a silhouette, both of which were outside.

Burton carried on walking along the beach. The sand further up had been warmed by the sun since just after sunrise and was extremely hot, so he changed tack and headed towards the sea, allowing the water to cool his feet. After paddling onwards for several minutes, he turned to walk back. Taking a line that he hoped would make it less obvious that he was heading towards Sir John's house, he started back diagonally up the beach.

He skirted the hedges and fences that marked the boundaries of the properties bordering the beach, looking carefully for clues as to who might have been watching him. He saw very little of interest before reaching Sir John's house, although he noticed that there were few footprints. Good, thought Burton, reasoning that it should be easier for him to find the footprints of whoever had been watching him. There was a trail of footprints leading from the Littles' gate onto the beach. They were smallish and he guessed they belonged to Melissa. They didn't seem to go very far but stopped a couple of metres from the stairs. There the owner of the footsteps had apparently turned round, as another trail led back to the gate.

A second set of footprints approached the house from the east. These were longer and broader, certainly a man's, and, by the look of them, a large man. They ended where the smaller prints stopped, and were just far enough away from them not to overlap, so he could not tell if one set was made after the other. At some points, though, they almost touched. Burton wondered if Melissa had met somebody there. A lover, perhaps? Was she having an affaire? This would provide her with a double motive, both the money and the freedom to enjoy it with someone else. But then, why meet them briefly here and not in the house, where they would be less likely to be spotted? Some feeling of guilt about meeting a man in Sir John's house, or fear, perhaps, that someone might be watching her, and that a stranger in the house might arouse suspicions? Or maybe she met not a lover but somebody she was employing to watch him, Burton, while he conducted his amateurish search of the 'crime scene'.

Burton started to follow the larger prints. They led first of all to the stairs, with unidentifiable sandy deposits on the steps, and then reappeared and led back along the beach towards where he had come from. He had not seen any prints at the place where he was dropped off in the taxi, so he knew that they had to originate somewhere else. He walked past another couple of properties before he came to a gap between two, which led back towards the road. On either side were high metal fences, which enclosed bushes and undergrowth. There was a sandy track leading towards the road, and Burton followed the footprints in.

As the track became harder and the loose sand scarcer, so too did the footprints become less obvious and more difficult to follow. Eventually they petered out into nothing, but Burton found some tyre tracks further up. They showed that a car had stopped and had then reversed across the track to drive out forwards. Burton looked carefully at the tyre marks, which resembled those of a military vehicle. The tyres had very deep symmetrical treads, and were probably from an off-road or rally model. Given the depth of the imprint, he guessed that they were relatively new. He imagined they came from a small pickup truck or a jeep, as these vehicles were most often fitted with this sort of tyre. His hire car had been fitted with light rain treads, which looked completely different. He surmised that a forensic professional would be able to come up with a lot more information than he, without training but with a bit of imagination, could come up with. On the other hand, he mused, perhaps such a professional would be far more constrained by what he could prove rather than what he suspected.

Burton found some footprints to the side of the tyre tracks, and they looked to him to be similar to the footprints on the beach. He knew it was tenuous, and far from being provable, but he was fairly certain that somebody had driven into this dirt track, had then walked onto the beach and had spied on him that morning. He suspected as well that whoever it was had visited Melissa Little while he was there.

Burton walked the rest of the way down the dirt track until he came to the road. The track was narrow at the entrance, which led onto a dual carriageway divided in the middle by a line of palm trees in a kerbed off area of thick grass. On the side of the road leading onto the track, the kerb was no lower than normal and he could see no new gouges in the stone.

Again he suspected a pickup or jeep had been used; a saloon car of similar size to his hire car would certainly have come into contact with the kerb stone and left some evidence of its presence.

On both sides of the road were driveways, and he recognized the entrance to Sir John's house, where he had been with Chester King a few days ago. He walked towards the house and peered through the entrance gate and through the greenery at the drive. It was empty; there was certainly no jeep parked there. The garage was probably big enough for two cars, but he doubted it would house both a car and a jeep.

Not wanting to be spotted hanging around outside, he turned and walked back towards the dirt track and followed it back onto the beach, turning towards the marina where he would be able to arrange for a taxi.

'Hello, stranger!'

Burton turned, startled at the sound of a voice breaking the silence that wasn't a silence; his mind had become so accustomed to the gentle rustle of the wind and the waves that he had filtered it out.

Melissa Little was standing on the beach, some way from the steps leading up to her property, smiling with glossy, slightly parted lips. The top of her face was shaded by a straw boater fastened garishly under her chin with a bright vermillion ribbon.

'Hello, there,' said Burton, jauntily, whilst desperately trying to think of a reason for his presence there. Despite the setback, he was grateful that he hadn't run into her earlier, when he had been lugging scuba gear around.

'Are you enjoying our beach? I'm sure I saw you earlier today coming in from a dive. What was it like? It was quite an unusual sight, I must say. We don't normally have many scuba divers around here. Most divers go in search of beautiful reefs full of fish, which are only a short boat trip away. Here, we only seem to have bare sand and, after the recent storm, murky water.'

Burton felt a flush rising on his cheeks, and determined to maintain control, had no option but to launch into an exuberant defence. 'Oh, it's always nice to dive in unusual places. I get a bit bored with colourful fish and pretty reefs. Give me bare sand and realism any day.'

'Well, perhaps we can dive together sometime. Although I have to admit, I'm a sucker for pretty sea life . . . '

'Sounds like a good idea. We'll rent a small boat and go out to one of the islands.'

'Mmm, but I'm not sure I trust you. You haven't even told me what you were really doing here.'

He decided to come clean. 'I'm actually here pursuing one or two leads we have on your husband's death. We wanted to check the immediate area to see if we could locate any further clues. I wasn't able to find any though.'

'Well, you're very committed. Coming here on a Saturday to search for clues — it's a shame not all policemen are like you.'

'Yes, well, I'm sure most are really. Very persistent, many of them. Anyway, there is one thing I would like to ask you about, if I may?'

'Yes, of course. Anything to help the police.'

Melissa seemed to enjoy repeatedly referring to Burton as a policeman, which confused Burton as she knew he was not employed by the police but by the British Foreign Office. He wondered if she doubted his authority to carry out the tasks he was. Still, if that was so, she would be right; he had none. But he couldn't really change his story now. And anyway, he was assisting the investigation in an official capacity.

'I noticed these sets of footprints here. They seem to join up with a set leading to your property. They start over there,' — Burton pointed towards the entrance to the dirt track — 'meet with smaller prints,

158

like yours, and then head onto your steps, and then back out again. Judging by the way the prints have been left, I'd rule out the possibility that the person stopped at the bottom of the steps and turned away. He'd have to be a contortionist.' At this point Burton pointed at a footprint heading away from the steps, the heel of which was almost in line with the edge of the gate.

Melissa laughed. 'Are policemen always so suspicious?' Again, that word. 'If you must know, these prints are Sean's. Sean is our gardener,' she added, seeing the lack of comprehension on his face. 'I'd have thought you'd have known that. After all, policemen do do research, don't they?'

She looked at him playfully as she said this, a smile creeping into both corners of her mouth.

'Yes, of course. What was Sean doing when he left these prints?'

'I have no idea. You'll have to ask him that. Surely it's not a crime for a gardener to leave footprints outside his employer's house?'

'But I think he left the prints here today.' Burton attacked triumphantly. 'He was here for the purpose of watching me to make sure I didn't find anything incriminating.'

Melissa burst into laughter. 'You are funny. And you're very definitely not like a policeman. Not like those policemen who stopped by when John had been drinking. Very serious they were. Not amusing at all. Anyway, Mr Burton, my gardener, Sean, works Saturdays. And Tuesdays. And Thursdays. I think he works at another house along here on Wednesdays and Fridays. Oh, and he normally takes Sunday and Monday off. Anything else you'd like to know about Sean, gardener and criminal mastermind?'

Burton said nothing.

'Anyway, he was here this morning. Working. Not spying on the élite of the British crime fighting contingent. At least, not as far as I know.'

With the last sentence came a mocking, questioning look. Somehow, she hardly resembled the woman that he and King had met previously, and he wondered if this had something to do with him rather than her. Maybe she, Melissa, was behaving in the same way, but the professional, assured, polite King had elicited a completely different response to the passionate, inexperienced Burton.

'And anyway, where's your sidekick? Mr King? I thought that policemen always had to investigate in pairs . . . '

Burton finally decided to play along. 'Only during the week. At weekends, we're allowed

160

out on our own. As long as we're well behaved . . . '

Melissa laughed. 'So you're going to be well behaved? How disappointing.'

'Well, I could make an exception. I don't think the police are watching me. Somebody else was earlier, but the police aren't now.'

'Are you sure you're not paranoid? It all seems a bit far-fetched, people spying on you and suchlike. Anyway, Michael — may I call you Michael? — it has been nice talking to you. I'm all alone now, so I don't get out much. Would you like to go out to dinner with me? I could pick you up at your hotel and we could go somewhere close by?'

'Yes, I'd like that. Although I thought the man should ask these things.'

'Yes, well, that may be true, but I'm sure if I had waited for you to ask, I wouldn't be going anywhere fast. Anyway, isn't it against the rules to go on dinner dates with suspects?'

'I'm not sure that you're a suspect as such. I mean, we're not even sure that a crime has been committed. No crime, no suspect. We are merely keeping open minds as to what happened.'

'Whatever you say, Michael. Where are you staying?'

'The Colonial.'

'OK, I'll meet you there this evening. Shall we say seven-thirty?'

'Good. I'll see you then.'

Burton turned and walked back along the beach. Before turning up the dirt track, he glanced over his shoulder, but Melissa had already gone.

10

After downing a Kalik Gold in Blackbeard's Cove, Michael Burton waited on a comfortable sofa in the foyer of the Hilton. He glanced at his watch and noted that Melissa was already quarter of an hour late, but somehow he wasn't at all surprised by this. He had himself turned up a few minutes late, comfortable in the knowledge that she wouldn't be there. Burton let his eyes wander around the colonial-style lounge, which was ostentatiously decorated with large gilded mirrors and impressive grey-white marble mantelpieces and plush carpets which, with almost British imprecision, just failed to fit in with the rest of the furnishings in the room.

A middle-aged couple was seated across the room from Burton, engaged in an animated conversation over a bottle of pink champagne, which stood in a silver wine cooler in the middle of the glass-topped table in front of them. The man, whose greying hair was carefully combed back, was wearing a double-breasted dark blue blazer emblazoned with large, heavy-looking gold buttons and a white shirt topped with a silk cravat. His wife

— at least Burton assumed they were married — was wearing a smart skirt and blouse. They looked every inch the well-presented English couple abroad, Burton reflected. He had always found it slightly strange that most foreigners regard English people abroad with one of two completely polarized views: either the quiet, reserved, well-dressed, polite, worldly traveller, or the ill-mannered, loud, xenophobic, rude, violent, drunken yob. And nowadays more often the latter than the former, he thought with some sadness. He wondered in which category he would be placed. He smiled at the thought of being labelled one or the other: as always, it was difficult, if not impossible, to generalize to the extent of being able to fit all people into any number of categories, let alone two. But then again, if so many people genuinely thought so, maybe there was something in it.

His reverie was disturbed by the arrival of a waiter, whose broad smile seemed to precede him. Burton looked up at him and smiled.

'Yuh all right, boss? Can I get yuh another beer?'

'Mmm, why not?'

Burton sat back and relaxed; if his character assessment was correct, it would be some time before Melissa showed up. A smartly dressed man wearing a colourful waistcoat, whom Burton first took to be a waiter, entered the room and made his way over to a beautiful grand piano which stood in the corner. The wood of the piano was deep mahogany, its surface a glossy sheen of hard polishing. It was an item that Burton had not really expected to find in a Bahamian hotel, but its presence was somehow strangely fitting here. The man lifted the lid of the piano and arranged himself on the stool in front of it before starting to play softly, fluently, with no sheet music or other distractions in front of him. The couple opposite broke off their conversation and listened attentively, clearly taken with the music. Burton wondered if they had asked for him to play, or if they knew that he was to play around this time and came specifically for that reason. Burton glanced at his watch to learn that Melissa was now half an hour late. This seemed less of an issue as the waiter trotted over with his beer, the misty condensation on the bottle testimony to both the coolness of the drink and the humidity of the air.

The piano music sounded familiar to Burton. As he listened, high staccato notes gradually slipped down in tone whilst building up in volume before ending in a frenzied yet controlled crescendo. He racked his brain desperately to come up with the name of the piece; he felt certain it was composed by Grieg, but was unable to work out why he knew this. He allowed his ear to tune in and his mind to tune out, hoping it would wander to the last time and place he had heard the music. He closed his eyes and concentrated, his perception of the music becoming stronger. He could almost see colours dancing in time with music as he tried to visualize the time so long ago that he had been playing the piece.

'Excuse me, do you mind if I sit here?'

The stream of reminiscence stopped suddenly. Startled, Burton opened his eyes and glared angrily at the source of the disturbance. His rage abated quickly on seeing that Melissa had arrived, and his frown was replaced by a wry smile.

'You looked as if you were lost in thought. I hope I didn't disturb you.'

'Not at all,' lied Burton. 'I was merely relaxing. And looking forward to this evening, of course. Yes, please sit down. Would you like something to drink?'

Melissa perched herself demurely on the edge of the sofa. 'Yes, please. May I have a glass of champagne.'

'Of course.'

Burton looked around for the waiter. He

saw immediately that the man knew his job. Having registered Melissa's entry and seen her sit next to Burton, he was waiting unobtrusively within easy eye contact for Burton, yet had not crowded the table straight away. Catching Burton's glance, he ambled over and took the order for the champagne.

An odd choice of drink for somebody who has just lost a loved one, thought Burton. He noted that Melissa was hardly dressed as a grieving widow either. She was wearing a smart and unobtrusive, but not unrevealing, black dress, which reached down to just above her knees, clung to her slim hips and widened around her bust, her plunging neckline displaying a profound fissure framed by a wide black 'V'. He felt his eyes wandering to her breasts and quickly looked away, reminding himself that she had just lost her husband. He wondered how she could sit so easily on the front corner of the sofa. It was soft and comfortable, with deep cushions that seemed to give under the slightest pressure, and which cried out for its occupants to lie back and lose themselves in their opulence. Yet somehow she defied the luxuriousness of the sofa and gave an impression of alertness, or readiness, or eagerness to move on, or all three.

'Did you have an enjoyable stroll on the beach this afternoon?' she asked.

'Yes, very good, although I didn't stay long after I saw you.' Burton was always amazed by the ability of people to start conversations on the most banal subjects, particularly people who had experience of moving in diplomatic circles. How often had he been to evening receptions, talking to people with whom he would not normally engage in conversation, trying desperately to find a topic of mutual interest? How often had he been forced to resort to, for him at least, the most uninspiring of them all, work?

The waiter arrived bearing Melissa's champagne in a tall champagne flute on a silver tray. He casually slid a small doily on the polished mahogany table in front of them and placed the glass carefully on top of it. Against the dark brown of the table and the black of Melissa's dress, Burton could see tiny bubbles effervescing from the top of the glass and catching the light.

'You've had a busy day, then. Diving in the morning, walking in the afternoon. You must be quite tired.' She looked across at Burton slyly and raised her glass. 'Cheers.'

'Cheers.'

'Do you mind where we go to eat this evening? I thought we might walk along to a small French restaurant I know, very close to here. Or would you prefer to go somewhere else? Do you like the French kitchen?'

Burton smiled inwardly at the use of the word 'kitchen'. 'I like most types of food, including French. That sounds perfect.'

They finished their drinks and stood up to leave. There was a momentary silence as the pianist finished the piece he was playing. Beyond Grieg, Burton had not been able to remember the name. The couple sitting opposite seized the opportunity to make a request. Burton noted wryly that the gentlemen requested a hackneyed classic from Mozart in a strong German accent. So much for his typical English countenance . . .

★ ★ ★

The restaurant was indeed very close to the hotel, a short walk along Marlborough Street towards West Bay Street. It was heavily influenced by both Bahamian and French cuisine, and undoubtedly aimed at the romantic end of the market. The large dark dining room was decorated, rather than illuminated, by a myriad of candles. Chandeliers adorned the ceiling and completed the traditional furnishings. As they entered, the *maître d'* scurried up to them obsequiously,

169

clearly recognizing Melissa from previous visits.

'Madame Little, good evening. I hope you are well. I was so sorry to hear about your husband. Sir John was a great man. We will certainly miss him greatly. Now, a table for two, I take it?'

'Yes, please, Manuel.'

The *maître d'* plucked two menus from the lectern at the entrance of the restaurant and headed off into the main dining area, which was very full with few, if any, empty tables.

'And where would you like to sit tonight? By the window, outside or upstairs?'

Although ostensibly talking to both Burton and Melissa, the *maitre d'* somehow managed to convey the fact that he was talking to his friend and patron Melissa Little, wife of his late friend and patron Sir John Little, rather than to the unimportant Englishman who happened to accompany her. Burton wondered how these sorts of people learnt this art, and how they practised it without being clobbered in the process.

'Actually, Manuel, we'd quite like to sit outside, if we can.'

'Of course, of course. A wise decision. It's lovely weather outside at this time of year.'

Without slowing down or changing course, he led them in a sweeping arc towards the exit to the patio. He called softly and sharply to one of the waiters, who immediately held the door for the three of them, and then scurried in front of them again to pull out chairs on a table laid for two people which, despite being in what Burton would have thought was the prime position, was free. Having pulled out the chairs, the waiter melted away, unseen.

'I called ahead to say that we might be eating here tonight,' Melissa said, noting the puzzled expression on Burton's face. 'They must have set aside a table in each area for us.'

The *maitre d'* placed the leather bound menus on the table in front of each of them. 'Can I bring you an aperitif?'

Melissa was quick to respond. 'For me, a Kir Royale.'

Burton took more time. 'What sort of beer do you have?'

The *maitre d'* began to reel off all the beers they had in stock, beginning with the locals and then embarking on a lengthy list of expensive 'premium' beers imported from Europe. Burton let him continue until he had exhausted his memory and, presumably, also the names of all the beers they kept, before ordering a local draft beer that had been mentioned at the start of the man's spiel.

'Very good, sir.' He managed a look that was genial, irritated and sanctimonious all at the same time and then shuffled off.

Melissa looked around appraisingly. 'My husband was a regular here. He loved the food, loved the atmosphere. I too have only good memories of the place. I wasn't sure if I should come back here so soon after John's death — I wasn't sure how it would make me feel. But actually, I think that it's good to carry on living, to go to the places one loves, rather than sink into a manic depression. I'm sure John would have wanted me to keep going.

'We used to come here very often on a Saturday night. Like tonight. Although he had retired, John would often have work to do during the week, or he would go and play golf early in the mornings, so we didn't go out much on weekdays. I would cook most nights, and we would drink some wine. John liked to eat fairly early, at least by Caribbean standards. Around seven-thirty. But on Saturdays he liked to go out and eat, and we would go to a restaurant and eat a fancy meal. And this was one of his favourites, if not the favourite.'

Melissa broke off as the waiter returned with her Kir Royale and Burton's beer. Seeing the unopened menus on the table, he

172

said he would be back to take their order.

'Life's going to be really different without John. It will take some getting used to. Especially here, in the Caribbean. I moved here for the first time with John, and have lived here with him ever since. Before I met him, I had only been to a couple of islands on holiday. My friends here are his friends. My acquaintances are his acquaintances. I know other people, of course, people I meet every day, but it's funny how quickly you build up a circle of friends who are all like-minded. Many of the women that I know are wives of John's colleagues working for the British Government, or friends of his from the golf course. Still, I suppose it's a small world, an island like this.'

'How did you meet your husband?'

Melissa opened the menu in front of her. 'That's a long story, and I'm going to need something to eat very soon. Let's order, and then I'll tell you.'

After a couple of minutes, the waiter returned, armed with a small notepad and a pen. Melissa ordered melon and ham, followed by a rare fillet steak. Burton chose snails, hoping they would be liberally doused in garlic, and joined Melissa with the steak. Burton chose a Châteauneuf-du-Pape, surprised that they had the heavy red wine. He

173

wasn't sure it would be better than many of the new world wines they seemed to have in abundance here, like the undiscovered ruby gems from South America he had tried in a hotel he had stayed in on his last visit.

Burton sat back and sipped his beer. His eyes met Melissa's, and he detected something unreadable in their blue grey sheen. He wondered if she was going to continue; he wanted to learn more about her, but didn't want to appear to be prying. After all, he was only an amateur sleuth and at the moment he was not even working anyway.

'Anyway, I was going to tell you how I met John. It was about ten years ago, at a polo match in England. John used to play polo as a young man, and maintained an interest in the game. I was hanging out with some of my friends from school, one of whom played polo regularly. I believe she actually represented England in a junior age group. I can't say that I had any particular fascination for the game itself, although I was at one stage a keen horse rider and still ride every now and then — it always looked as if they rode those poor ponies mercilessly into the ground. Tell me, Michael, do you like polo?'

'Er, well, I don't know much about it, to be honest. I like other sports though. I've played a bit of cricket and rugby, though not recently.'

'Oh, John loved to follow the cricket as well. Always glued to the television for days when there was a test match. Anyway, at the time John was just separated from his long-term girlfriend, so I guess he was on the rebound. I was not long out of university, and definitely not looking for love. I was sitting with my group on some blankets, and John and some friends came traipsing past and John knocked over my glass of champagne. He gallantly insisted on buying me another, and came back with a bottle not a glass. We got chatting and he asked me if I'd like to go to dinner with him. I didn't want to appear too interested, and I had anyway arranged to dine with friends, so I declined, but I gave him my number so he could call me, which he did the following day.

'I'd woken up with a bad headache, and had struggled through the day, and then I had this chipper voice on the phone asking me if I could make it to dinner that night. I told him I could barely make it to my own kitchen for dinner that night, but I'd be happy to meet him later on in the week. In fact, it was the following weekend that we met up for the first time since the polo match. We went out to dinner, and things moved on from there.'

She paused to take a sip of her drink, holding the pink frothing liquid to her full, equally pink lips. Burton watched her throat contract as she swallowed the liquid. She replaced the glass carefully.

'John was obviously a lot older than me, and I wasn't particularly looking for a relationship, but he was charming and clearly held a reasonably high position in the Foreign Office. He was based in London then, after having been stationed in the States and before he was offered the ambassador's position in Jamaica. The life of a diplomat's wife seemed very appealing to me at the time.' Melissa smiled sadly, as if to say that experience had cured her of this illusion. Burton wondered if the smile was also partly meant for him, as a more junior employee of the FCO who might ultimately rise to the role of ambassador. If only she knew how tedious he found it all and how unambitious he was in that respect.

'So how long did you stay in London? When was he given the ambassadorship?'

'We were in London for a little more than a year. We saw each other regularly, but I lived still with a girl I knew from university. I had managed to land a job as a correspondent for a South American newspaper in London, which was interesting work and paid quite well. I was perfectly happy doing that, but then John announced that he had been

176

offered the ambassadorship. Well, it was quite a shock at the time, I can tell you. At first, I was unsure whether I actually wanted to go, but the Caribbean was so far away that it meant that I would not be able to visit very regularly. If I stayed in England, it would effectively mean the end of our relationship. And, after all, who wouldn't jump at the chance to be a diplomat's wife in Jamaica?'

Melissa smiled and took a sip from her drink. 'That was seven years ago. John had about ten years to go until mandatory retirement, but he was able to take early retirement after only five years. I think it was good for him. He was still able to busy himself in certain aspects of his work, giving advice on issues he had worked on and people he had dealt with, but it gave him a lot more free time to go out and do things. I don't know about you, but he never seemed to have much time when he was working.'

Burton drained his beer and cleared his throat. 'Well, er, I probably have a lot more free time than Sir John did. He held a far more senior position than I do, and I can imagine that the demands on his time were fairly severe.' As he said this, he thought of the current ambassador, Sir Anthony Reardon, and wondered if what he was saying was entirely true. Reardon did very little, as far as

Burton was aware, apart from delegate his duties to lackeys who worked like dogs. Like Burton, for instance.

The sommelier arrived bearing the bottle of wine, which he opened with a competent and practised flourish after displaying the label to Burton. He poured a tiny amount into the large, glass in front of Burton and stood to attention. Burton swirled the wine quickly, watching it as it coated the glass and ran down. He sniffed and was rewarded with a complex aroma, which was suitably finished off when he took a small nip to taste. He nodded to the sommelier, who then poured generous measures for Melissa and himself.

'What will you do now?' Burton asked, keen to get Melissa talking again.

'I don't know. I haven't really thought about it. As I said, most of the people I know here I know through my husband, and I don't necessarily have a lot in common with them. But they're nice people, all the same. I may stay here on the island — I like it here a lot — but I'd have to think of something to do. I'd get very bored here on my own, without a job or something else to keep me busy all the time. I may consider working for a newspaper again. If anyone will have me . . . '

'Oh, I'm sure there are plenty of people who would want to employ you. I'm not sure how many South American papers have correspondents here, but I'd have thought that there are plenty of other opportunities.'

Their starters arrived and Burton was pleased to note that his *escargots* were positively swimming in garlic. He took a piece of bread and used it to soak up the glorious buttery mixture.

'Well, at least you won't have many financial issues.' Burton said this gently, not wanting to dwell on the fact that she would be very well off following her inheritance of Sir John's estate. He felt Melissa's eyes burning into him as he finished the sentence, and he knew he had gone too far. But he desperately wanted to see how she would react.

'Yes, I suppose you're right.' Melissa spoke quietly, sadly, having quickly regained her composure. 'But I've not really thought about that at all. I'm obviously very upset that my husband is dead, and his body has not yet even been released for burial. I'm not planning my future at this stage.'

Burton steered the conversation away from Sir John and Melissa, and towards more neutral subjects. The starters disappeared and were replaced almost seamlessly with the main courses, thick slabs of fillet steak that were genuinely rare. A large bowl of thickly cut home-made chips accompanied the steak. The food was delicious.

Once the waiter had poured out the last of the wine, he asked them if they would have another bottle. Burton looked to Melissa, who smiled and shook her head gently.

'Shall we move on somewhere else?' she asked, once the waiter had left. 'I know a very nice little pub a short cab ride from here.'

Burton was feeling a little groggy and had in fact hoped that they would call it a night at that point. Tired after his underwater excursions that morning, he knew he would be fairly dehydrated; he'd drunk little water but several beers during the course of the day. However, he enjoyed Melissa's company and was happy to experience a nice local pub that he might not otherwise find on his own. He heard himself answer 'Yes, why not?' and motioned to the waiter for the bill.

Outside, the doorman from the restaurant motioned to the first in a line of cabs waiting in the drive and a small people carrier pulled up. They climbed inside and were greeted with a strong smell of car freshener, obviously there to hide a more illicit smell.

Melissa said something Burton couldn't catch to the dreadlocked driver, who looked vaguely surprised but nodded affirmatively anyway. The car roared off at the speed

Burton had subconsciously known it would, taking the right turn onto West Bay Street and then onto West Street. Burton was surprised when they didn't turn off onto Marlborough Street, heading back towards his hotel and Nassau city centre, but instead continued along past the police station where he had been the day before. The roads became increasingly characterized by residential areas of varying homeliness and, as they reached the end of the road, they turned left past what looked like a small area of parkland. He must have looked concerned as Melissa took his hand and squeezed it.

'Don't worry, we're almost there. You'll love this place. It's small, cosy, not too noisy and you'll feel just like a real Bahamian. You'll be able to chat with the locals about your legendary nights out in the places where the tourists never go.'

They turned off right into an even smaller road, but the taxi pulled up almost immediately. Burton fumbled for his wallet, but by the time he had found it, Melissa had handed the taxi driver a note. In return, she received a large smile and a muted 'Thanks, ma'am.'

The pub looked fairly dodgy from the outside with barred windows and stone walls. It seemed to Burton to be just the sort of place one wouldn't visit wearing a knee-length black dress, but once inside it was refreshingly clean and tidy. The place was sparsely decorated, with simple wooden tables and a rickety bar, but the people seemed friendly and many seemed to know Melissa, at least by sight. A few of them nodded in recognition as they passed, and the barman seemed to treat her with noticeable respect. Burton was surprised that a woman like Melissa would frequent a bar like this although, whilst he would be the first to admit that it was the sort of place he would never have found as a tourist, much less dared to enter, the atmosphere was good and it did have a laid-back, comfortable feel about it.

Most of the drinkers were perched up against the bar. They were dressed in colourful but faded T-shirts and shorts, the unofficial uniform of the locals when not on tourist duty. Melissa and Burton took a small table in the corner and Burton went up to fetch a beer for himself and a glass of wine for Melissa. He was by now severely regretting the beers he had downed during the day — it always catches up with you, he thought ruefully. Pushing these thoughts out of his mind, he took a long swig of beer and sat down opposite Melissa, and continued listening to the ubiquitous Bob Marley album playing in the background.

They chatted about various subjects and Melissa went to the bar to refill their glasses. Burton was starting to feel a little groggy again but managed to go up and get a third round in. He sat down and felt worse and worse. Bob Marley was still playing — or was it some other reggae band? — and the room started to spin and the colours became blurred. He couldn't recognize Melissa anymore and then everything seemed to go black.

★ ★ ★

His temples were pounding and he felt as if knitting needles had been inserted into his eyeballs. Suddenly something smacked into his jaw. He opened his eyes and saw a pale unshaven black face in the darkness. The mouth in the face moved and his ears tried to discern the words. Then a booted foot hit his jaw again and he tried to scream but couldn't tell if any sound was coming out of his mouth. He closed his eyes again and screwed them closed and hoped the pain would go away.

11

Burton's head throbbed with the noise of every car that passed. As the traffic built up the throb became almost constant. For a long time he lay still, trying not to move, as any attempt to do so sent new waves of pain coursing through his body and ignited new fires in his head. He screwed his eyes tightly shut and tried to go back to sleep.

His closed eyes began to register more brightness and somewhere inside his mind his subconscious connected this with it getting lighter. But why was it getting lighter? Had he forgotten to close the blinds when he went to bed that night? He listened carefully for clues, still unwilling to risk opening his eyes and allow the pain to career through his head.

His bed felt strangely hard, and he wondered if he had actually made it home the night before. What on earth had happened? What had he been drinking? His mind raced with the horror he was feeling. Even in his pained and weakened state he was overcome with pure fear. Not back to the bad old days of beer and whisky and smoke-filled late nights, half of which he was unable to remember the following morning when he awoke, sometimes not sure where he was, with unexplained injuries and a feeling of self-loathing that bordered on thoughts of suicide. Those days when the night before was a humiliation of sudden, snatched memories in an otherwise mysterious and irretrievable void, each one an invariably stupid action executed by a man whose brain was on autopilot, whose common sense was dissolved in an admixture of alcohol. A man whose drinking added colour to the grey, vague expanse of everybody else's evenings, and a man who experienced his mornings in black and white, good and bad, beautiful and ugly. Those stark mornings were character-ized by a period of unknowing anticipation, his puritanical side hoping vainly that he had got away with whatever it was, that he had survived the night free of humiliation and embarrassment. This forlorn hope was invariably destroyed by laughing friends gleefully reliving the highlights of the evening, whilst Burton himself laughed along ostensi-bly, whilst inside his heart wrenched at each ridiculous act he had managed to accomplish whilst in his state of inebriation.

The thumping pain in his head reminded him of those mornings, of the deadly serious promise not to drink again which threatened to evaporate already by the same evening, of the subsequent harsh self-recrimination, followed by periods of abstinence until the next time he fell spectacularly off the wagon. He thought it was all behind him: it was years since he had lost control and allowed the drink-fuelled alter ego free rein; now, he wasn't so sure.

He heard voices and laughter. This was odd: either he had left the door open or he hadn't made it back to the hotel at all. He tried to bury his head into the pillow but felt only coldness and hardness. He felt a prod in his side. The fear of further humiliation welled up inside him. Agonizingly he opened one eye and found himself looking into the face of a small Bahamian child wielding a long stick and poking him with it. The child appeared to be standing on a grey wall that Burton was leaning against. It took a while for Burton's brain to rotate the image, but then he knew he was lying on the street.

As he opened his eye, he heard peals of high-pitched laughter followed by a staccato patter of feet as the children scattered at the sight of the target of their merriment awakening. A deeper laugh resonated and Burton shifted his head to see where it came from. He heard his face scraping against the concrete but could not feel anything beyond

186

the pulsating agony in his head.

For a couple of seconds he lay with both eyes open, allowing them to focus on the scene in front of him. His left eye felt sticky, and he imagined that this meant that it was bloody. All his senses were dominated by the excruciating headache.

It was early morning. The light was cold. He appeared to be in a shabby-looking residential area. A couple of men were looking at him from a distance. They were locals, dressed in jackets and hats, and laughing at him. He sensed though that they were cautious about approaching him — he did not feel threatened by them. He didn't blame them for their perceived caution; he must appear to them a strange, dirty apparition, a foreigner in their world who didn't fit in at the best of times but was now lying in the street barely conscious.

He tried to sit up and was suddenly assailed by various other pains with different origins. His arm gave way underneath him and he crashed back down into a lying position. He gingerly tried to move his limbs and discovered a plethora of different injuries he seemed to have picked up. His left arm, with which he had tried to raise himself, throbbed and ached. His ribs, which he managed to press carefully with his right

187

hand, felt badly bruised. His legs hurt as he moved them, but he felt only elation when he had tried and succeeded in moving everything. He was bruised and wounded, but nothing appeared to be broken.

He had to work out where he was and what had happened. He had clearly been beaten up, but by whom and for what reason he didn't know. Even as this thought ran through his head, his right hand moved to his pocket to check his wallet. It wasn't there, although even as he looked he caught sight of the discarded wallet on the ground a couple of metres away from him. He assumed that all the cash would be gone; if he was lucky, his cards and other documents would have been left.

In the past he had always been lucky: despite his drunken antics he had mostly survived with a few scrapes and a bruised ego. It seemed, however, that his luck had changed; now he had more to show for his lack of self-control.

He rolled onto his back and then onto his right side, before using his good right arm to elevate himself to a sitting position. He looked down at his torn trousers and saw that his knees were bloodied and bruised. Once sitting, he ran his right hand over his face and probed the injuries there gingerly. A thick trail of dried blood led from his nose to his upper lip and he seemed to have a gash above his left eye, where a stocky clump of blood had congealed. A glance in a mirror in the near future would be a nerve-racking experience, he thought to himself.

Putting his weight again on his good right arm, he eased himself first of all into a kneeling position and then cautiously tried to stand up. With the second attempt he made it, and stood still for a second allowing the burning sensation in his legs to subside. He took several painful steps over to where his wallet was lying and contemplated reaching down to get it. He was surprised when one of the onlookers moved forward and gestured that he would pick it up. Burton nodded, and for a fleeting second expected the man to pick the wallet up and run off with it, but found it being held out to him gently. He pocketed the wallet and nodded this thanks.

'Where am I?' he tried to ask the man, but only a hoarse whisper came out of his mouth. Hearing this, he tried again, concentrating just on the word 'where'.

'Grant's Town,' said the man. He showed a shy, toothy grin and added, 'Not where yuh wanna be, man. Not good for tourists. An' yuh is beaten up good. Where yuh wanna go?'

Burton thought for a moment. Although

the man seemed friendly, in his present predicament he did not want to tell him where he was staying. Besides, he probably couldn't say the name of his hotel anyway. 'Centre,' he managed to croak.

'Nassau centre?'

Burton, whose normal response would have been to ask sarcastically which other centre he might be wishing to go to, nodded painfully.

'OK, man, you gotta go this way.' He gestured one way down the street. 'Then yuh got t' go down the big road. Yuh can get a bus there. Take yuh t' the centre.'

'Thanks,' whispered Burton as he struggled off in the direction the man had indicated. He hoped with unbridled fervour that the man was not having a joke, compounding his woes by sending him off in the opposite direction to where he needed to go.

As dawn approached the light became warmer and ruddier. The cold grey of the concrete roads developed a rosy glow and the colours of the houses became slowly more vivid. The noise levels started to rise slowly, as the city began to awaken. The sound of engines, which at first had periodically disturbed the silence, now replaced it as background noise. This was reflected in the number of cars passing him on the street. Burton noted happily that the road ahead of him looked like a main road, so he was probably going in the right direction.

With every step that jarred his body, Burton began to ask himself how he managed to get into this situation and curse his weakness for doing so. He noticed warily that his subconscious had decided that the situation had changed and moved on. First, he was worried about getting out of the difficulties he was in; now, he thought he was safe and was cursing his stupidity in getting into the trouble in the first place. He told himself that he wasn't safe until he was back in the hotel and tried to concentrate on getting there.

At the corner of the street, Burton looked carefully in both directions. He was not certain which direction he needed to go but spotted a bus stop on his left. His sense of direction told him that he actually needed to go straight on, but he would need to get on a main road running perpendicular to this main road in order to take a bus. He walked slowly towards the bus stop he could see, which was in any event the closest. If he wasn't able to get a bus from there, he hoped he would at least find some information telling him where he could.

Unfortunately, the bus stop contained little

in the way of information. There was, however, an old lady waiting there. Burton asked her which bus he would need to take in order to get back to the centre.

The lady said nothing but pointed to him and wiped her brow above her eye. Burton understood that she was trying to tell him that his face was cut. He nodded his agreement, and thanked her, and asked her again about the bus.

'Number 2,' said the lady, pointing to a column on which the bus stop sign was fixed. There was a small, rusted plate with bus numbers on, most of which were illegible. Burton looked carefully and was just about able to make out the number 2 and the words 'Bay Street'. That was enough for him. He thanked the lady again and tried to make himself comfortable. There were no seats, but he didn't regard that as a problem as he wouldn't have wanted to sit down in his condition anyway — getting up would be a painful and slow process he really didn't want to have to go through.

Burton stood watching the traffic become increasingly heavier until at last he spotted a yellow bus with a white top. It was little more than a large minibus but a black number 2 on a white cardboard square was visible propped up behind the windscreen. The bus itself was a rickety affair which looked as if it probably wouldn't get them much further than the next junction, but as long as he didn't have to get out and walk, he didn't really care.

It was only when he had followed the old lady on board and told the driver his destination that he realized he had no money with him. The hope afforded to him by the bus seemed dashed at the last minute. Burton remonstrated with the driver, trying to get him to allow him to ride on the bus, but he could see it was going nowhere. He turned, painfully, to exit the bus when the old lady came forward again and offered the driver money for Burton's ticket. The driver accepted it and gestured him back into the bus. Burton nodded his thanks again to the lady and took a place near the window. He wondered how he could pay her back, but knew that it would be impossible to try to explain to her that he had money back at the hotel. He shook his head slowly. In his mind, his humiliation was complete. Not only had his drunken exploits led to his being mugged and beaten up, he had to rely on a little old lady for a bus fare that was almost certainly worth a hundred times more to her than to him.

Burton tried to distribute his weight on the seat in the least painful manner, but once the bus drove off he found himself thrown around by a combination of poor roads and indifferent driving. Despite his discomfort, he was finally able to breathe a sigh of relief as the scenery became simultaneously better cared-for and more familiar. When they passed a turn-off to the left, Burton saw the police station one block away, and almost shouted with joy.

Once he knew that he was close by, he left the bus at the first opportunity, not wishing to risk driving a long way past the hotel. He was about 400 metres from the hotel and walked this distance slowly but surely, as he imagined an exhausted runner might complete a marathon, knowing that the pain and suffering was almost over.

Burton held it all together long enough to get to his room and then collapsed on the bed. As his tired body snatched at sleep, he found his mind slowly drifting off despite the excruciating pain. He finally gave in to the urge to close his eyes and fell into a deep, troubled sleep.

★   ★   ★

The piercing noise seemed to drive into his skull from all directions. He rolled over and covered his head with the pillow, but still the noise wouldn't let up. Eventually he re-linquished the protection of the pillow and, with blurry, tired eyes, tried to locate the source of the disturbance. A couple of lights on the telephone beside his bed were flashing, so he guessed that was to blame. He lifted the receiver for a second and then replaced it. The noise stopped. He settled back down to sleep.

Almost immediately, the noise started again. Admitting defeat he reached for the receiver a second time, this time holding the offending object to his face.

'Yes?'

'Michael, hello, it's Melissa. Are you all right?'

Burton's first reaction was to move the receiver away from his ear as Melissa's voice rang out. Almost immediately afterwards he was hit by simultaneous pangs of suspense, embarrassment and regret: what had he done? Had he got away with it? How much did she know? How much should he tell her about what happened?

'Er, yes, well, I've felt better. Bit of a headache.'

'Is that all? Oh, that's good. I was worried about you when you headed off last night. You were certainly very drunk. You do drink a lot, don't you? I suppose all Brits do, but it really was quite excessive. I pointed you in the right direction, but you appeared to want to stay out. Did you go for more beers?'

Burton started to think as fast as he could in his delicate state of mind. As usual in this particular situation, his main concern was damage limitation, primarily in the form of not giving away any more information than he had to. She didn't appear to know what had happened to him, so he didn't really need to tell her, but if she saw him any time soon she would be able to see that something untoward had happened. He would surely see her anyway in the next few days. He might as well come clean.

'Yes, I rather think I did. And I ran into some trouble while I was out. Nothing serious, but I appear to have rubbed somebody up the wrong way. And received a few hits in the process.'

'Oh no! What happened? Are you hurt? Who did it? Why?'

There were too many questions and Burton's head started to ache again badly. He managed to stammer, 'No, I'm all right, just a bit tired,' before putting the receiver down again and slipping back into unconsciousness.

12

The phone rang again. It seemed like only a few minutes since it had last rung. Why couldn't these people leave him alone? Burton turned over and reached out for the handset, which he reluctantly held to his ear. To his surprise, he could hear Chester King's voice faintly.

'Where the hell are you? Why aren't you here? Do you know what time it is?'

King's voice sounded almost comical, faint as it was but clearly belonging to a very irate detective. Burton wondered why it was that recently people kept bombarding him with multiple questions simultaneously. He tried to remember what the questions all were but could only recall the last one.

'No.'

'What do you mean 'no'?'

'Well, er, no, I don't know what the time is.' What did King think he meant?

'All right then, smartass, I'll tell you.' This was a new Chester King, a riled and angry Chester King, one Burton hadn't encountered before. 'It's quarter to twelve. We were supposed to meet at 9.30 — more than two hours ago. I didn't insist on an early start so that you could enjoy your weekend and not have to get up too early, and what do you do? How do you pay me back? You're lying in bed and it's almost midday! What's wrong with you?'

Burton pondered the fact that King, unshakeable in moments of high drama, had lost the plot so dramatically just because he was late. And he had seemed fairly relaxed when Melissa was less than punctual. He was pretty late, though. And he felt absolutely awful.

'Look, I'm sorry. I'm really not feeling very well. Can I meet you a bit later? Give me some time to wash — '

'I'll see you in my office at one. Don't be late.'

'Well, all right then.' Before he had finished his sentence, he heard a click in the receiver as King put the phone down.

Burton lay back. He felt terrible, but he knew it would help him to get moving. He climbed out of bed and stretched his aching limbs before heading for the shower to wake himself up. He looked at his face in the mirror and cringed with embarrassment: his left eye was swollen, black and bloody, his upper lip swollen and his right cheekbone bruised. His body was a mass of blackened contusions and purplish-brown bruising. He closed his eyes for a moment and opened them again, but the damage still remained. He shook his head, watching the blue eyes swivelling to maintain focus on his reflection. Despite it all, he couldn't help feeling that he was lucky not to have sustained any permanent damage.

Burton took a quick lukewarm shower; he didn't feel up to anything that was too hot or cold, and he felt a lot better afterwards. As he dried himself, he noticed that the white hotel towel was faintly lined with traces of blood. He touched various parts of his body and face until he had found out that it was the cut on his lip that had started to bleed again. He dabbed it gently and looked again at the face in the mirror. What the hell was he going to tell King?

★   ★   ★

'What on earth happened to you?' King asked as he entered the office and shut the door behind him.

'I ran into some problems on Saturday night.'

'Who did this?'

'I don't know. Look, it was my own fault. I went for a couple of drinks and was wandering around at night. I got lost. I must have annoyed somebody. I don't remember what happened, so I can't finger anyone. Probably best to forget about it.'

King's face, which at first registered surprise, had passed quickly through concern and was now positively stuck on disapproval. He looked downwards slightly and shook his head. 'As you wish. I'm not impressed, though, Michael. You do know that I'm supposed to be reporting on you to your Mr Reardon, don't you? Anyway, I'm not going to mention this, but please make sure it doesn't happen again.'

'Of course. And, thanks.'

'Don't mention it. Now, let's get on with it. We can't let this delay our progress, of which there has been very little so far. I mean, where are we in this case? We have little to go on and, frankly, there's little or no evidence that a crime has been committed here. We, the Bahamian Police, have accorded more attention than usual to this drowning, although of course all such deaths are investigated. However, a reasonable amount of police time has already been spent on this, and I'd like to ask what the British perspective is on the case at the moment.'

Burton was still standing in the middle of the room, in front of King's desk. King had not asked him to sit, but sat back comfortably in his own chair with his eyes fixed expressionlessly on Burton. He was wearing his trademark lightweight suit, this one a sandy colour framing a white shirt with a distinctive beige tie adorned with wide blue and red stripes, which reminded Burton of the Fusiliers tie although he could not see how King could possibly have served in the Fusiliers. Anyway, he wasn't in the mood to discuss ties. He indicated one of the chairs in front of King's desk, asking belatedly, 'Do you mind if I sit down?' then making himself comfortable.

'Go ahead.' King responded redundantly, looking at Burton frostily. 'Now, the British perspective, if you please.'

Burton hadn't been expecting this question, but had a pretty good idea of how he felt they should be approaching it. What he definitely didn't want to do was return to Jamaica with an inconclusive 'not enough evidence' report. And he knew that Reardon wouldn't want that either. Trying to ignore the all-consuming pain in his forehead, he mustered up all the concentration he could and launched into an unprepared pleading for continued action.

'Well, we wouldn't be comfortable concluding the investigation now. Whilst I appreciate that to date we have uncovered little evidence of a crime, there are facts about Sir John's death which have not been explained and, as such, still leave an element of doubt over what happened, and how, and why. Sir John's death was wholly unexpected, we have yet to uncover a clear motive for suicide, and the provisions of the great man's will were not exactly what we had anticipated. For a start, there's the not insubstantial amount left to some mysterious practitioner of a dark art. He is one player in the game who would have a motive. Then there's the residue of the estate, a significant amount in total, which was left to Sir John's wife, who quite clearly therefore also has a motive.

'Of course, having a motive doesn't mean that either of them did anything. For almost every fatal accident that happens, I'm sure you could find several people who would have had a motive to kill the person involved, but that doesn't mean that they *were* involved. No, that's not what I'm saying. However, I still feel that there are enough loose ends here, enough unknowns, coupled with at least two people we know of with a motive, to continue the investigation.'

King looked faintly bored and said nothing. There was a moment of silence. Burton felt more or less obliged to resume.

'You asked for my view. I gave it to you. I think we should be increasing our investigative efforts, not bringing them to a close. So did you, last week. Now, obviously you're concerned that I'm not taking this seriously and have been involved in some scrape at the weekend. Fine. But don't let that cloud your professional judgement. This case is not solved, and whilst it may not be that high on your list of priorities, I'm sure if you check with your foreign affairs department, they'd be keen to put a little more effort into strengthening relations with the UK.'

King smiled slightly at the veiled threat to escalate the matter to the politicians. 'And so what do you suggest we do?'

'Well, I think we should try to find out a bit more about this obeahman. Maybe he had something to do with Sir John's death. On the other hand, maybe not, but at least we can cross him off our list if he's been in group meditation on Haiti for the last year.'

'All right. And how do you propose we go about this?'

'The man lives on Cat Island. I'd start by going there and trying to find him. We could find out more about him, his organization, and, of course, how and why Sir John Little was connected to them. After all, it's not every respected diplomat who is connected with what is regarded in some areas as dubious religious practice or even black magic.'

Burton stopped and looked at King, who in turn looked down at an open diary on his desk. Burton felt relieved to have got this off his chest, and was also secretly quite pleased with himself. He had turned up in a pretty dire situation, missing the morning and arriving looking like he'd lost a boxing match, but he felt that he'd defended his position reasonably well when challenged to do so.

'I have a lot on at the moment,' said King. He turned over a couple of pages. 'The earliest I could afford to take the time to visit Cat Island would be next week. Unfortunately, I have several cases which require intensive preparation for upcoming court hearings.'

'I could do it.'

King looked up again. 'You?' he said, laughing. 'You want me to let you go on your own to Cat Island to question this obeah-man? Why on earth would I do that? If he was involved, I can't see how it would help us. He wouldn't talk to you anyway. He probably wouldn't talk to me either, but as a native policeman I'm sure he'd be more likely to.

'And if he did talk to you, what would we have? You aren't authorized to take a statement, so we'd have hearsay only. No, I can't condone it. At best, you'll just warn him that the police want to see him, at worst, you'll get yourself hurt. I mean, look at you, you can't even take care of yourself in Nassau.'

Burton felt the colour rush to his cheeks, but managed to calm himself. 'Let me go and see what I can find out without interviewing him. I can poke around a bit and gather information on the organization he belongs to, see if locals know him, stuff like that. Then we can decide whether to go back officially on the basis of what I find. That way we can save time, as we won't have to interview him if nothing indicates that it is necessary, and if we do interview him, we will be better prepared and will already have some background information.'

Burton could sense King wavering. He pounced for the kill.

'What have we got to lose? You're busy with other cases, so we're not going to make much progress here. As you pointed out, I can't interview people on my own, so I can't do that here either. I could go over for a day, you could try to work on your cases, and then we'll touch base again when I come back. My budget will cover tickets.'

He didn't really know if his budget would

cover it. He envisaged some tough conversations with Reardon about expenses, but then this was nothing new — as far as he was aware, the only thing Reardon actually did do was make sure that nobody else spent his budget. Anyway, he could afford to pay it himself if his expense claim was refused.

King considered the proposal quietly. Finally, he relented.

'All right, Michael. You go to Cat Island and try to find out as much as you can without interviewing the man himself. You will go in your official capacity as liaison officer on a simple fact-finding mission. You will have no authority to represent yourself as a policeman, or to formally interview anyone. Do I make myself clear?'

'Yes, absolutely. So what are we going to do now?'

'I'm going to work on my other cases. You should book a flight for tomorrow and then go and get some sleep. You look terrible.'

13

Burton allowed himself to be pushed back into his seat by the acceleration as the pilot opened the throttles on the twin-engined Embraer Bandeirante E-110. The aeroplane leapt forward on the runway like a startled deer caught in headlights on a dark road. The scenery, at first stationary, accelerated past until the pilot pulled back on the stick, and then the ground fell away sharply in a rapidly diminishing patchwork quilt of different textures. The stormy weather had passed over, and the sky was a clear, deep blue.

The plane, fitted out for nineteen passengers, was about half full. The majority of those aboard looked like locals, although he guessed an elderly couple sitting towards the front were tourists. A dark-haired, tanned woman who looked to be in her early twenties was sitting on the same row as Burton. Burton had her down as an ex-pat living in the Bahamas, but was unable to confirm his suspicion as his brave attempt to strike up a conversation was met with a cursory one-word response complemented by a frosty glare which encouraged him to refrain from asking any more questions or attempting to engage in trivial conversation. The girl's fashionable sunglasses remained firmly on her face throughout the flight as she flicked through a glossy, woman's magazine. Burton could hardly blame her for not wanting to talk to him; although he had slept for hours and now felt much better, when he caught sight of his battered, bruised and unshaven face reflected in the aeroplane window, he realized that he still looked an unsavoury character.

The flight was a short forty minutes, with the captain announcing their descent and approach into New Bight Airport only minutes after they had stopped climbing. Far below the opaque blue of the sea was speckled with islands big and small, from uninhabited lumps of rock to the bustling centres of the towns spread at intervals along the main highway on the long, thin island of Eleuthera. From his vantage point of the right-hand side of the plane, he could see the smaller, lesser-used airfield of Arthur's Town on the northern part of Cat Island.

As they descended, Burton could see that there was little wind: washing hanging in back yards decorated the dreary background with unmoving coloured squares whilst the fan-like palm trees near the shore were motionless. They appeared to be coming straight in to land on the west-to-east runway. A pretty stewardess rushed round to check that all the passengers were strapped in and then took her seat at the front of the plane, next to the elderly couple, with whom she exchanged a few pleasantries.

The plane touched down and they stepped out to be greeted by warm humidity and a strong lingering smell of kerosene. Being an internal flight there were few formalities and Burton was soon looking for a car hire company. He found one which had, amongst an eclectic selection of hire cars old and new, an old MGB convertible in battleship grey. Burton had to have it and embarked on a long discussion with the lady at the desk, whom Burton suspected was also the owner, trying to persuade her that this street fighting Englishman was not a high risk hire. He suspected that he did not do this particularly well as, although he walked out of the ramshackle shed with the keys of the MG, he had left behind a substantial deposit secured by credit card and was paying a daily price for which one of the other car hire firms would probably have let him keep the car. Still, he considered it a small price to pay for having a decent car on the open road.

Burton opened a tourist map he had

picked up at the hire car desk and spread it on the bonnet of the MG to have a quick look for the addresses he had written down. He had two for the obeahman: one in Arthur's Town in the north, and one in New Bight itself. As there was only one road heading north to Arthur's Town, he figured that he was unlikely to require the help of the map to get there. However, the street map of New Bight would be helpful to find the first address.

The black canvas roof of the MG was slightly damaged in places and had been patched, which meant that it took a little longer than he had expected to fold it away. Mindful of his credit card and deposit, he took care not to force anything. Once done, he took a step back and admired the car. The black upholstery of the seats was cracked and weathered, and the carpets worn, but the coachwork was in a surprisingly good condition. Burton loved the classic lines of the car and the old-fashioned but beautiful spoked wheels. He climbed in and listened to the deep purr of the engine as he turned the key in the ignition. Although only a 1.8 litre engine, the outdated silencer technology allowed a throaty roar to escape. Burton looked around quickly and then headed off.

As he approached New Bight, Burton

could see that it was a sprawling, disorderly looking town, with a plethora of coloured houses in varying states of repair. Some smarter buildings were placed sporadically throughout the town; they looked like churches or other places of worship. Many of the houses were adorned with lightning rods, which Burton understood were prescribed by obeah conventions and supposed to protect against ghouls and evil spirits.

Burton decided to park the MG on the outskirts and then walk around the town. He would be able to learn a lot more by walking as he wouldn't have to spend time concentrating on navigating. Besides, he didn't really want to draw attention to himself in the MG, which stood out like a sore thumb in a world of American pickups and Japanese saloons. He wouldn't have been surprised if he had been told that this was the only MG on the island. Although it had seemed like a good idea at the time, he now realized that it was tantamount to carrying around a huge billboard advertising his presence.

Walking through the town, Burton had the impression that it was a miniature Nassau, the whole town being less than two miles in length. He looked at his street guide and, having determined the general direction and memorized a couple of landmarks that he should be able to see on his journey, folded the map and stuck it in the back pocket of his jeans.

Most people he saw in the streets greeted him warmly, perhaps happy to see a tourist taking time out to visit New Bight rather than heading straight down to the south of the island to the more interesting dive sites. On one corner, a dishevelled man wearing a woollen hat that looked as if it may once have been colourful but was now so grimy that the colours were no longer discernible said something under his breath to Burton that the latter assumed was some kind of insult. Burton ignored him and walked on. He didn't want to be picked up by the local police for arguing with a local and have to rely on Chester King to get him out — particularly after their last meeting, which Burton was unable to describe as cordial. Seeing Burton's restraint, the man jeered loudly but was rewarded only with Burton's retreating back and not the rise he had clearly hoped for.

He passed a small Baptist church that he knew marked the road before the one he needed to take, which would lead him to Fernandez Street. He went up to the door of the church and pushed it gently. It was open and he went in. His eyes took a while to adjust to the darkened interior of the church, but he could already hear that it was empty. A faint smell of incense hung in the air and, as his eyes acclimatized, he could see the flames of a number of candles burning. Burton had read in the library that the Spiritual Baptist religion sometimes contained elements of obeah, though the information he had found had not always been the sort of material that he immediately and completely believed. The church was sparsely furnished and, as he had expected, he could see no signs of anything abnormal, nothing that would make him think that it was linked in any way to the practice of obeah.

Burton left the church through the same door he had entered, his eyes shocked by the brightness outside. He continued walking and turned off the next street. The houses became more ramshackle as he walked along, and he spotted a couple of pubs with barred windows and faded adverts for beer painted on their walls. A shiver ran down his spine as he recalled his last visit to such an establishment.

Fernandez Street, a narrow road just about wide enough for two cars to pass, was completely empty. It was not wide enough to park cars and there was nobody in sight. Looking at the numbers on the side of the road he was on, Burton ascertained that the obeahman's house would be on the other side. He could already see it though: a relatively large house in keeping with the rest of the area as far as the style and décor was concerned. On the door the obeahman had painted his own advertisement: a large black cross on a white oval background.

Despite the fact that he had come specifically to look at the man's house, Burton felt his hair stand on end as he looked at the door, and couldn't help experiencing a genuine feeling of fear. He wondered why it was that people were generally far more afraid of things they didn't understand than things they did. If he was attacked by a man in the street, he would size up the man and decide, as mankind had always done, whether to stand and fight or take to his heels. It perturbed him to think that a man might look an easy victim but be able to harness other forces and cast a spell on him which he could not understand and could not fight against. For him, obeah was an unknown. Difficult to categorize as a religious practice but equally difficult to describe as sorcery, the very nature of obeah remained a mystery to him.

Trying to stop his imagination running away with him, Burton reminded himself that, like many other ancient and mysterious arts, obeah developed many years before during the colonial periods of occupation in the Caribbean, and consisted mainly of intelligent men performing tricks to play on the gullibility and fear of other slaves enabling them to rise to the forefront of their groups and obtain not insignificant power by so doing.

It was at this moment that the door of the house opened. A tall man stood in the doorway, dressed in a loose robe. He had to stoop slightly to look out of the door and the forward tilt of his head gave his gaze an angry, severe demeanour. Curls of dark hair hung around his face. Burton felt the man's eyes on him as he walked past the house, not daring to look across at the doorway and hurrying on as quickly as possible.

His heart thumped as he continued walking, and it was several metres later that he found the courage to look back. The door was closed. Nothing moved in the windows.

Breathing deeply, he continued on to the end of the road. There, he turned round and headed back down Fernandez Street. He kept his eyes fixed on the obeahman's house, but the man he had seen before was not visible and he saw no other movement. Once he had passed the house, Burton walked to the end of the road and looked back. Again, he could see nothing.

He returned to the MG, his mind racing. Was it the obeahman he had seen? Or was it somebody else? Should he have spoken to him? He was mindful that King had specifically told him not to speak to the man, but he felt he could have got away with it.

Burton started the car and headed onto The Queen's Highway, a paved road of reasonable quality which runs the length of the island from Springfield Bay in the south up past Arthur's Town in the north. The road was good enough to drive reasonably fast and as soon as he had passed the airport on the way back, he opened the throttle, going through the gears, pushing the car all the way to fourth. Most of the slight bends in the road he could take without braking, employing at most a light comfort lift off the accelerator before turning. He concentrated on getting to Arthur's Town as quickly as possible, looking ahead and anticipating the speed he could carry through the bends. Once or twice he felt the rear of the car slide, which he corrected with a gentle turn of the wooden steering wheel. To his left the sea stretched endlessly away from the shore, whilst the thin strip of land on his right flashed past quickly.

It was about thirty miles to Arthur's Town and he made good time, arriving in half an hour, despite having slowed through the small towns he had passed on the way. Arthur's Town was much smaller than New Bight and, despite the moniker of 'town', it resembled little more than a small village. Leaving the car just off The Queen's Highway, Burton walked around until he came to the second address that he had for the obeahman. The door was adorned with exactly the same motif as he had seen in New Bight. He felt invigorated by the drive and, perhaps because he knew that the man was in New Bight, he felt confident and curious to find out more here. He looked across at the house, seeing little more than the cross on the door and two darkened windows. Having passed the house, he walked to the end of the road and then crossed over to walk back on the same side.

As he passed the first window, he tried surreptitiously to look inside. It was too dark compared to the bright glare outside, so he could see nothing. He still didn't feel quite confident enough to stop and stare, but he did slow down past the second window. As he glanced in, he heard the door open. He quickly straightened his head and walked on. Out of the corner of his eye, he could see a tall man looking out of the door. He was slightly stooped and he was looking blankly through dark curls of hair which hung around his face. Burton was amazed and stopped to stare at the man, who held his gaze with cold, black eyes. His heart thumping for the second time that day, Burton realized it was the same man he had seen in New Bight.

He looked away and crossed the road as fast as he could, looking back only when he had gone some distance. As he suspected, the door was closed and the man gone. How had he got there? There was no other road up to the north of the island and Burton had not been passed by any cars on the way. Anyway, he doubted very much if anyone could have covered the distance quicker than he had done; he hadn't been hanging around and even in a much faster car the time saving would be minimal. Was it a different man, dressed up to look the same? But he was quite certain it was the same person: everything about him was familiar. Whilst looks can be copied relatively easily, there was something about the gait, the way the man had been standing, the inclination of his head, how he held himself, that persuaded Burton that he wasn't mistaken. Could he have flown there? Then he'd need to have had a light aircraft at the ready, a pilot possibly, unless he flew himself, also at the ready, a car to get to the airport. And all this would have to have been accomplished in less time that it had taken Burton to drive there. Was it even possible? As he walked back towards his car he tried to calculate how long it would take if he had driven there himself, and flown in a plane that was ready and waiting. He'd had to have been able to take off straight away, which wasn't unlikely as New Bight was not a busy airport, but even then he couldn't be sure. In any event, if it was possible, it would be one hell of a feat. What did that leave? Had he used a powerboat? Was *that* possible? There was little wind today, so that would mean few waves, so a boat would be able to go much faster. But to beat a car? Burton had his doubts. What else could it be? Did he have a twin, someone with the same looks and characteristics? Or had he used a spell? Could he transport himself?

Burton shook his head. Again, he was letting this whole thing get to him. There had to be some explanation; he just didn't know what it was yet. He quickened his stride as the car came into sight. He looked at his watch: he didn't have a great deal of time to get back to New Bight to catch the return flight.

As he put the key in the ignition, he noticed that his hands were shaking. He was angry with himself for letting it get to him, but noted all the same that he should take it a little easier on the way back. He gunned the

MG, executed a three point turn and turned back onto The Queen's Highway, heading south.

He couldn't get the appearance of the same man in both places out of his mind. If there was a logical explanation, and this had all been engineered to frighten him in some way, they would at the very least have needed some time to prepare their conjurer's trick, in whatever way it had been arranged. And that he didn't understand: he hadn't booked his flight yesterday, even though King had advised him to. He knew from experience that the flight to Cat Island wouldn't be full so he had just turned up in the morning half an hour before the flight left. He hadn't told anyone at his hotel where he was going, just grabbed a taxi and left. So nobody could have had more than an hour's notice of his arrival, even if they had been in touch with the ticket desk at Nassau Airport and been informed as soon as he bought his ticket. Unless, of course, they had been told by King . . .

Burton's thoughts were interrupted by a large black jeep that suddenly filled his rear-view mirror. He glanced down at the speedometer and saw that he was doing a reasonable speed. Whoever it was must be in a hurry, he thought. The thought of racing them along the road fluttered through his mind but he dismissed it as puerile and pulled the MG further into the side of the road, waving the jeep jovially past.

As it pulled level, Burton felt as if he was being stared at. He turned to his right to look at the occupants of the jeep but, as he did so, it pulled ahead. He watched the vehicle as it overtook, cursing himself for being so jittery. What was wrong with him? He was seeing spooks wherever he looked.

The jeep passed and started to turn in to return to the left side of the road. It was the brake lights that saved him. As it pulled in, the driver stood hard on the brakes. Burton saw the red warning lights and started to brake himself, but he realized quickly that with the old brakes and his reaction time he wouldn't make it and instead wrenched the wheel to the right to go past. At the same time he knew that it wasn't an accident and that he had to get by as fast as possible. As he braked with his toe, he used the heel of his foot to give the accelerator a hard blip and shoved the gear stick forward into third. Then he booted the throttle and the MG shot past as the jeep also turned to the right. For a second Burton thought it was going to catch the side of the MG, but he had just cleared it before the jeep moved out into the middle of the road and filled his mirrors again.

Burton watched the rev counter creep into the red before changing up to fourth and flooring the accelerator again. He felt strangely confident now the mystic element of the unknown had been removed. Now they were in a car, as was he, and he was confident of his ability to stay ahead of them, whoever they were. He was glad he had pushed the car so hard on the way there; he now knew how it would perform, and had a good idea of the road ahead and how fast he could take the bends.

The jeep was gaining on him. Like many American cars, it was probably fitted with a heavy V8 engine, which would make it faster and more powerful than the MG. It was also almost certainly an automatic, which was probably the reason he'd been able to get past in the first place — there would have been a lapse between the driver putting his foot down and the kick down of the automatic gears which had allowed the MG past. But on this straight road, there was little chance of keeping the jeep off his back.

Burton watched the road ahead of him, looking for somewhere to turn off. On smaller, twistier roads he'd be able to leave the heavier, higher jeep behind him. For the moment he could see nothing, and concentrated on getting as much speed as possible from the MG, and maintaining it through the bends. He glanced in the mirror and saw that the jeep was dropping back slightly in the corners, gentle as they were, so he would have a clear advantage on a smaller road.

Ahead he noticed a small road turning off to the left. He decided to allow the jeep to draw steadily closer as he approached the turning and then brake and turn off at the last moment, hoping the jeep would miss it altogether. By the time the jeep had stopped and come back to follow him, he'd be well away. But he had to be careful he didn't let it get too close and run into his back.

He looked ahead, and, judging the distance to the turn, lifted his foot slightly to allow his speed to bleed away. He moved his eyes to scan the road ahead, checking the distance to the turn, and the rear-view mirror, monitoring the approach of the jeep. With each glance, he adjusted his right foot on the accelerator accordingly.

Now! Burton braked hard, blipping the throttle with his heel and changing down as he did so, releasing the brake when the tyres locked up and then re-applying it to kill speed to make the turn. When he thought he had as much speed as the MG could handle through the corner, he released the brake, balanced the car on the throttle and turned left.

The MG sailed through the bend, throwing Burton against the right hand door, his seatbelt locking and holding him still. The MG started to drift sideways in the middle of the corner. Burton corrected, lightly steering away from the apex until the tyres found grip. He tried to look over his shoulder to see where the jeep was but the locked seatbelt held him down. He sensed rather than saw the black mass hurtle past the turning and continue on The Queen's Highway. He could hear the screeching of the other car's brakes over the noise of the MG jumping over potholes on the dirt track he'd turned onto.

He immediately saw his error. He would easily be able to keep the MG ahead of the jeep on a narrow, twisty road *if* that road was a good quality, paved road. The potted dirt track he was on would favour the jeep — he would never keep the MG ahead and he'd break it in the process. He'd messed up. He'd have to get back on the main road.

He braked to a standstill, feathering the brake lightly so he didn't skid on the dust. Then he shoved the MG into reverse and executed a passable J-turn so he was facing back towards The Queen's Highway. He accelerated immediately back towards the road, hoping to catch the driver of the jeep unawares.

He was lucky. The jeep was just approaching the turn-off when Burton's MG burst out of the side road onto the main highway. He accelerated all the way through the turn and the rev counter was touching the red in second gear before he had straightened up. The jeep, facing the wrong way, grew smaller in the rear-view mirror. Burton smiled to himself. By the time they'd turned it around and were following, he'd have a reasonable lead and they wouldn't get to him before he reached the airport.

Smith Bay flashed past on the left, followed by Fernandez Bay, and then he was driving back into the car rental area inside the airport secure area. Burton tried desperately to stand still and remain calm despite the adrenaline which continued to course through his body as the car rental lady looked the car over. He was amazed that he'd got through the whole episode without hitting anything, but he was fairly certain that he had done so, and the lady found nothing. Smiling his thanks as his credit card was returned, he set off at a fast pace towards the terminal.

The stewardess was shepherding people towards the plane when Burton ran through the terminal to the departure gate. He opened his stride, not wanting to get left behind. That would be a big disaster that he really didn't need. He called out to the lady on the desk who was checking tickets. She took one look at the crazed white man with a bruised face running towards her and called out to him, 'Don't worry, sir. The plane won't go without you. Take it easy.'

To Burton, the words sounded beautiful. He slowed to a jog and covered the rest of the distance to the desk. 'No need to run,' the girl assured him. 'Now, may I see your ticket please?'

Burton handed her his ticket, which he had been holding as he ran over. He grimaced as it stuck to the sweat on his hand, but the girl smiled as she unravelled the crumpled paper ticket and handed him a boarding card.

'It's the gate right in front of you, sir. We expect to take off on time' — she looked at the time displayed on the departures monitor — 'in about ten minutes. The stewardess will show you to your seat. Have a nice flight and thank you for choosing Cat Island Air.'

'Thank you.'

Burton pushed open the doors and walked towards the plane. The stewardess was directing people up the stairs and telling them where they could find their seats. As he reached the bottom of the stairs, he heard, 'Up the stairs, please, sir. Your seat is on the right-hand side towards the back.'

As he placed his foot on the bottom step, Burton looked around and noticed the black jeep pulling up on the other side of the airport fence. There was no mistaking the modern look and the smoked glass windows. He climbed up the rest of the steps and turned to look when he reached the top.

He was looking to the west, where the sun was slowly moving down in the sky. Between the clear blue of the evening and the dark blue of the sea was an orange line across the horizon, broken by the silhouette of the jeep. With the backlighting provided by the setting sun, Burton could make out the silhouetted figures of two men inside. Burton threw them a flippant salute before turning and entering the aeroplane as the stewardess started to climb up the steps after him.

14

Burton woke early the following day. He felt invigorated after the activity of the day before; the drunken stupor of the weekend was almost completely forgotten. The face that looked back at him in the mirror after he had showered still looked battered and bruised, but the swelling had gone down and his eyes, now alert, had lost their yellow bloodshot sheen. He went down to the restaurant and breakfasted heartily on eggs and bacon and coffee. He was, uncharacteristically for the last couple of days, early for his meeting with King, so he ordered more coffee and took it into the lounge with him. He sipped the hot, bitter liquid thoughtfully.

The past few days had raised quite a few questions in his mind about Sir John's death. He was now certain that there was more to it than a simple case of accidental drowning, he just didn't know what. But he felt as if it were his duty to uncover what had happened, to obtain justice for Sir John.

There was no doubt that someone had been watching him diving off the beach where Sir John had taken his last swim, and that he had been pursued yesterday on Cat Island. He had also been beaten up on Saturday night, but, given that he could remember nothing of this, he was prepared to accept that it was unconnected; that he had merely looked a little too deeply into the glass and that this alone had led to his woes — after all, it wouldn't be the first time that he had forgotten an entire evening.

What little he could remember of Saturday night had at least shed some light on the relationship of Melissa and Sir John. He had no problems imagining Sir John as the charming ex-polo player but he wasn't sure about the role Melissa had cast for herself. He found it difficult to picture her in awe of the much older diplomat and moving to the Bahamas for the sun and the money. She seemed independent almost to a fault, and he guessed that, even if it was for the most part true, she must have had an ulterior motive that she didn't want to share. And, as he had no corroboratory evidence for any of it, he could only guess whether the story was true or not. Maybe she had fabricated the whole thing. For all he knew, she could be a hooker who had landed Sir John one night and had been blackmailing him ever since, taking the lot; not just the cash, but the man himself, his money, his lifestyle, and even his life. But he couldn't quite bring himself to believe this either. And even if it were true, he would still be no closer to solving the mystery surrounding Sir John's death.

He remained puzzled by the events of the day before. How the man he had seen had got himself from New Bight to Arthur's Town he could not answer, but that, and the subsequent antics on the road, led him to believe that they were prepared for his visit. Somehow, they had known he was coming. And only Chester King knew that he was planning to visit the island on that day. Could King be involved? Burton liked the detective, but there was no question that he seemed less interested in the case now than he did in the beginning. Burton had initially accepted that King, who seemed to epitomize puritanical self-control, was disgusted by Burton's behaviour when he turned up four hours late, hung over, most likely still stinking of alcohol, and beaten. But maybe there was something else? Was somebody getting to him? If so, who? Or did he have another motive? Although King was not mentioned in Sir John's will, it was not impossible that one of the other beneficiaries had some kind of relationship with him, or even some sort of hold over him. Could he be involved with Melissa? Could he be a closet obeahman himself?

Burton sighed. He had only questions, not answers. He decided to work together with King as before, but not to trust him too implicitly. He would mention the black jeep in the hope that King could help identify it, but he wouldn't give him all the details of what had happened. Not that he had any meaningful details: no registration number, no view of the driver. Anyway, he couldn't very well not co-operate with King and start his own investigation, but equally why should he risk keeping him in his confidence when he wasn't convinced of his veracity?

Burton drained his coffee. It was time to go and meet King.

★   ★   ★

Burton decided to walk to the police station. The unsettled weather of the last couple of days appeared to have passed, and in the resplendent sunshine it was hard to believe that it ever rained here. Although still early in the morning, he could feel the heat starting to build, bringing with it the promise of a stifling day.

The city was alive with its habitual early morning rush-hour hustle and bustle, although that concept in the Bahamas was a mere shadow of what one could expect in a city like

London, where a journey of twenty minutes could take more than an hour at the busiest time of the day. Nevertheless, a steady stream of traffic was standing unmoving on Marlborough Street, and Burton could feel the heat increasing with the exhausts of the cars, just as the fresher air from the sea was scented with their fumes. It was a short walk to the Bay Street police station and, looking at the traffic, Burton could easily imagine that the journey would take longer by taxi than it did on foot.

The desk sergeant greeted him as he walked through the door. By now, he was an accustomed visitor. He could imagine the police laying bets on what he would look like the next time he showed up, following his shock appearance on Monday afternoon looking as if he'd gone a painful twelve rounds with somebody in a much heavier weight division. He acknowledged the sergeant, who, without being told whom he was coming to visit, told him to 'Go on up, sir, Mr King is in his office', and headed off up the stairs.

King was walking in the corridor. 'Ah, Michael, you're looking much better today. And you're early, too. What a surprise. Can I get you a cup of coffee?'

Burton accompanied King to the coffee

machine — no fresh brew this morning — and selected the least offensive sounding offering, a 'Colombian' espresso. They walked back to King's office.

'And how was Cat Island? Did you find anything interesting?'

Burton thought for a second before answering. 'Yes and no. I didn't learn anything new from the visit. I located both the addresses we had been given. They both look like they belong to the obeahman, but I haven't been able to verify this in any other way.

'I think I saw him. Do you know what he looks like?'

King shook his head. Burton looked carefully for any signs that he might not be telling the whole truth, but King met his eyes and looked, if anything, faintly uninterested.

'I saw a tall native man. At both addresses in fact. The same man. I'm not sure how he travelled from New Bight to Arthur's Town, but he did so in less time that it took me, and I was driving fairly smartly. I don't suppose you'd have any idea how one would travel between these two towns, or villages I suppose would be a better description, in such a short time?'

King shook his head again, but Burton fancied he could now see a flicker of interest in his eyes.

233

'After I'd seen the man for a second time, I was pursued by a black jeep. I don't know the registration number, but it looked brand new. American manufacturer. Can we check the police records for registrations of similar vehicles? There can't be too many cars like that on Cat Island.'

'No, probably not. And we can check with the records office to see what we have. The problem is that the car might not be registered to someone with an address on Cat Island. It may be registered elsewhere and have been moved to Cat Island by ferry or the mail boat. Moving vehicles between islands does not require any kind of clearance, and I suspect that Customs would have no record of it. The ferry company might, but we don't know when the jeep would have been shipped or by which company, so we'd have to do a blanket check on all the companies in the past, say, two years. It'll take some time, but I think it's worth trying. Even then, we won't know for sure — somebody with a large enough boat could have moved it themselves, and obviously we'll miss anything moved before the date we start checking. Or somebody shipped a red jeep and then sprayed it black. But we'll have a go — maybe we'll turn up something useful.'

'Thanks. It might come to nothing, but I

think it's worth checking. Anyway, what we haven't gained in information, I think we've gained by experience. There's definitely something going on here. Somebody was watching me when I went diving on Old Fort Beach, and yesterday somebody chased me on Cat Island. Somebody is worried about us finding something out.'

King laughed. 'And I suppose somebody poisoned your food on Saturday night? Come on, Michael. I don't think we can start reading too much into these occurrences. There's no law against watching somebody diving, if that's what the person was doing — if there was somebody there at all. I seem to recall that you found no direct evidence that someone was there watching you. And as for the alleged car chase, well, there is some level of secrecy involved in the practice of obeah. Maybe you were just being politely warned off from disturbing them too much. Obeah stems from the times of slavery, and those who practise it have, understandably, a mistrust of the well-heeled white man hailing from the old colonial power. After all, I'm investigating this case too, and nothing untoward has happened to me.'

That's because you're not really very involved in it, Burton thought. Or, he mused immediately afterwards, perhaps it was because King was too involved in it. He said, 'I understand that, but in my mind these events are enough to cast some suspicion on the death of Sir John. We have very little to go on right now, but we've not completed the investigation and I'm not satisfied that we have spent enough time on it. At the same time, I understand that we have no evidence of a crime, and that you have a lot of cases on at the moment, which are as important as this one. I just ask that we spend a little more time to try to get to the bottom of it.'

King considered for a moment before responding.

'Very well, Michael. We requested a liaison officer from your diplomatic mission here because of who Sir John was. We didn't request this so that you would leave dissatisfied with our investigation; we requested it as a good-will gesture to your country so that you will be satisfied that we have investigated the matter fully, and also to help us, as you might have information about Sir John that we don't have access to ourselves. You have asked us to continue the investigation: I am more than happy to do so in the interests of maintaining good relations between our two countries. But I can't say I'm convinced that we are going to find anything, or, for that matter, whether there's anything to find.

'Anyway, if we are going to continue, we need to have some idea of how we're going to approach it. The fact is that we still do not know if Sir John Little committed suicide, whether he drowned accidentally, or whether he was killed. In addition, we have absolutely no evidence to back up the theory that he was killed, and the accidental drowning or suicide theory is backed up by the eyewitness statements and the rest of the evidence. There were no marks on his body or anything else to suggest forced drowning. In my view, we should not use further resources trying to find physical evidence of forced drowning. Do you agree?'

Burton nodded. He could sense that this discussion was going in a direction he did not want it to, but there was little point in arguing against King's impeccable logic.

'Now,' continued King, 'we are left with accidental drowning and suicide. He used to swim regularly, which makes it harder to believe that he drowned accidentally, but it is not impossible. We do know that he wasn't drunk, something that accounts for many an accidental drowning. The main reasons to believe that it was not suicide seem to stem from the fact that he left no note and is not believed to have had suicidal tendencies. On the other hand, we know that many suicides don't leave notes *and* we have evidence, from a policeman no less, that Sir John appeared suicidal after drinking. So, the question here is whether we spend any more time trying to differentiate between accidental drowning and suicide and, if so, how do we go about it. What are your views, Michael?'

At this point, Burton's mobile phone began to play *Mission: Impossible*. Burton apologized and fished the guilty piece of equipment out of his pocket, setting it to silent mode. Before he slipped the phone back into his pocket, he looked to see who had called him. It was Reardon. Great, he thought, that's all I need: the serial delegator checking whether his minions are carrying out their orders properly.

Making a mental note not to call him back until he really had to, Burton looked up and met King's disapproving look. Holding King's stare, Burton responded, 'We searched Sir John's house thoroughly for a note, but we did not find one. I don't see much to be gained by searching further. Besides, Melissa is still living there, and she's bound to tidy things up. If she finds something, we have no reason to believe that she wouldn't tell us about it. Anyway, as you said, not all suicides leave notes. If he had left one, he would most likely have left it somewhere where it would be found. So, he either didn't leave one or somebody else found it first and destroyed it. If the latter, we won't find it now. And the only reason that I can think of for removing a note is that it contained something somebody didn't want us to know.

'We didn't look at Sir John's laptop though. If there was anything that was worrying him, we might be able to find some clues there. Information he had stored on his computer could help us to understand whether he was indeed in a situation in which he might have contemplated suicide. Also, if there was a note and it was destroyed because it contained something someone didn't want us to know, perhaps there will be a clue about it on the laptop.

'I suggest we visit Melissa and ask to be allowed to take it. I'm sure you have people here who can find information that might be hidden. I can call her and find out if she's amenable to our having the laptop for a while.'

'All right, Michael, it seems a reasonable place to start. I do want to make clear to you, though, that we will not continue to look at this indefinitely. Obviously, we were happy to allow the British to appoint a liaison officer and are happy to have you present' — King shot a friendly smile at Burton as he said this

— 'and, equally, we want you to be satisfied that we have done all we can in order to uncover anything untoward. We can't, however, continue to the point where we ourselves could be accused of wasting resources. Accordingly, I wish to make a proposal: you can continue along the laptop route for the time being. At the same time, though, I will be drafting a preliminary report summarizing the position. We, you and I, will go through this report tomorrow and discuss where things stand. If, in my opinion, we do not have reasonable suspicion that a crime of some sort has been committed, then we round off the investigation. Are you comfortable with that?'

The idea of digging his heels in and trying to pull in the weight of Reardon flashed across Burton's mind, but he quickly discounted it as it would mean having to talk to Reardon, who, on reflection, he was sure had only given him the task to get him out of the Kingston office. Anyway, what King said made sense: he was only there by invitation and not in a position to dictate terms. And something told him that he was better off having King as a friend than an enemy. Bottling his dislike of diplomatic charades, he said, 'Yes, no problem at all. I can assure you that we are content with this position, and satisfied with how the investigation has been conducted thus far.'

★ ★ ★

It was early afternoon when they left for Sir John's house. Burton had called Melissa who, after enquiring after his health in a concerned fashion, had readily agreed to them taking the laptop. The drive over was for Burton the complete antithesis of his last car journey on Cat Island. King's calm confidence behind the wheel gave the impression that, whilst he was ready for anything to happen, he preferred to take things easy on the road. It's a pity more Bahamian drivers aren't like him, thought Burton.

When they arrived, the door was opened as before by Sarah, the Bahamian housekeeper. She welcomed them like long lost friends, explaining that she had the laptop ready but that Lady Little was down on the beach if they'd like to see her.

'No, it's all right, Sarah,' said King. 'We'll just take the laptop. No need to bother Lady Little. But would you mind if we asked you a few questions?'

'Me? Well, of course, sir, but I'm sure I don't know anything.'

King laughed. 'Why, Sarah, I'm sure you

know a lot. But, actually, all I wanted to ask was whether you had noticed anything about the way Sir John was before his death. Was his behaviour in any way different from normal?'

The kindly, grey-haired lady answered without a second's hesitation. 'Not that I noticed, sir. Not that I noticed.'

'And what about Lady Little? Has she been acting differently recently?'

'Since the death of Sir John, do you mean? Why, of course. She's distraught, poor woman. They've been together for years, sir. I've worked here for them both for years as well. It's terrible. Terrible.'

'Er, yes, quite. But I meant before Sir John's death. Just before. Did you notice anything about Lady Little's behaviour then?'

'Well, let me think.' She thought for a moment. 'I don't believe so, sir. I don't believe so. Why do you ask?'

'Oh, it's just routine, Sarah. We always ask these questions when somebody is missing, or there's a death. Sometimes we can glean ideas from the most innocuous changes in behaviour. Anyway, we won't take any more of your time. Thank you, and please thank Lady Little for allowing us to take Sir John's laptop. Tell her that we will bring it back as soon as we can. Goodbye, now.'

* ⋆ ★

'What did you think of Sarah's responses to my questions?' King asked, as they drove back. 'Particularly the last one.'

'Well, I think she is very loyal to her employers. I don't think she would say anything bad about either of them. Curious, though, that she had to think before telling us that Melissa hadn't behaved any differently before Sir John died but she didn't when you asked about Sir John himself. I suppose she wasn't expecting questions about Melissa, only Sir John.'

'Yes, I imagine it was something like that. It's amazing how much somebody like Sarah will know about her employers though. Often people have all sorts of secrets that only the house-keeper will know about. The difficulty is getting them to talk. Many of them are fiercely loyal, and it's clear that Sarah falls into this category. She certainly won't say anything disparaging about Melissa. Unless, of course, Melissa had something to do with Sir John's death and we were able to demonstrate this to Sarah. Then her loyalties would be split.'

Burton nodded. 'True, but my guess would be in that case she would side with Melissa. After all, Melissa is still her employer at the moment, and Sir John is already gone.'

'Maybe. Who knows? Anyway, we'll get this computer to the building on East Street. That's where all the boffins hang out. We'll see whether they can find any interesting data.'

★ ★ ★

It took the officer from the computer centre about two minutes to crack Sir John's password. They'd pulled up Sir John's record from the police database and the officer was poring over the information they'd gleaned trying to guess what he'd used. Striding impatiently around the room, Burton was about to call Melissa to ask her if she knew what it was, when the shout 'I'm in!' went up and he rushed over to have a look.

'Here we go,' the officer, a youngish-looking Bahamian with cropped hair and a small, thin moustache, was saying as his hands danced over the keyboard. 'Month and year of his birthday, followed by month and year of his wife's. Not particularly secure. But now we'll see whether he had any reason to need to be secure.'

Despite the air conditioning sounding as if it was working overtime, the room was warm and the fans on the computers were cutting in regularly. Burton was surprised that the computer operator was wearing uniform — dark-blue trousers with a thick red stripe and a white short-sleeved shirt with his stripes on the shoulder — but, like many of his compatriots, he looked utterly unaffected by the heat.

'So what am I looking for?' asked the officer, his hands poised over the keyboard waiting for instructions.

'I don't really know,' replied Burton. 'We are looking for any information which may shed some light on his death. Particularly anything that may give someone he knew a motive. Could be anything really . . . ' Burton realized he wasn't being particularly helpful but he really had no idea what Sir John would have kept on his computer.

Sir John's desktop screen was cluttered with files, most of which appeared to be word processor documents ranging from letters to Sir John's tailor, to plans for tee-off times at the local golf club. There were also several spreadsheets and a folder containing photos. A warning message from the anti-virus software popped up. Burton guessed the computer hadn't been used for some time and it had not been updated recently.

'Can we look at the recently opened documents? And perhaps see which applications were the last to have been used?'

'Yes, sure.' The young man's fingers moved over the keyboard, and then came the response. 'A couple of Word documents, a spreadsheet of his accounts, not much else. I don't think he used the computer that much. I'll open them and we can have a look.'

Burton watched as the spreadsheet opened on the screen. Sir John had clearly kept a good record of his income and outgoings. Burton looked down the list, but he didn't notice anything out of the ordinary. Most payments were run-of-the-mill: golf club membership, utilities bills, shopping accounts and suchlike. There were a couple of anomalies, which were most likely payments to individuals. Sir John, however, had not noted down anything more than 'cash payment'.

Burton's eyes shifted to the incoming column. Again, nothing leaped out at him: there was a monthly pension payment, rent on a property in Jamaica and dividends on investments. No unexpected payments were logged. But then, what if Sir John didn't have any shares, and the 'dividends' were in fact payments from the obeahman?

'Can we check all these payments?' he asked King. 'I mean, cross-check with credit card statements, bank accounts, share certificates?'

'Well, yes and no.' King answered, somewhat enigmatically in Burton's mind. 'If we had the necessary documents, then yes, we could cross-check. At the moment, however, we have been allowed to look at Sir John's computer by virtue of the fact that his widow has given us permission. In order to view other corroborating documents, we would either have to ask Melissa if these documents are lying around and, if so, whether she minds us looking at them, or we'd have to subpoena Sir John's bank or other financial institutions for their records. I don't believe we are in a position to issue the latter, and I'm not sure we want to bother Melissa again at the moment. Perhaps if we reach a situation in which evidence of these payments is critical to the case, we can follow one of these two routes. Now, though, it would be a fishing expedition at best.'

Typical conservative, by-the-book King, thought Burton. He said, 'OK, I can understand that. What about the Word documents?'

These proved to be a couple of letters, one a strongly worded complaint to a plumber, the other a request for confirmation of a meeting date with a lawyer. No further information was available. A complete dead-end, thought Burton. Unless, of course, an irate plumber had decided to take matters into his own hands and had settled on his customer paying the ultimate price.

'OK, gentlemen. You're welcome to keep on looking if you want, but I've got other things to get on with. Let me know if anything crops up.' King's face was a study in controlled frustration as he left the computer centre.

Burton walked towards the window and gazed out. Outside it was serene and quiet, the Bahamians engaging in the traditional lull in activity common in so many hot countries. He racked his brain for ideas: he was getting nowhere fast, and he knew that King wanted to pull the plug on the whole thing. But he also knew, or rather felt, that something wasn't quite right. His intuition told him that there was more to this than an accidental drowning. His reverie was broken by the voice of the young officer working on the laptop.

'Oh look, that's interesting. Hey, sir, come and have a look at this! I think I've got something.'

Burton rushed over and looked at the screen.

15

King answered the phone after about ten rings. Burton guessed he was waiting for the noise to stop but, when it didn't, finally succumbed. He'd left work hours before, but he somehow knew King would be working late. He could picture the detective in his office, the only lit room in an otherwise deserted police station, working at his report when everybody else apart from the desk sergeant had long since departed. How different it would be from the plush yet minimalist interior of his hotel room. Burton lay relaxed on his bed, staring up at the pristine white ceiling. He asked, 'How's the report going?'

'Fine, thank you, Michael. I'm sure I will have something ready by tomorrow. Nice of you to check though.'

King's voice, laden with sarcasm, sounded faint and weary, but Burton wasn't sure whether that was because he was tired, which he thought was unlikely as King never seemed to show signs of fatigue, or whether this was something for which they could thank the Bahamas Telecommunications Corporation.

'That's good. I just got back from the

computer centre at East Street. It took us — or rather your computer whizz — quite a long time, but I think we might have something else for you to add to your report. Something that might change the complexion of the case somewhat.'

'Oh yes, what might that be?'

Burton swung his feet off the bed and stood up. He walked over to the window and looked out over the harbour. The mail boat had just arrived at Potter's Cay and workers scuttled like ants over the concrete, which glowed golden in the warm evening glow. Behind, the bridge to Paradise Island was a dark silhouette superimposed on a streaky pink and orange sunset. The diagonal slash of the black bridge against the pastel background reminded Burton of a Japanese print. He would enjoy the next few minutes.

'Well, it seems that Sir John wasn't the IT ignoramus that we all had him down for. In fact, it rather appears that he was quite a skilled operator. Not an expert, apparently, but also not a complete nitwit. He even had the guy in your computer centre stumped for a while. Certainly surprised me as well, I can tell you.

'Anyway, Sir John seems to have been in possession of some information that he clearly didn't want his wife to know about.

Now, from what we found it looks like he was the only one to use the computer, but he obviously felt concerned enough about the information in question to take steps to hide it, probably because he knew that Melissa might find it. Apart from the housekeeper, she was the only person we know had access to the laptop. So anyway, he set up an encrypted 'hidden' partition on his hard disk. He used some sort of open source file encryption software. You can download it from the Internet — relatively straight forward for somebody reasonably in the know, but I definitely hadn't had him down for this. Anyway, he didn't quite do enough to fool a professional.

'He left the encryption programme on the computer, for one thing. Sort of gave us a clue that that's what he'd been up to. Also, and this is what really gave the game away, he apparently couldn't remember his password. He had a very strong password, mind, which obviously meant that it was very difficult for anyone to guess or for anyone to crack. Not like the main password to log on to his account, which was essentially weak.

'So he saved a Wordpad file with his password along with all of his photos in his 'Cuban Holiday' file. Changed the file extension to .jpg and used a standard icon so no one would notice that it wasn't what it seemed. If you open it normally, owing to the incorrect file extension, you get gibberish. Your computer officer looked at the gibberish and somehow divined that it needed to be opened with Wordpad. Or he just guessed. Or he tried all the programmes on the machine. I don't know. Anyway, he got us in.

'And there was some interesting reading, and viewing, in the encrypted file. We found letters to a private detective, invoices etc. Some of which correspond to the amounts on the spreadsheet. And photos, lots of them. Of Melissa and an as yet unidentified male who was in any event not her husband. We think these were taken by the private detective, who was hired by Sir John to gather evidence of his wife's affaire.

'There are also letters to Sir John's solicitor, explaining the situation, summarizing the information he had, and asking her to act for him. He was planning a divorce. There's lots of evidence of this, all very clear. The solicitor kept very quiet about it though. Not a word when we were in her office. Not a sign to us, or to Melissa, as far as I could see. I'm not sure why she didn't say anything. She was Sir John's solicitor; I don't think she did any work for Melissa. Couldn't have done, I suppose, if she was to represent Sir John in the divorce proceedings. Wouldn't that be a conflict of interest?'

It was intended as a rhetorical question — Burton was in full flow. King, sensing this, remained silent, waiting for him to continue.

'Then again, the housekeeper lady didn't mention anything either. But she might not have known. I don't know how discreet Melissa was with her lover. Clearly not discreet enough for a detective — who has, after all, had professional training to find out these things — but perhaps discreet enough to keep her housekeeper in the dark. Anyway, the housekeeper seemed too loyal to spill the beans — I don't imagine she'd have said anything if she knew. What do you think?'

There was a short pause. In the silence, Burton could almost hear King's thought processes before he responded.

'Yes, this is an interesting development. Although it raises almost as many questions as it answers. As you point out, we don't know if the cleaning lady knew about the affaire. But we also don't know whether Melissa knew that Sir John knew about it either, or that he was planning to divorce her. It gives her a possible motive, though, either way: if she knew that he wanted to divorce her, she might have taken steps to ensure that this didn't happen; equally, she may have been in the dark about the divorce but wanted to elope with her lover and feared that Sir John wouldn't have agreed to a divorce.

'Well, Michael, you do seem to have uncovered something of value. Now we need to think about what we're going to do with it. I think we should invite Melissa Little over to the station for an interview.'

Yes, I think we should as well, thought Burton. He said, 'I agree that would be appropriate. When?'

'Well, I'll have to call her. I don't want to arrest her if I can help it, so I'll ask if she's available tomorrow morning to help us with our inquiries.'

Burton smiled at King's usage of the hackneyed phrase he had heard so often in connection with the police in England. Obviously, some of the phraseology had rubbed off on him during his stay in the UK.

'OK. I'll see you tomorrow morning.'

Burton smiled as he hung up the phone. This whole divorce thing had to mean something. Melissa must be involved. And she must have set him up on Saturday night. Made sure he was nicely drunk and then paid a couple of local thugs to beat him up. The face of the man he remembered seeing on Saturday night flashed through his memory. He suddenly knew what he had to do: find the man and get him to admit that Melissa Little had paid him to beat him up.

Burton rushed over to the desk in the corner of the room and started to fish around for the city map they had given him at the front desk when he had arrived. He spread the map on the desk and quickly located the restaurant where they had eaten. It was just round the corner from the hotel. Trying to remember the events of the evening was taxing: he recalled now that he had felt unwell even when they left the restaurant, but dredging his vague memories for any information of any value seemed futile at first. He sat down, closed his eyes and tried to picture what they had done when they had left the restaurant.

He remembered getting into a car and heading along West Bay Street and then away from the coast. He pored over the map, looking at the possible routes they could have taken that were consistent with his memory, such as it was. He was fairly certain that they hadn't passed the main police station, so East Street was out, but there were several roads running more or less parallel that they could have taken.

He racked his brain for images of the forgotten night in a sea of uncertainty. The few he could find were of the pub and some

255

objects on the street. He could vaguely remember the way he walked back, but none of the street names meant anything to him.

He sat back and tried to put together what he did know, which wasn't much. He knew that they had been in the taxi for some time and that it had been a bus journey of about half an hour to get back. He could vaguely remember that he had taken a number 2 bus, but the bus routes weren't displayed on the map he had. He would have to work out approximately where to go, and then verify this by checking the bus stops on the way to confirm that the number 2 went along that route.

After a while, Burton decided that he must have been Over-the-Hill, in or around Grant's Town. It was the only area that fitted with the pattern of journeys that he had taken, unless he had got the timing of the journeys seriously wrong, or they had been hugely delayed because of traffic. He was fairly certain that the latter wasn't the case, as he had no recollection of sitting in a stationary car.

Having decided that this evening's activities would mean a visit to Grant's Town, Burton began to formulate a plan. Clearly, any communication with King about this was not a viable option, so he would have to go it alone. He decided that he would walk there: it would take quite a long time, he guessed about an hour, but he wanted the exercise after having spent the day looking at a computer screen and he also wanted to familiarize himself with the neighbourhood. He was fairly confident that, once confronted with the scenery itself, he would remember far more of the void that his Saturday evening currently was.

He had no plan for once he was in Grant's Town, and could think of nothing better than to walk around looking for things he remembered, particularly the pub, or people he recalled. A flush of anger coursed through his body and he flexed his muscles, acknowledging that what he really wanted to see was the person whose face remained etched on his memory. Now he wanted to see him again; now he wasn't paralysed by alcohol; now he was ready. The thought of imminent revenge spurred him into action.

Although it was still warm outside, he didn't know how long he would be out so he changed into a pair of jeans and a dark-coloured sweat-shirt. He put on a pair of trainers and picked up the map. He wasn't planning to take his wallet or anything else with him, but he took some small change in case he wanted to take a bus or taxi back.

Looking at the map, he tried to memorize his route, as he didn't want to have to keep stopping and checking where he was. He always had the feeling that this sent out signals of vulnerability, which on this evening in particular he didn't want to do. He rehearsed until he knew more or less his exact route, and the major roads in the whole neighbourhood, and then he folded the map into a small square and stuffed it into his back pocket. He looked at his watch. It was almost eleven o' clock. It was time.

★　★　★

The evening had cooled considerably since he had left the hotel, and Burton was glad of the sweat-shirt he had worn. Despite the persistent heat of the afternoons, the nights could be biting as the warm air spilled off the island, chased by the cold air moving in from the sea. Burton had elected to follow one of the main streets up towards Grant's Town, but avoiding East Street. Not that he rated the chances of running into King leaving the office after a hard night's work particularly high, but he wanted to see if the surroundings jogged his memory.

Deciding finally to take Blue Hill Street, Burton tried to recognize various features as he walked. Nothing seemed familiar, but he hadn't really expected otherwise. There were bus stops on the road he was walking along, but the rusted signs gave little away. Finally he found one on which he could identify a number 2, and he knew he was on the right path, at least for his journey back. He hadn't been looking out much on the way there, as he had been talking to Melissa throughout the journey.

As he walked in the cool evening air, Burton ran through the events of the Saturday night. He was still somewhat mystified that he had lost track of the evening when he could not remember drinking that much. At least in the restaurant, Melissa had matched him drink for drink, and yet he had already felt a bit woolly when they had left. He'd had a few beers beforehand, which may have made a difference, but still . . .

As he neared the junction with Wulff Road, he had the impression that things were starting to look more familiar, although it was still only a general impression rather than any kind of concrete recollection of any particular features.

Burton turned into Wulff Road, hoping to recognize one of the streets heading off towards Grant's Town. He passed East Street and continued until he came to the next road he had memorized as allowing him to get through to Robinson Road. As he turned in, he saw a couple of men walking along the other side of the road.

'Hey, baby, what yuh doin?' Burton heard, and assumed they were talking to a woman walking with them, although he could see no one.

Using his peripheral vision, he tried surreptitiously to make out what was happening, but could see only the two men. When they started to cross the road towards him, he knew that it wasn't a friendly greeting. He stopped and turned to look at them, his fists clenched in anticipation of seeing his previous sparring partner. He was disappointed. Neither man resembled the face he had seen. One was a tall, thin man with dreadlocks, the other squat and broad. Burton stood his ground and stared. The adrenaline pumped through his body, as he took in his would-be attackers. The shorter one was broad with fat, not muscle, and the thin man looked gaunt. They both looked spaced out. Despite being outnumbered, Burton chose fight over flight and squared up to their approaching. He saw the glint of a knife in the thin man's hand and quickly adopted a boxing stance, eager to strike before the knife came into play. His eyes moved upwards and held the thin man's stare for a second before the man looked away.

'Hey, man, take it easy.' The blade of the knife retracted and the thin man slipped his hand into his pocket. 'Yuh want some ganja, man? Ah thinks yuh need some, all that aggression. Wot yuh doin' walkin' here at night? Are yuh confuddle up, man? Here? Ain't no place for a tourist. Yuh lookin' for a broke down or summin'?'

'No thanks.' Burton straightened up. They were playing it cool, but he had seen the look in the thin man's eyes before he had glanced away. There was no doubt in his mind that they had meant to attack him, but had changed their minds when their prey turned out not to be defenceless, as they had thought. Part of him wanted to lash out at them anyway, teach them a lesson for picking on the vulnerable and stealing from them, as had undoubtedly been their intention. Smack them around a bit so they wouldn't do it again. But he had not come on a one-man vigilante mission to sort out a suburb of Nassau, so he let it ride. And besides, he didn't want to make the same mistake they had made and underestimate his enemy, expending his energy on someone other than his target for the evening, or, worse still, carrying an injury into the latter confrontation. He stood still watching them.

'OK, man, whadever.' The two men continued past Burton towards the main road. Burton watched them go, waiting until they disappeared from sight. They chattered as they walked away, and once they were out of earshot the evening was almost surreally silent.

Burton continued along in the same direction. He knew he was in the right place, as the cafés all sported barred windows, the shops were run down but well frequented and here and there functional but unattractive garages and workshops were peppered around the neighbourhood. He saw a small café with barred windows on the other side of the road that immediately struck him as familiar.

Not wanting to enter it, Burton crossed the road and walked past the café, glancing in as he did so. He recognized the bar against the far wall and the tables dotted around.

Burton walked past, trying to remember where he had gone after leaving the café. He seemed to remember Melissa indicating the way he should go. If he was right, and Melissa was somehow involved, it was fair to assume that she did not have his best interests at heart and had probably advised him to go away from his hotel, further into Grant's Town. He decided to head further in the direction he was going.

Burton wandered around the area, walking a simple square pattern, so he could find his way back without having to look at the map. There were few people on the streets, but whenever he came across anyone, he felt their eyes checking out the out-of-place tourist, trying to decide whether he was lost and vulnerable. He kept walking confidently without looking around more than was necessary to check to see if any of them were the man he was looking for.

Then he saw him. He was sitting on a doorstep outside a shop, which was closed and barred. The thin, cruel face was unmistakable. Burton recognized the man immediately, but even if he hadn't, the man obviously recognized him, as he suddenly got up and ran away. Burton sprinted after him.

The man ducked left and right in the small alleys, and then out onto a larger street. Burton no longer knew where he was, but he kept the man in sight, and was soon gaining on him. The man ran into an alley and Burton followed him, tripping over some rubbish as he turned in. He regained his balance, putting a hand against the wall, but when he looked up the man was gone.

Burton kept running, looking for a turning. He could see none, so he raced on until he spotted the man in front of him. They were

263

now running downhill, and he had a lot of ground to make up. He sprinted as hard as he could; he didn't think the gaunt man could outrun him, but he was already breathing heavily and he could feel his heart thumping.

Further and further they ran, and Burton was spurred on as he saw the distance between them decrease steadily, as if Burton had hooked his fish and was slowly reeling him in. His quarry must have felt this as well, as he suddenly veered across the street to turn onto another largish street at the junction.

Burton saw him preparing to turn and, when he did so, dived at him full length in a rugby tackle. His shoulder hit the man hard about mid-thigh, his head tucked behind the running man, and the force of the hit lifted them both up into the air.

The man hit the ground first, hard, and then Burton crashed down on top of him. He heard a gasp, and the man rolled onto his back. Burton was slightly winded by the fall but the man he had landed on looked like a rag doll hit by a car. The man moaned slightly and tried to sit up. A slave to adrenaline and revenge, Burton caught the man under the jaw with a vicious uppercut. He heard the crack of his fist against the man's chin, followed by a second crack as the man's skull pounded against the pavement. The man's eyes went glassy and unseeing and all movement stopped.

Despite the immediate relief of having had his revenge, Burton immediately regretted the punch. He needed information, and unconscious people don't say much, so now he would have to wait for him to come round. He looked around and was not comforted by what he saw. He was in the middle of what was certainly not the safest neighbourhood, and he was with an injured local man whom he had just rendered unconscious. Not good.

Burton checked again but could see no one. He knew he had to get off the street, so he picked up the man in a fireman's lift and carried him back into the alley. Dumping him unceremoniously on the ground, he leaned against the wall, struggling to get his breath and his heart rate under control. He tried to regulate his breathing, slowly drawing deep breaths and trying to relax.

It was a good ten minutes later when the man began to stir. He groaned and moved a bit. Burton walked over and prodded him a couple of times with his foot. Finally, the eyes opened, slowly at first but then jerking wide open as they came to rest on Burton.

'Don't say a word.' Burton crouched as he spoke, brandishing his fist. What he didn't want was for the man to call for help, so he was prepared to hit him if he tried to do so. The man clearly saw this; his face paled and panic filled his eyes.

Burton remained still, waiting for the man to regain control. The pale face, so unusual in a dark Bahamian, seemed to fluoresce in the dark.

'Who told you to attack me last Saturday?'

The man's face remained unmoved. Burton could not tell if he had understood him, couldn't answer the question, or was scared to do so.

'If you tell me the truth, I won't hurt you anymore. Do you understand?'

The man nodded, his eyes transfixed on Burton.

'Who told you to do it?'

The eyes glazed for a second, and Burton could almost sense confusion replacing fear.

'Who made you do it?'

He gave the man a way out: he could claim he was forced to attack Burton. Again, though, as far as Burton could see, the man only registered confusion. Burton began to doubt whether he had been set up after all.

'Why did you rob me last Saturday?'

The man remained silent, but now he looked merely scared.

'Look, I came here to find out why it

happened. If you tell me, I won't hurt you again. But I need to know. I don't want to have to beat it out of you.'

This seemed to hit a chord. The man stammered and then said, 'Money.'

'Somebody paid you to do it?'

'No, no, no. I wanted money. An' then I see yuh staggerin' down the street, can't even stand up proper, so I thinks that I can make some easy money. I can roll a drunk tourist an' 'e won't even know nuttin' about it in the morning. That's easy money, man. Easy money.'

The man spat on the ground next to him. He looked up and continued bitterly, 'Looks like I was wrong. It wasn't easy money. I picks on some crazy tourist who comes an' robs me back. Well, I ain't got yuh money no more, man. I spends it long ago. Look.'

Finally, a smile crossed the man's face as he turned out his pockets. Burton might have had his revenge, but he wasn't going to get his money back. With this knowledge, the man became more animated.

'What was yuh doin' here anyway, man? Pissed up tourist crawlin' round here? That's crazy, man. Yuh is real crazy.'

Burton leant back against the wall. He had the feeling that the man was telling the truth. The fact that the man genuinely seemed

267

convinced that Burton had come back for the money seemed to be the confirmation. Nowhere could he detect any sign of lying.

'All right then. Be off with you.'

Burton watched as the man got unsteadily to his feet and scuttled off. He waited until he was gone and then walked out of the alley in the opposite direction. He checked the map he had brought with him, but as he suspected, he'd long since left the area that was covered by the tourist map the hotel had given him. He had no idea where he was, but he knew he'd come downhill, so he headed back up.

The enormity of the whole situation finally began to dawn on him. It was now the early hours, and he was tired and miles away from his hotel. Judging by previous experience, it wasn't the safest part of town. It was going to be a long night.

16

The persistent ring of the telephone woke him. Burton picked up the handset of the offending article and greeted it.

'Hello?'

'Good morning, Michael. I see your time-keeping is back to normal. I was expecting you here earlier today, but no matter. I've asked Lady Little to come to the station at eleven. She was happy to do so. Are you able to make it, or do you need some more beauty sleep?'

'No, no, I'll be there at eleven.'

Burton hung up the phone immediately. He wasn't about to get involved in a discussion about punctuality seconds after waking up. He checked the alarm clock at the side of the bed. It was almost ten o'clock, and he noted that the alarm had been set for half past eight. He'd obviously slept through an hour of the irritating buzzing noise the thing made, and wouldn't be surprised if he received complaints from the neighbouring rooms.

He'd had about four hours' sleep, having finally arrived back at the hotel a little before six. He'd walked for nearly an hour before he'd been able to discover where he was, and then he went the shortest way back. No buses were working at that time, and he saw no taxis, so he'd had to walk the whole way. He was physically, and mentally, exhausted.

He stood under a cold shower trying to wake himself up. The ambient temperature was so hot that the cold water out of the tap was lukewarm. Still in an exhausted stupor, Burton made his way down to the restaurant and fed himself coffee until he felt able to face King.

★　★　★

It was just before eleven when Burton reached the police station. As he walked towards it, he spotted Melissa coming in the opposite direction. He waited for her outside the front door.

'Good morning.'

'Good morning, Michael. This is a pleasant surprise. I've come to see Detective King. Although I suppose you already knew that?'

Burton treated this as a rhetorical question. 'Come on, let's go inside. I think Detective King is waiting for us.'

The desk sergeant greeted them and waved them through, either knowing or assuming that both of them knew exactly where they were going. He was certainly right to do so in Burton's case, but he wasn't sure Melissa was that familiar with the inside of the police station. Or maybe she was.

'So, have you any idea what this is all about?' she asked and they climbed the stairs.

'No, not really,' Burton answered. Somehow he felt much more comfortable not telling barefaced lies but giving vague answers that could be construed to be true. 'I think it might have something to do with information which was uncovered from your husband's laptop by the police computer forensics team. Anyway, I'm sure Detective King will explain to us both what we need to know when the time is right.'

King met them at the top of the stairs carrying a thin, buff-coloured folder, of which he seemed to have an endless supply, and showed them into an interview room located down the corridor from his office. Once they were perched on hard, uncomfortable chairs around a cheap plain wooden table, King took the lead.

'Lady Little, as you may have guessed, or as Michael may already have told you, we have asked you here to discuss certain information that we found on your husband's computer. Now, you allowed us to take the computer, and you agreed to come here to answer our questions. I would like to take this opportunity to tell you that you are not under arrest, and that you may leave at any time should you wish to do so. I would also like to draw your attention to the fact that this interview is being taped.' King indicated an old cassette player on the desk between them, the sheer size of which meant that Melissa could hardly have avoided seeing it anyway. 'Do you have any questions about the interview?'

'Yes, I do.' Melissa's voice was cool, unemotional, but her face registered concern. 'This all seems a lot more formal than I had expected when you asked me if I'd be happy to come down here and answer a few questions. Am I in danger of being arrested? Do I need a lawyer?'

'Well, of course, if you would like a lawyer, you're free to ask to have one present. At the moment, though, we are simply asking questions. You are not a suspect in the case at present, so we are not planning to arrest you.'

For the first time, King sounded less than confident. Burton smiled inwardly at his clumsy attempt to encourage Melissa not to call a lawyer.

'So I can ask for a lawyer at any time if I want one? Any interview will be terminated at that point until my counsel arrives?' Melissa was calm, quietly probing to ensure she had fully understood her rights.

'Yes.'

'OK, then I'm happy to continue without one at present. Ask me whatever it is you need to ask.'

Melissa's face had ceased to look troubled in any way, and she exuded confident curiosity rather than anything else.

'Right. Yesterday evening, one of the forensics officers in our computer centre found an encrypted file that Sir John had used to store some sensitive documents and photographs. We have looked at these and would like to ask you about them.'

King opened the buff folder, and took out printouts of the photographs and the letters Sir John had drafted to the lawyer and the private investigator. He arranged the photographs so that each was visible to Melissa, and laid out the two letters next to each other.

'As you can see, we have uncovered evidence of your affaire, and also of Sir John's intention to divorce you. This gives you a motive for wanting him dead. You didn't want a divorce, didn't want to lose your position in society. You were worried it would leave you with no money, destitute in a strange land. Tell us, please, Lady Little, who is the man in the photographs? Are you still seeing him? Was he involved in Sir John's death? Or were you?'

Melissa sat back, gave a cynical half laugh and looked from King to Burton and then back to King again. 'Is that it, gentlemen? Is this why I am here?'

Neither man responded.

'If my husband hadn't just passed away, I might find your incompetence amusing. As it is, I find it merely insulting.'

Burton had the feeling the interview wasn't going well.

'The answer is yes, I am still seeing the man in the photograph. Or at least I was until he left the island several weeks ago. But I'm still in contact with him. He's my brother. He came over to visit me from England.'

Melissa sat back and stared at them, as if daring one of them to say something. Once again, Burton had the impression that he was listening to a truth that didn't fit in with his suspicions. He looked across at King, who looked faintly embarrassed. Burton cleared his throat.

'Er, I have some questions.'

King and Melissa both looked at him.

'If the man in the photographs is your brother, why were you meeting him surreptitiously? Why did Sir John *think* you were having an affaire, if you weren't? Why didn't he know your brother was visiting you?'

Melissa smiled. 'I can see that it looks slightly strange. I didn't tell my husband, as I didn't want the two of them to meet. You see, my brother is an odd sort: he dropped out of university and went travelling around the world; has never had a regular job and earns his income by dubious means. I'm not really sure what he does to support himself, and I'm careful not to ask. When he's not flush with money, he starts scrounging from anyone he knows: family, friends, acquaintances, anybody.

'When he called me to say he was coming over, I was concerned that he would want money from me, or, worse still, from my husband. As you know, my husband was a rich man. He was also a very kind man. I didn't want him to be harassed by my brother, and I certainly didn't want him to give my brother any money. Although he had enough, John was no longer working and shouldn't have been giving money away. Anyway, my idle brother should have been earning his own.

'So I kept them apart. I met my brother only when I knew that John was playing golf. In hindsight, this may have been the wrong thing to do: one of my husband's friends from his chess club saw us in town. Confused sibling affection for an altogether more amorous kind.' Melissa sighed regretfully. 'He informed my husband that I was having an affaire.

'Unfortunately, John didn't come straight to me, but decided to employ a private detective to spy on me.' There was audible bitterness in her voice as she spat out the word 'spy'.

'The detective duly reported that I was seeing an unknown man, and provided lots of photographic evidence, of course.

'Idiot! If he had done some real investigating, rather than just taking photographs, he'd have found out who he was and wouldn't have had to upset John.

'Anyway, my husband looked at the evidence, decided I was having an affaire and spoke to his lawyer about a divorce.' Melissa looked up at Burton and King. 'You know the lawyer. Mrs Wells, Agatha Wells. A nice lady, very bright and very practical. Anyway, she at least managed to talk some sense into him, pointing out that all he had to go on was a few photographs and even if I was having an affaire, he would have to talk to me about it before filing for divorce. After all, I'm sure any self-respecting judge would have been livid if John had wasted his time with this ludicrous action.

'So my husband confronted me, and I explained about my brother, who he was, what he did, why he had come and why I hadn't mentioned it. Needless to say, there was relief all round; John was happy, I was happy, and I believe Mrs Wells was happy. Although she didn't get any fees for the divorce, my husband was eternally grateful for her advice and told her so.

'And that, gentlemen, is more or less it. I wasn't having an affaire, my husband knew that I wasn't having an affaire, and so did his lawyer. Feel free to ask her, if you want somebody to corroborate my version of events.

'I know you're only doing your jobs, well, at least one of you is doing your job' — Melissa stared at Burton — 'but I really think you should do some detecting of your own before dragging me here to bandy about wild accusations that you can't substantiate because they're not true. From some dried up ex-copper making a living as a private detective I can understand sloppiness of this kind, but not from you.' Now her gaze transferred to King.

'Now, if there's nothing else you'd like me to help you with? Tying your shoelaces or something? Then, I'd like to leave.'

King and Burton stood up as Melissa did.

'Thank you for coming to the station and helping us, Lady Little. We're very sorry about the inconvenience.' King was talking to Melissa's back and she walked to the door and let herself out, slamming the door behind her.

Burton looked across and King and raised his eyebrows. The other man shook his head. 'I don't blame her. I wouldn't be too impressed if I were her. On the other hand, we have got answers to our questions. And they sounded fairly solid answers to me. We will check up with the lawyer to tie up any loose ends, but somehow I don't think it's really necessary. After all, we've already spoken to her and she didn't mention anything.

'No, I don't think there's much future in pursuing this line of inquiry. I will finalize the report I've been working on, and we can discuss it later today.'

★ ★ ★

King's report made light reading. Burton had to admit that the detective had put together a very concise document, which nonetheless seemed to cover all salient points of the investigation in adequate detail. The style of the writing was clinical and detached, and

Burton found himself feeling as if he was looking at the case objectively and from a distance. The report concluded that there was insufficient evidence of any crime having been committed, which was how Burton had known it would conclude and the direction in which he had been drawn, logically and unemotionally, from the very first page. It was, he thought to himself, a masterpiece of suggestive writing.

Burton laid the report down in front of him and thought about what to do. He faced a conundrum: the facts and inferred logic in the report were inescapably correct, yet his gut feeling was in total disagreement. He was fairly certain King had not been given the authority and rank he possessed for flying off on wild goose chases following unsubstantiated hunches, and he knew he would face an uphill struggle trying to persuade him that there was more to it than a simple accident. Still, he considered, doing so would be fulfilling the role given to him by the Foreign Office, and exercising the discretion he had been given in doing this. And if Sir John's death was in any way criminal, then the perpetrator should be brought to justice.

Burton glanced at his watch. He was meeting King in half an hour to discuss their next move. He went through the report again, trying to find a chink in King's armour, marking the parts he felt were assailable.

The door opened and King's head appeared. 'Are you ready, Michael?'

'Yes, I'm coming.'

Burton followed King from the interrogation room in which he had been sitting to the detective's office. King indicated a chair for Burton, but remained standing himself, looking out of the window.

'What do you think of the report?'

'Well, it's certainly factual and correct. But I still have a gut feeling about this case. There's something not quite right about Sir John's death, although I can't quite put my finger on what it is.'

King turned back to face him. 'And what do you suggest we do about your feeling? Assign a few more officers to the case? Ask Scotland Yard to help us?'

King's voice was thick with sarcasm, and for the first time since Burton had met him, he looked drained and tired. He realized that King must be juggling some fairly heavy workloads. He looked around the room slowly, taking in the scruffy piles of notes in towering piles that now formed the landscape of King's desk. These had not been there when he had arrived. Things had changed. The detective was inundated. The gesture of loyalty to the old colonial power had been made when they weren't busy, and now more pressing matters had come up, the investigation of a former diplomat aimed at currying favour with a foreign state was getting in the way of real work. Burton saw in an instant that there was little point in a protracted discussion.

'No, OK, I understand. Do you mind if I take away a copy of your report? I will need to make my own report, which will obviously refer to yours. I'll try and finish this off in the coming days, but it makes sense for me to write it here. Then, if I have any questions, or think of anything else, I can bring them up with you.'

'OK, Michael, you can take away that copy. Let me know when you want to bring it back. Now, if you'll excuse me, I have plenty of other things to get on with.' He gestured at the columns of paper on his desk.

'Of course. Well, thanks and goodbye for now.'

Clutching King's report under his arm, Burton left the police station feeling very few ill effects from the undisguised brush off he had been given.

17

Burton set King's report down on the table in front of him and sat back. In front of him were two empty pots of coffee and one cup. He was sitting in the lobby of the hotel, where he had met Melissa several nights before. After a fitful and sleepless night, he had devoured a large breakfast consisting of everything from succulent fresh fruit to the always slightly disappointing cooked breakfast, which only really tastes good when cooked to order by a competent chef.

Only the low chattering noise of children playing outside disturbed the silence in the lobby, which was at present peacefully under populated. It was a sunny day and most guests were enjoying the fresh air before the real heat settled in; then, only the real sun worshippers would be out.

It was almost impossible to find inaccuracies in King's masterpiece of factual precision, but Burton still remained steadfastly unconvinced by the theory that this was a simple accidental drowning. King's report detailed facts, and from these facts drew conclusions that were probable. There appeared to be no facts that supported a probable crime, and King's summary was therefore that there was insufficient evidence to pursue the case further.

Despite admitting there was a lack of evidence, Burton was of the inexplicably strong opinion that either Melissa or the mysterious obeahman had something to do with it. Maybe, he thought to himself, they both had something to do with it. Maybe it was some kind of conspiracy in which both beneficiaries had planned Sir John's death and were now covering for each other. But were they really covering for each other? Or was there simply no evidence that either of them had anything to do with it?

Burton sighed. He was getting nowhere. He decided to go for a walk on the beach and headed up to his room, swapping the report for a towel and sunglasses, which he stuffed into a smallish rucksack along with his wallet and phone, all whilst trying to slip on a pair of light sandals. As he left the hotel room, he reflected that this combination of actions probably took much longer than the combined time of each separately.

As he walked along the beach road, Burton's mind kept turning over the puzzle he was facing. With the information he had, he could do nothing. Yet he wasn't satisfied with doing nothing and felt that he needed to take some action. The only thing he could think of was to go and have another look at Sir John's house, although he wasn't really sure what he would find, or even what he was looking for. He wanted to talk to Melissa, but was fairly certain that neither he nor King would be particularly welcome guests after the fiasco of the day before.

Burton decided to walk. It was a fairly long way and he could take a bus if he needed to, but he liked walking and fancied that he could walk the whole way there. Then he could call a cab to bring him back, or take the bus.

The sun rose higher in the sky as he went, and soon he felt the scorching sun on the back of his neck and his shoulders. He had put on sun cream earlier, but he knew that it would be insufficient to save him from the relentless rays. He opened his rucksack and put his towel over his shoulders, using it to protect his neck. The extra insulation meant that he felt warmer, but at least he no longer had the feeling that his neck was slowly cooking. He ducked and dived along streets, hugging the edges where the buildings afforded some shade, then back on the beach he quickly moved into the shadow of the thick-trunked palm trees that cast fan-shaped shadows across the path.

As Burton headed out of the town, the traffic lessened and a sort of half-silence descended; he could hear the dull, uniform background noise only when he listened for it. The empty streets glared silver as the sun reflected off them harshly. Every now and then flashes of indiscriminate piercing brightness would glint off cars traversing the strip, their coughing, rumbling engines breaking the pregnant silence.

An hour or so later, it was too much. Although he still rather fancied the walk, it was nearing midday and there was no respite from the unrelenting sun. Thoughts of mad dogs and Englishmen cascaded through his mind, but nevertheless he decided to take the bus. The bus stop was bare and unforgiving, and he concealed himself under a palm tree with a view of the road. When the bus approached, he ran to the stop and flagged it down. The driver grinned at him as he climbed into the bus, clearly in awe of the crazy tourist walking from one town to the next at the height of the hot day.

Burton left the bus a couple of stops before he needed to, in order to give himself some time to think about his approach to Melissa. He cut through to the beach side, rather than walking along the road, and was immediately glad that he had done so as he felt the gusty wind rolling in off the sea. Although it was a warm, humid breeze, it at least provided some cooling qualities.

Burton decided that he would knock brazenly on Melissa's door, using the pretext of coming to see how she was after the events of the last few days. It was not inconceivable that he would visit to check up on her, or even to apologize for the mistakes that had been made during the investigation. He began to rehearse words in his head, thinking each time how empty and inadequate they sounded. He looked down as he walked, his brain running through various different scenarios, his eyes following the gentle undulations of the sandy beach.

A set of slim, tanned feet with painted nails crept suddenly into Burton's view, and his eyes wandered from sandy ankles past toned brown thighs to a brief yellow bikini which accentuated the owner's hips, flat stomach and rounded breasts before settling on a regular, beautiful face framed with long, dark hair. He barely registered that it was Melissa until a smile of recognition appeared on her lips. It was clear that a different approach from the one he was practising in his head would be required. At least, he thought, it was a smile of recognition rather than a frown.

'So, what brings you out here?'

Melissa's tone was even and emotionless, neither pleased nor displeased to see him.

'I was just going for a walk along the beach. I thought I might visit you to see how you were. I know the last few days have been difficult.'

'Yes, they have. But I understand that you and Mr King have your jobs to do. I don't hold it against you.' Now, she smiled. 'I might have wished that things had gone slightly differently, but in the end it's the result that matters. If you have reached the right conclusion, then how you got there is not so important.'

Burton wondered whether they had reached the right conclusion. In fact, he thought to himself, he was fairly certain that they hadn't reached the right conclusion. But King thought they had, and it was King's investigation. Melissa was happy with it, and it was, after all, her husband who was dead. His own mind was still full of doubt, but now didn't seem like the best time to bring it up. Instead he responded, 'The end justifies the means? Do you really believe that?'

'In this case, I do. Your investigation is finished, and there are no lasting consequences of the steps you have taken. To bear a grudge would be wrong. We were getting on

287

well together not so long ago. It seems a shame to ruin a friendship over a couple of mistakes. Do you want to come up to the house? We can have a drink. And let bygones be bygones.'

'Yes, sure. That sounds like a good plan.'

Melissa walked next to him along the beach, stopping close to her beach entrance to pick up her towel, which had been tossed casually on the sand. She shook it and wrapped it round her waist before heading off up the steps. Burton followed, ruminating on how differently his visit had turned out.

* * *

Melissa set a bottle of champagne on the table, its shapely dark green form mottled by a mist of condensation which had bloomed rapidly since it had been taken out the fridge. She pointed to the bottle. 'Would you like to do the honours?'

Burton pulled the cork and poured some of the champagne into the fluted glasses that Melissa had brought. He asked cautiously, 'Are we celebrating something?'

'No, not really. Given what has happened over the past weeks, I don't think I have a lot to celebrate. I like champagne, though, particularly during the day. It's so light and cool. But, in a way, we are celebrating something — that we're on speaking terms again.' She smiled broadly. 'I'm glad you decided to go for a walk on the beach today.'

'So am I,' Burton replied, thinking to himself that it was actually very true. He liked Melissa and, although he had initially decided to come because he mistrusted her, he was wondering whether he had in fact got it all wrong. King thought so, and Melissa seemed to have brushed everything aside as if it was inconsequential nonsense. Maybe it was. Maybe it was just a stupid accident that Sir John had drowned.

Melissa had showered quickly when they had arrived, and was now wearing a pair of designer jeans and a light white blouse. Burton had used the time to look around the kitchen briefly, but had found nothing of interest. She seemed at ease, and sat down on the sofa next to him. Her wet hair fell in curls around her shoulders framing her lightly tanned face, on which a friendly smile appeared. 'Cheers', she said, holding out her glass.

'Cheers.' Burton sipped the champagne appraisingly. The bouquet was delicate, floral and light. The liquid was cool in his mouth, but not too cold so as to mask the flavour.

Burton wondered what he could get away

with. 'So, do you know the obeahman? The one Sir John was involved with?'

'No, not at all. I know of him, though. My husband was a man who shared a lot with me — he never tried to hide the fact that he was involved with an obeah group, and that he practised the faith. Or at least was somehow involved — he didn't tell me that much, but then again I didn't really ask. I wasn't really interested. It didn't take up a lot of his time. He went once or twice a week. No more than that.'

He wondered whether there was anything in the obeah stuff he had read. If Sir John had fallen out with them, could they have put a spell on him? A spell that would make him lose control whilst swimming, for example? He had the feeling that his thought processes were starting to go around in circles. If the obeahman had cast a spell on Sir John, the chances were high that nobody would ever be able to confirm this, and higher still that they'd never be able to prove it. And if they did, was there even a law against it? As far as he knew, laws against witchcraft had gone out about the same time as the preordained sink or swim ordeal by water that so many unfortunate witches had fallen foul of in the middle ages.

Burton decided to drop the whole thing.

Why not leave it alone? He'd been given a task, he'd carried it out, and now it was over. It was time for him to relax and think about other things. He looked at Melissa's authoritative face, across which he had lately seen flashes of uncertainty, but which now bore all the confidence of days gone by.

'So, what are you going to do now?' he asked.

'Well, I don't really know. Now this is over, at least I won't have to worry about it anymore. I can grieve like any normal widow. And I can put my life back together and do something with it. I'll probably stay here, at least for a bit, until I know what I'm going to do. What about you? Are you heading back to Jamaica soon?'

'I suppose so. I don't think the British taxpayer will continue to support me over here for much longer.'

Burton drained his glass. Smiling, Melissa refilled it, holding the bottle professionally with her thumb in the heavy base and twisting it as she finished pouring.

'Well, don't go too soon. Or at least, come back often if you do.' Her hand brushed against Burton's thigh. In his mind he struggled to work out if this was merely a friendly gesture or if there was something more in it. His thought processes seemed slow and unwieldy. All he could really grasp was that he was tired and comfortable and sitting with a beautiful woman on a sofa alone in her house. He just wanted to collapse into her arms and hold her warm body to his and allow sleep to take over as he breathed the subtle floral femininity of her scent. But he was unsure: the last thing he wanted was to get back to Jamaica and find himself subject to a complaint that he was abusing his position or something similar.

But the signs were all there. His mind tried to order them, but seemed to be unable to complete the sequence. Once again he felt Melissa's hand on his leg, and he looked at her upturned face. He moved towards her slowly, waiting for her to move away. She swayed towards him and their lips met.

He was becoming very weary. His eyelids drooped as his mouth closed on hers and her tongue explored his mouth. He blinked and opened his eyes widely, involuntarily recoiling slightly from her. She looked surprised, uncertain, and her glossy, painted lips parted in a sensuous smile. He leaned across and kissed her again.

★ ★ ★

The lamp on the ceiling floated in and out of focus. Burton blinked and looked again. The lamp continued to move and the ceiling seemed to reverberate in time with a thudding in his head. He closed his eyes again and went back to sleep. He dreamt he was lying in Melissa's arms, basking in her feminine warmth and floral scent. He was warm and comfortable and happy. He loved her.

18

Burton opened his eyes. The blurred white light that filled his vision started to separate itself into different shapes and sizes, different colours and hues and brightness. He could sense that he was making progress towards bringing the whole scene into focus, but every time he tried to speed up the process, the bright wash returned. Gradually he was able make out objects in the room, which appeared before him out of a blurry haze. He recognized the lamp on the ceiling above the sofa and remembered where he was. He looked next to him, to Melissa, his lover, in whose arms he had fallen asleep.

Melissa was lying next to him on the sofa. But she didn't look well. She was sprawled out on her back, with her head hanging over the arm of the sofa. Her face was bruised, bloodied and expressionless. Burton's eyes moved down from her face and took in the rags of her torn blouse, which were hanging off her arms, her still fastened bra lifted clumsily to reveal her shapely breasts, and her ripped jeans, one leg of which was still around her left ankle. On the floor by the sofa were her knickers, which were torn and bloody. Burton felt like retching as he looked at her legs, which were naked and spread wide; both thighs were bruised on the inside, and her shaved pubic hair was matted with blood. She wasn't moving.

Burton started. His head thumped with the movement and his body felt heavy and uncooperative. His heart thudded. He looked again at Melissa and felt the bile rise in his throat. Beneath her bloodied pubic region, he could see tracks of a dying white liquid on the front of her thighs and dripping down to the back. He felt sick.

Had someone broken in and raped her and beaten him up? Even as the idea crossed his mind, he knew it hadn't happened. The only pain he could feel was the throbbing in his head. Unless someone had clouted him on the head, he hadn't been touched. Gingerly he felt the back of his head but could find no wound. Involuntarily, he looked down at his own legs and saw his shorts round his ankles. Small smudges of dried blood were apparent on his thighs. Oh God, he thought. What have I done?

He looked again at Melissa, struggling to comprehend what had happened. He had raped her. He would go to prison for years. He tried to ignore the pain and think. What should he do? He'd have to turn himself in. If he didn't, Melissa would go to the police, and he'd be caught anyway, most likely in a matter of days, if not hours. He had no experience of being on the run. If he left now, he might make it to some small island and have some hope of evading capture, but for how long? And anyway, how long would he have before Melissa reported him?

The thought crossed his mind to silence her to prevent her from talking. Even as the idea entered his head, he was sickened by the fact that it had done so. Unable to come to terms with the commission of a heinous crime, he was now plotting another even more so. He shook his head in disbelief. No, he would have to face the music when she came round.

As he glanced back at her, his already thumping heart seemed to miss a beat. Beneath her bruised features, vivid purple bruises adorned her neck. How had he missed those? It took some time for the fact to sink in that he may already have committed the crime the very idea of which had unnerved him just moments before.

In desperation, for deep inside he already knew, he tried to find Melissa's pulse. His movements were clumsy and ineffectual. First he tried her wrist, again and again. Then, when he could find nothing, he put his fingers against her slim, ravaged neck, more in hope then expectation. Again he fumbled and tried several different sites on her bruised neck. He left his hand against the side of her throat for what seemed like hours, but was in reality less than a minute, desperately waiting for a glimmer of hope. He knew after a couple of seconds, maybe had indeed already known, that he'd killed her.

It was often difficult to locate a pulse, particularly a weak one, so he gently moved Melissa's head onto the arm of the sofa, tilting her head back to open her airway. All the while aware he was merely going through the motions. Nothing he did now was going to change anything. For twenty seconds, though, he held his ear by her nose and listened and felt for a breath, whilst watching her chest to see if it was rising. He heard nothing, and felt nothing. There was no sign of life at all.

Burton leaned over the side of the sofa and was sick. His head shuddered as he retched violently, and the back of his neck felt like it was on fire. He hadn't eaten much and his body struggled to get rid of the little that was available, at first the remains of his breakfast and some champagne, and then just sour-tasting bile.

Burton closed his eyes and tried to think rationally. It was all over. He was a rapist and a murderer. What could he do? He no longer faced any kind of dilemma about whether to call an ambulance. If she'd still been alive, he wanted to believe that he'd have called one straight away, but he acknowledged grudgingly that even that might not be true. Only minutes before he had been contemplating finishing her off, now he was pretending, even if it was only to himself, that he would have called the ambulance as soon as possible.

They'd find him easily. Even if he cleaned everything up, he knew that the forensic teams would find traces of him all over the place. If he had enough time, he could probably clean up most of the evidence, but then what? Dispose of the body? Do a runner? No, he knew it was all over. He could do nothing but report the murder and turn himself in.

He took his mobile phone from the table and typed in King's number. He was about to press the dial button when a sudden doubt entered his mind.

He didn't have to turn himself in, he thought suddenly, he could simply end it all here and now. Why go through a trial in which he would obviously be found guilty? He would probably end up being advised by a

298

lawyer to plead temporary insanity, or some equally feeble excuse for a crime against humanity. He'd be able to look forward to being gang-raped in a Bahamian prison if he was found guilty, or being committed to an indefinite period in an asylum if found not guilty by reason of insanity. No, he couldn't live with it. His family would be devastated when they found out what he had done. His family would have to live with it; he couldn't. He would not have to go through anything, and his family could perhaps take solace from the fact that he had punished himself, taken an eye for an eye instead of facing some ridiculously inadequate sentence for such a heinous crime.

Once he had decided what he was going to do, it was easy to decide how to do it. He didn't have any pills, or a gun, and he was scared that trying to slit his wrists wouldn't work and he would be rescued and subjected to ritual humiliation, a perverted rapist who couldn't even kill himself properly. What he did have was a beautiful ocean within walking distance. He'd always loved the ocean; it seemed oddly fitting to him that he would end his life there.

He stood, staggering for a second as the movement made him feel lightheaded and faint. He dropped the phone onto the sofa.

Without looking around again at Melissa'a body, he pulled up his shorts and picked up his T-shirt from the sofa. Putting it on, he walked towards the French windows. He looked out and realized he must have been unconscious for some time. From the imminently setting sun he guessed that it was early evening. But it didn't really matter what time it was, he thought to himself; it was time.

He opened the window and walked out into the humid air. The air-conditioning had been keeping the house cool. He left the door open: somebody might notice it and come to investigate, in which case Melissa's corpse would be found sooner. The corpse spelled not only the end of Melissa's life, but his as well. The thought embittered him. He set off towards the sea.

19

The setting sun was disappearing into the aquamarine ocean across from Old Fort Bay. One end of the beach, where the sun still warmed the sand, was an untidy patchwork of towels and sunbathers. Despite the now rapidly cooling air, people were determined to make the most of the last rays, before the dark-grey storm clouds, which were gathering in the distance, brought in the rain. Almost nothing was visible in the expanding shadow which had swallowed half of the shore and was slowly completing its conquest.

Burton walked dejectedly, each step shovelling a spray of sand in front of him. He felt a chill run through him as he entered the shaded section of beach.

Without the direct heat of the sun, it was suddenly much cooler. He could feel the beginning of the nightly land breeze, which would pick up during the evening as the island cooled down and became relatively cold compared to the sea. He breathed deeply, savouring the clear air and sensing a hint of diesel fumes.

He walked for about five minutes, moving

away from the house and, in his mind, away from the events that had taken place there. He glanced around but the beach was surprisingly empty. He strolled on towards the water.

His feet entered the foamy surf that was climbing slowly up the beach, and he felt immediately the cool touch of the dominant sea. Striding defiantly over the small waves, he felt his body stiffen as it sought to acclimatize. The water now reached his knees. As he walked on steadily, he looked around behind him. There were few people on the beach, and those that were paid him no attention at all. In the distance, he could discern the buildings of the Ocean Club. The shadow was slowly advancing; the sun's golden pendulum was split in half by the horizon.

Burton breathed deeply as his crotch submerged and the sudden change in temperature momentarily took his breath away. He was aware of a heightened sense of touch, as if his nerves were intensifying everyday feelings. He dived, curving his body to slip under the waves, before starting a strong crawl away from the shoreline. He kept his submerged eyes closed and swam as fast as he could before snatching a breath here and there, not following a regular pattern but swimming until he could no longer hold his breath.

He turned onto his back, panting slightly from the exertion, and watched the sun as it sank further behind the rolling azure expanse that he knew was to become his grave. He glanced again at the beach, his eyes scouring it for signs of something, anything that might change his mind, although he was not sure what that could be. There was more to it than simply his own life, his position, his reputation and indeed his liberty, but those of the organization which he represented and those of his family.

Although anathema to him, he began to breathe in the ocean greedily. In his mouth, the water tasted dank, salty and bitter, and he fought the urge to retch. His nose stung as droplets of sea water found their way in. It required huge willpower to continue ingesting the foul-tasting liquid, but he managed to persevere until he felt his lungs were full.

The next thing he knew, he was coughing and spitting out sea water, and there was suddenly brightness where there had been darkness. He felt his chest expand involuntarily as his lungs drew in as much air as they could. Drops of salt water irritated his throat and started more coughing fits.

This wasn't going to be as straightforward

as he thought. He stroked further away from the shore, further away from life, again holding his breath until he could no longer do so, but now allowing himself to gasp water whilst still swimming. Somehow he always seemed to recover, his only achievement a salt water induced coughing fit.

He wondered vaguely how long it would take them to find his body. Would King be told to investigate his death as well as Sir John's? Would they even care about him? After all, Sir John's death had only been investigated because he was important and he, Burton, would hardly qualify for that. Suddenly, a bizarre thought entered Burton's mind.

Burton stopped swimming and started to tread water, thinking desperately. They wouldn't look for his body unless there was a reason to do so. If they found Melissa's body, and the surrounding carnage in Sir John's house, they would try to piece together what had happened, and then they would probably want to find his body in order to obtain his DNA, which could be compared with that of Melissa's murderer. But what if Melissa wasn't dead? What if, somehow, he was wrong? If there was no murder scene, nobody would know why he had drowned himself. They probably wouldn't even investigate.

After all, they wouldn't have investigated Sir John's death if he hadn't been an ex-diplomat, a VIP. An important man.

He looked back at the beach, looking for a clue, something to suggest that there might be an element of doubt. Then he saw it. Sir John's house was still visible far away across the beach. Burton could just about see the French window, which he knew he had left open. They were now closed. He remembered thinking that someone would notice more quickly if it was open. But not this quickly. Had Melissa closed it? Was she still alive? Had she set a similar scene for Sir John, which had precipitated a similar reaction to his own? Or was he merely clutching at straws?

Burton started to swim back towards the shore. His unwillingness to give up his life was stronger than his fear that she was dead and that the scene had merely been discovered much more quickly than he had anticipated. If that was the case, he would be arrested immediately, and would no longer have the option to take one last swim.

As he swam, different scenarios flashed through his mind. But in reality, he already knew. He tried to work out how Melissa had managed to convince Sir John, a clever and respected diplomat, and Burton himself, not completely without intelligence, that she was dead, and that they were responsible for her murder.

Burton was now convinced that the obeah-man and Melissa had conspired together. He must have put together some potion that induced gullibility in people taking it. How this might work and how and when it had been administered he did not know, but he was going to find out.

★ ★ ★

Burton walked up the beach outside Sir John's house. The French windows were closed and it looked like all the other windows were closed too, not uncommon for a house with air conditioning. He crept quietly up to the kitchen window and looked inside, but could see absolutely nothing out of the ordinary. He then moved around to the sitting room.

Burton's heart was hammering. He stood still and tried to calm himself down but to no avail. There was no fear, he noted, but merely the anticipation of finding out whether he was right, or whether he really was, definitively, a rapist and a murderer. He took a deep breath and looked through the window, scanning the scene for what seemed like minutes in order

306

to be sure he had seen everything.

The sitting room was exactly how it had been when he had arrived. There was no body, no blood and, he noted wryly, no vomit next to the sofa. It had all been a set-up. This was the final confirmation; Burton was absolutely certain that had been what had happened to Sir John as well. It was no accidental drowning, it was suicide. But it was no normal suicide. It was a kind of induced suicide; one compelled by Melissa providing the stimulants she knew would provoke this reaction. It was, finally, a simple application of the laws of cause and effect. Bitch, Burton thought to himself.

He started to walk around the house, looking in through all the windows, but the house appeared deserted. He wondered if she had left to visit somewhere, to at least have an alibi for the time when Burton was going for his last swim. Although, he mused, she wouldn't really need an alibi — that was the whole point. There weren't many people on the beach now — not as many as when Sir John drowned — but surely someone would have seen him going off on his own for a swim. She probably waited for a while after he had gone, watched him enter the water and then set about cleaning up.

Burton arrived back at the sitting-room

window without having seen anything. He picked up a stone from the garden and used it to smash one of the smaller windows. Then he listened carefully for noises that might suggest somebody had heard and was running to see what the disturbance was. Hearing nothing, he opened the window and climbed in, taking care not to cut himself on the jagged glass fragments. Once inside, Burton made for the telephone. He dialled King's number and impatiently listened for the ringing tone. The ringing he had anticipated was pre-empted by a loud click which seemed not to come from the telephone but from behind him. This was confirmed by the words which followed.

'Put the phone down. Now.'

He half turned to look behind him but stopped as he felt a hard prod in his back.

'Now, or I blow a hole in your spine.'

Burton set the receiver back in the cradle slowly and carefully, hoping that he had held the line long enough for the number to be recognized. The pressure in his back was relieved, and he turned to face Melissa.

She was dressed in a ludicrously inappropriate flowery yellow summer frock, holding what looked to Burton's inexperienced eye like a massive calibre revolver. Her hair was pulled back, which gave her face a stern, serious look. Pink flip-flops completed the incongruity.

She moved back cautiously, obviously wanting to keep some distance between them. He'd have done the same, thought Burton, had he been the one holding the gun.

'Move over there and sit down.' Melissa gestured towards the sofa.

Burton sat down on the sofa. Melissa sat down opposite him on a small wicker chair. She rested the hand holding the gun on her thigh.

'So, you worked it out, did you? Perhaps you're not as stupid as you look, although I still think you are. It was going swimmingly until now, if you'll forgive the pun. But then you had to keep butting in. To give you credit, though, you were the only one who had any idea everything wasn't what it seemed. That policeman wouldn't have suspected a crime if he'd had a signed confession. He would have believed anything just to get the case off his workload.'

Burton sat back. As he did so, he felt something hard underneath him. He was about to pick it up when he remembered he'd dropped his phone on the sofa before he'd left. Melissa must have missed it when she tidied up. He tried to remember more — it wasn't easy, he'd still been quite groggy, but he seemed to remember trying to call King. No, he hadn't actually called him. But he had entered the number. He knew then what he had to do: he had to keep her talking and somehow press the green button on the phone. He didn't know whether he'd wiped the number, or whether the phone would forget the number after a while, but it was worth a try.

'Oh, I don't know. I think Mr King is definitely someone who's smarter than he looks. Anyway, it won't take a genius to work out what happened if you call the police in to investigate a corpse on your sofa with a large bullet hole in it. You'll have gunpowder residue on your hands, you know. They'll be able to prove you shot me. Why not give it up?'

Melissa laughed condescendingly. Burton moved both hands slowly next to his thighs.

'Do you really think that I hadn't thought of this possibility?' she asked condescendingly. 'Do you expect me to turn myself in? Think about it. When the police come over, they'll find the dead body of an intruder. An intruder who broke the window of my house to get in and shouldn't have been anywhere near here in the first place. Also, coincidentally, someone who has been harassing me constantly over the past few days, trying to pin my beloved husband's suicide on me. And given those facts, what do you suppose the police will make of it?'

Burton touched the phone with his right hand. He held Melissa's stare, trying to look as if he was concentrating on what she was saying whilst he pictured the phone in his mind. He knew he had to dial first, and then turn the volume down. The last thing he wanted was for Melissa to hear King answering the phone. He rehearsed the sequence of key presses in his head.

'When I tell them that I shot you to save myself, that I feared for my life, what do you imagine they will think? When I tell them how you hounded me, how you invited me out to dinner whilst investigating me, when you weren't even a real policeman. Do you think they'll think I'm a calculating, murderous cow, or do you think they'll feel sorry for me?'

He identified the screen of the phone and slid his finger down to the top buttons. The green dial button was the second one down on the left, he was sure. He pressed it once, and then pressed the lower volume button on the side of the phone several times, before moving both hands forward slightly to cover it. He hoped any audible answer would be muffled by his leg.

'Because I think they'll see it as self-defence.

The poor, bereaved widow who, having endured the unwanted attentions of a love-starved, would-be Romeo from the arrogant echelons of the Foreign Office, finally had to defend her honour when it got out of hand. They might feel I led you on, but that's hardly a crime, is it? And even that I'll deny.

'What do you think, Michael? Is it a believable story, or not?'

Burton shifted slightly in his seat. He felt the phone vibrating very slightly. Melissa's hand was resting on her thighs holding the gun pointing steadily in his direction. He said resignedly, 'Well, I must say, you seem to have all the bases covered. I thought I might have rumbled you with my reappearance, but apparently that's not the case. Unfortunately.'

'Yes, Michael, it is unfortunate. For you, anyway. But tell me one thing: when did you know? Did you play along with the story from the beginning just to catch me out, or did you realize later on?'

If I'd known earlier on, I'd have brought the police, thought Burton. But thinking that King might be listening, he said, 'Well, I knew about it beforehand, of course. I had my suspicions that you were responsible for Sir John's death, and I told King that I was coming here to your house and that he should meet me here as soon as possible. I told him

312

you might try to kill me. So you see, Melissa, it's all over.'

Burton wondered if this was good enough. He hoped so. If King was listening, he now knew where to go and why and how urgent it was. If he wasn't, well, he hadn't lost anything.

Burton felt her inquisitive eyes scanning him. He looked away. She said, 'Nice try, Michael. But I don't think so. I wasn't expecting you to show up, but I was swimming when I saw you walking on the beach. I watched you for some time, and there was nobody with you then. When we came back in, and I went up to change, I looked out front to see if there was anyone out there. That's the great thing about these gated communities. Strange cars don't just turn up outside your house every now and then. When I looked out this afternoon, there were no cars apart from the neighbour's Cadillac. Certainly none I didn't recognize. And I doubt any policemen from Nassau would walk here for a stake out — it's miles from anywhere. Besides, if King knew about it, he'd be here by now. He wouldn't risk losing you and having to report to your boss that his employee will be coming back in a box.

'Of course I know Reardon,' Melissa

continued. 'My husband used to work with him. And I'm not sure he will be that distraught when you fail to report for duty, even though it means he'll have to find another serf to do his work. But we're moving away from the point: which is, when did you know? I think you only just found out. I think you left here with the intention of permanently drowning your sorrows but something changed your mind. And I'd like to know what it was.'

I bet you would, thought Burton. 'And why should I tell you?'

'Because I'll make sure the first shot is a good one. Otherwise I might wing you a couple of times and have you bleed out. Exsanguination is a long, slow, painful death. And messy, too. Which neither of us want. I need an answer. I'm a perfectionist, Michael. I want to know where I went wrong.'

'All right, I'll tell you. I did suspect you before, I think you already know that. But I didn't have any proof that anything untoward had happened. Obviously, this was because you had covered your tracks very well and left us very little to go on. But something didn't feel right to me. A man who goes swimming every day *could* have an accident and drown, if for example he'd had a seizure or a heart attack or something. Equally, a man who never swam, or was a very weak swimmer, might drown whilst swimming in unfamiliar waters. Or a swimmer might drown if he was drunk, or affected by some other toxic substance. But in this case we had a man who swims regularly, in the same place, with no obvious sign of any kind of seizure or attack, or toxicity. Or, at least, the medical examiner found no indication of this on the body.

'So what happened? We discounted a medical condition, and there was no sign of a struggle, so we discounted forcible drowning. We were left with suicide or a bizarre accident. Eyewitness accounts seemed to back this up. I never believed either, though.

'Once we'd heard the will, I was immediately suspicious of the obeahman. Some kind of spell to make Sir John lose consciousness, or think he was a lead weight or something, and he might drown without the need for any physical interference. Then there was the man watching me from your house whilst I was diving. It was at that point that I realized you were both in it together. Everything else fell into place. The men trying to force me off the road on Cat Island, and the night with you I just survived. Both of you were trying to warn me off without giving any obvious clues.

'You did a very good job of sowing the seeds of doubt in my mind though. For a while I really believed I was wrong. And then here, earlier, I guess you just did the same to me as you did to Sir John. Possibly because you thought I was on to you, or at least stirring things up where I shouldn't have been, which is ironic because as I was sitting here I was beginning to think that I had made a mistake, and that there was nothing in my suspicions.

'But when I found myself swimming out to sea, having committed what I considered to be a hugely out of character crime, my suspicions returned. Basically, because it all seemed so similar to Sir John's last swim. Then I looked back and saw that the French window had been closed.' He nodded towards them. 'That was the clincher. I knew that I'd left them open. I didn't remember much of the scene that took place here, but I did remember that, because I'd been thinking that the body would be found much more quickly if they were open. Amazing, the details one remembers at the strangest moments.

'So what did you use? Was it a spell, or some ancient obeah potion in our drinks? How did you know it would work?'

Melissa smiled. 'So you don't know as much as you think you know. You're wrong about the obeahman, Michael. I don't know

316

him from Adam. I never trusted that pseudo-voodoo stuff. That was John's realm. He was obsessed by it: I was amazed by it all. John was your stereotype Western civil servant. Very British, very stiff upper lip, very colonial. And then suddenly he was best mates with the local obeahman. I think he tried to assimilate with the locals too much, and didn't know when to stop. Whilst his predecessors were scared and afraid of the obeahmen, John was different. He was the local's friend; he was the man who had truly integrated: the hero of the Foreign Office. Or so he saw himself.

'I saw him as a foolish old man whose undistinguished career in the Foreign Office had culminated in a mediocre position of power in an ancient former colony in the Caribbean, of all places. Put out to grass, I'd call it. Anyway, he'd decided to embrace the indigenous culture and obeah with it. Worse still, I knew he had changed his will to accommodate his new obeah friends, and I suspected that, given time, the whole document would have been rewritten in their favour. So, you see, I had to act. But I certainly didn't do so in co-operation with the man who was slowly worming his way into my husband's last will and testament. I don't know why his men tried to force you off the road, but it's a shame they didn't succeed. It would have saved me some trouble. They were probably just trying to protect their privacy, something people like you have little or no respect for.

'To be honest, I didn't understand the whole obeah thing, much less want to rely on it for help with a venture of this nature. Quite apart from the fact that they were competing with me for my husband's inheritance. I certainly wouldn't be trying spells and black magic potions when I could use something far more reliable, more scientific. Something that, whilst not guaranteed to work, at least in my view provided a good probability of success.

'So I used gamma-hydroxybutyric acid, or GHB as it's more commonly known. It was ideal for my purpose: it's colourless and odourless, and, though salty, hard to taste when added to strong alcoholic drinks,' — she looked at Burton — 'as I'm sure you'll confirm. It's difficult to detect in the body. It's a naturally occurring substance, already present in humans, and found in beer and wine. Even if they tested you now, they probably wouldn't find any, because they wouldn't be looking for it. Even if they did, you've drunk a fair amount of beer recently so it could have come from there. The amount might be slightly more than normally found, but perhaps your body produces extra — who knows?

'The hypnotic and amnesiac effects of GHB aren't as good as those of Rohypnol, but I have found them to be more than adequate when the drug is given with alcohol and no food is imbibed. Rohypnol is too easy to detect in the system: I'm sure that your medical examiner would have fairly quickly found the vestiges of the drug if I had used it on John. I did consider it, as an accidental drowning wouldn't normally give rise to a check for Rohypnol, but I knew that they would at least check for alcohol and if Rohypnol was found, it would certainly prolong the investigation.

'I'm sure John never tasted the drug in his whisky, and it worked surprisingly quickly. It's quite weird waiting for someone to lose consciousness and then trying to ascertain whether they are fully aware when they wake up or not. That's one of the tricks of the dosage, though. You need to get just enough for the victim to feel euphoric and just about go to sleep. Too much, and you will induce a deep sleep, which is obviously not ideal in the circumstance. Firstly, you have to wait until they wake up, and secondly, they might sleep off the drug and wake up alert.

'The effects of the combination of GHB and alcohol can last a good couple of hours, and have a rather debilitating effect on the victim, as I believe you are aware. John probably never really recovered from the whisky and GHB cocktail he drank — it was probably all a surreal blur of actions until he drowned himself about an hour after I had set the scene.

'I have to admit, there was a certain amount of pride involved when the plan I had conceived worked out the way it did. The idea actually occurred to me when John was brought home in a state of extreme inebriation by a couple of policemen. One of them accompanied him to the door, and said that they were very concerned about him — he had apparently been distraught and displaying almost suicidal tendencies. So knowing that John might be harbouring latent suicidal tendencies, I decided to bring them to the fore.

'Although I had planned it all very carefully, I didn't know exactly what would happen. I was relying on placing John in a situation from which there was no escape, and giving him several 'outs'. I didn't repeat them for you, but when I drugged John I left a kitchen knife on the table, thinking that if he didn't immediately consider suicide, the knife might give him the idea. As it is, you both decided on drowning. Why was that, do you think?'

Burton remained silent. The woman was clearly unhinged. She was talking about the murder of her husband, and the attempted murder of Burton himself, as if it was a scientific experiment into the behaviour of drugged individuals.

'John might have acted in a completely different way, I couldn't tell. All I tried to do was create a situation in which I thought he would want to take his own life. My analysis of his character was such that I felt that, if I placed him in a situation in which he could be led to believe that he had committed a violent, and above all sexual, crime, he would feel unable to live with himself and take the only way out. And the whole plan was surprisingly successful. With you as well, up to a certain point. Maybe I underestimated the dosage, maybe you were too lucid, I don't know. The door was certainly a mistake.

'I thought I had the dosage spot on though. When we went out on Saturday, I gave you some during the course of the evening, just a few milligrams here and there. I did it for two reasons: Firstly, as you know, I wanted you to be less aware than usual so I could send you off into Grant's Town, knowing that you would at worst get mugged and at best killed. Unfortunately for me, whoever mugged you decided not to do away with you completely. Secondly, I wanted to see your reaction to the amounts of the drug I had given you, for exactly the sort of occasion as today. As I said before, the trick is getting the dosage right. Obviously, you can estimate the dosage based on build and weight, but people react differently and it's really helpful if you have some empirical evidence of the subject you wish to drug. My data was collected that Saturday night, but it is difficult to estimate accurately the exact effect the drug is having. The plan to drug you was definitely Plan B. Plan A was that nobody would be overly suspicious and the whole thing would blow over without any further action on my part. But as you became more and more intrusive, I prepared an alternative approach. When you came nosing around again today, I knew I'd have to act, so I merely repeated what I had done before with John. The shame and guilt of a violent rape and murder appear to be too much to bear for you Foreign Office types. John didn't even check my pulse or breathing. I didn't think you would either — GHB causes considerable confusion. In any event, I was relaxed and not breathing, and you were clearly unable to carry out the checks properly. In fact, your efforts to perform first aid were comical, although you did seem to have a good idea about what you wanted to do. Maybe John didn't care whether I was dead or not. Violent rape on its own was probably enough to push him over the precipice — it didn't matter if the victim survived.

'It almost worked a second time. But no matter that it didn't, it's all over now.'

Burton noticed Melissa shifting the gun on her lap. More time, he thought. I need more time. 'Aren't you forgetting something?' he asked.

'Am I?'

'If you shoot me now, if there's a body here, it'll be a crime scene. The forensic teams will search the whole place from top to bottom. They'll find evidence of the scenario you put in place. They'll find the fake blood, and the ripped clothes. I can understand that nobody would have checked had I done what you expected and topped myself, but it didn't work out that way. But now they will check everything, whatever happens. And they'll get you, Melissa. You're going to gaol, and you'll stay there for a long time.

'But if you don't shoot me, it won't be a crime scene. The forensic team won't come. They won't find anything. Not unless I tell

323

them what happened and they decide to look. But I won't tell them, Melissa. It will be our secret. I promise.'

Melissa smiled sweetly. 'Nice try, Michael. I'd have done the same if I'd been in your place. But you know I can't let you live. How could I trust you to keep your word? And what would stop you from starting to blackmail me from the very first moment you declined to mention it to the police?

'And, anyway, I'm rather proud of the clean-up job I've done. The clothes are gone. The blood, not fake by the way, is gone — cleaned away with strong detergent. Fortunately, the tiled floors here lend themselves to thorough cleaning. And I've already gone through one dress rehearsal clean-up, a week ago. Since then I've had neighbours, friends and even police officers visiting without even a shred of suspicion. No, my guess is that, after they've picked up your body and mopped up the blood, there'll be absolutely nothing to incriminate me at all.'

Melissa lifted the gun. Burton started to rise so he might have some chance to reach her once she had decided to shoot, but was checked by a gesture with the gun. 'Don't move, Michael, or I'll shoot now. On second thoughts, why not get up? It's only a matter of seconds now anyway.'

Burton knew that he'd never be able to get up and reach Melissa before she shot him. He decided to play his last, weak card.

'Isn't it going to look a bit odd that you shot me whilst I was sitting down? Surely that will jeopardize your claim of self-defence?'

'Not at all, Michael. It was like this: you broke in, I stopped you and made you sit down on the soft sofa so you wouldn't be able to jump me. Then you made a move towards me and I shot you. They'll never be able to tell whether you were sitting quietly rather than actually trying to stand up. Of course, I'd rather you moved somewhere else so I wouldn't have to ruin the sofa, but I doubt you'll play along with that. So this is it, Michael. You were a worthy adversary. To a point. Farewell.'

Melissa's finger tightened on the trigger.

20

Burton closed his eyes, wondering if he'd hear the sound of the shot before he felt it. What he heard, though, was a loud splintering sound followed by running feet and then the welcome voice of Chester King.

'Drop the gun, Melissa. Put it on the table in front of you and take a step back.'

Burton opened his eyes. King stood calmly by the door, a blue-black automatic pointing at Melissa held steadily in his outstretched right hand. Two uniformed officers had fanned out to his side and held their service revolvers at the ready.

Relief flooded through Burton's mind as he took in the situation, looking from the tall Bahamian in the pastel blue suit to the beautiful, cold woman in the floral dress. He tried to stand up but found he was shaking uncontrollably, so he remained seated on the sofa. He looked across at Melissa as she calmly placed the gun on the table and stepped backwards as directed. The look on her face did not resemble that of a person who had just been caught red-handed about to commit a murder.

'Thank God you're here, officer. Please arrest

this man immediately. He broke into my home and threatened me. I didn't know what to do. Fortunately, my husband kept this old gun here.'

Burton was dumbfounded. He finally managed to free himself from the grip of the sofa, jumped up and shouted, 'That's ridiculous. She tried to kill me. She was going to shoot me. It's her you should be arresting. She's crazy. She killed Sir John too.'

King was unmoved. Two more uniformed officers entered the room. The flashing red lights on their car outside sent waves of red wash over the ceiling of the living room. King slid the hand with the automatic into his jacket and withdrew it empty-handed. He held up his other hand.

'That's enough, both of you,' King said curtly. 'I know you will each have very different stories, and we will be listening to these shortly. In the meantime, we will carry out a forensic examination of this place to find out what happened. Our teams are already on their way. These officers will be taking you down to the station until we need to interview you.'

Burton and Melissa were shepherded towards the door by the remaining officers. Burton started to resist, angry at being treated like the criminal he was not, but thought better of it and instead walked obediently away from the scene.

21

'So, Michael, what are we going to do with you?'

King looked at Burton across a desk in one of the interrogation rooms in the East Street Police Station. It was a dark, windowless room with a chipped wooden table in the middle and two folding plastic chairs on one side and one on the other. On the table was a tape recorder, which whirred away almost imperceptibly, and three empty coffee mugs. King sat back, unbelievably looking comfortable on the cheap, flimsy chair on which he was perched.

Next to him was a taciturn hulk, introduced briefly as Detective Smith, who had barely said a word since they had arrived. He was a Caucasian, deeply tanned, a good inch or so shorter than King, but probably twice as broad as the lean Bahamian. The plastic chair on which he sat, similar to both King and Burton's, looked taxed to its limits, and he was doubled up uncomfortably with his knees under the table, almost as if somebody had folded him up and forced him into position there. His hair had been cropped and his face was unshaven, both areas covered by equally dark stubble. Lightweight, wire-rimmed glasses were perched on his nose, looking oddly incongruous with the rest of the man.

Burton hadn't seen him before, and guessed he had been given the role of second investigator to King's flamboyant lead. Perhaps it was a role he was used to playing, allowing the more talkative King to forge ahead whilst he watched and listened and learned. His huge bulk, silent demeanour, and slow, careful movements, made him appear unintelligent, but his eyes were quick and cunning, and Burton felt that he wasn't merely present to make up the numbers. The lenses of the glasses showed almost no distortion, signifying to Burton that they were weak. He wondered briefly if they were plain lenses, used for reasons other than to correct vision.

'What do you want me to say or do, Chester? I've already told you what happened. You were present for most of the time I've spent with this woman. You know me; you know her. Who do you think is lying to you?'

'What I think, whilst important, is not the issue. What matters far more is what I can prove. And I have to say, I have almost nothing to prove that Lady Little did anything wrong. She was holding a gun, which was registered to her husband, and for which he had a licence. As he is now dead, in theory the licence is no longer valid, but all I can charge her with is possession of a firearm, for which, given the circumstances, she will probably receive a caution and maybe, just maybe, a small fine.

'You told us a tale of mocked-up rapes and staged murders, of fake blood and torn clothes. Our forensic teams found no torn clothing anywhere on the property. We found no evidence of burnt clothes. We checked the bins in the street. We checked the neighbours' bins. We found no fake blood. We did, however, find traces of animal blood. We believe it was cow's.'

'That's it! She said it wasn't fake blood. So she used cow blood!'

'Well, Lady Little accepts the finding of cow's blood. She also challenged us as to how much we could say was present. And I have to tell you, Michael, we can't say for certain that there was any more than mere splatters. Either there was very little, or it was cleaned up extremely well.'

'You know her, Chester. She would have cleaned it up well. Come on, it's obvious I'm telling the truth.'

'Unfortunately, Michael, it is anything but obvious. Lady Little claims that the animal blood is the result of a ritual carried out regularly by her husband. She was never around, says she made sure she went out and knows nothing of what went on, but it seems that he met every now and then with like-minded individuals. And it's not unfeasible that they were carrying out rituals that involved cow's blood.'

'What about the time the blood was spilt? Can't your forensics experts' — Burton heard his own voice spitting out the word 'experts' with as much sarcasm as he could muster — 'tell how long the blood was there? Because it wasn't there yesterday, Chester. Not the top layer.'

King paused, a look of resignation briefly passing over his face. 'There were layers, Michael. At least two, but that's all our people could tell. They can't tell how long the blood spatters have been there. It's a miracle they found them. The whole place had been scrubbed with detergent.'

'Well, doesn't that tell you something? The fact the whole place was scrubbed clean?'

'It does and it doesn't. It raises suspicions, but it gives us nothing concrete. Nothing we can pursue further. It's a free world, Michael. If you want to clean your house on a particular afternoon, you are entitled to do so.

'You also claim that she gave you a drug. Our doctors took a blood sample and tested it, but found nothing. You even told us what to look for, but there was no trace of it.'

Burton snorted with frustration. He cut in, 'That's because it's a drug that is undetectable. I told you that!'

'You, on the other hand, broke into her house. That, we can prove. She claims you threatened her. I can't prove that, but nor can I prove your story which, if you don't mind me saying, will come across as slightly fanciful in a court of law. You claim that she drugged you and made you believe that you had committed a heinous crime, the most heinous of all in fact, murder, after which you tried to kill yourself, incidentally in the same fashion that Sir John Little did last week.'

'You know she did, Chester. Come on! You must have heard it on the telephone — the whole conversation went on with you on the line.'

King laughed. 'Actually, I had to listen really hard just to work out who was talking. I heard a few words — those you said intending to direct me to Lady Little's house, which was good thinking by the way — but even if I had caught every word, and believed it implicitly, it would be inadmissible in court. It would be hearsay and, worse still, there would be no way of even verifying who said what. It could have been a setup for all I know.

'Aside from the possible possession of a firearm without a licence, Melissa has done absolutely nothing wrong that we can prosecute her for. She didn't shoot you, merely apprehended you for entering her property, which she was well within her rights to do.

'Anyway, Michael, I'm sure you appreciate the problem. Whilst I may well believe you' — King emphasized the 'you' — 'I would have a job proving any of your story. Lady Little, on the other hand, could request that we press charges for breaking and entering, which we would more or less be obliged to do, and the evidence is such that you would probably go down for it.

'So, now we come to the nub. Lady Little, who has steadfastly maintained the same story throughout some rather aggressive questioning' — King looked across at the silent detective, who met his glance — 'has offered not to press charges if you, and we, drop what she refers to as 'this silly story that I had something to do with my husband's death'. It's an interesting conundrum, Michael. Normally, a suspect will make a deal with the police, either giving them information about other criminals or accepting a lesser plea instead of trial for an offence carrying a more stringent sentence. Here, Melissa is using you as her bargaining chip. She is probably betting that we won't want to allow you to be prosecuted, as you are a visiting guest of our police force at present, or maybe she thinks that we have developed a personal friendship which would mean that I would not want you prosecuted. She would, of course, be right on both counts, but actually it is not my decision. It's up to the public prosecutor to decide. She will, as likely as not, agree with our recommendation, though. So the question is: are we going to accept Melissa's offer?'

The other detective broke in for the first time. 'We think she did it, Michael. We think you're telling the truth.'

Burton was surprised at the man's accent: he had a slight Caribbean lilt to his voice, but even in the short two sentences he had uttered it was clear he was American.

'She looks remarkably similar to a lady we knew some time ago in Florida. She was then the girlfriend of an American banker, who travelled often to the Cayman Islands. She went by the name of Marisa. This banker was a lot older than Marisa, and he died, seemingly of natural causes, only days after rewriting his will in favour of his wife-to-be, Marisa. The new will was later declared invalid, as it failed to satisfy the formal requirements of a will in the state in which it was drawn up. Our banker decided to make a holographic will, by which I mean that he wrote the will himself without using the services of a lawyer. This is fine, but in Florida, unlike some other states in the US, a holographic will must still be witnessed by someone other than a beneficiary of the will. I suspect our banker was unaware of the legal requirements in Florida, or else he was aware of them and didn't actually want to leave everything to her.

'Anyway, the will was challenged by the banker's family and declared invalid. That's not unusual — it happens fairly often when family members are cut out of wills and feel aggrieved. The really strange thing in this case, though, was that this Marisa did not attempt to have the decision reviewed, nor did she make any claim against the banker's estate.

'Colleagues of mine who worked in the District Attorney's office said she would have had a very strong case, if not for the reinstatement of the will that was declared invalid, then certainly for a high value claim against the estate. But she wanted none of it.

'We didn't know what to make of it. Was she a genuine good girl, who wasn't

335

interested in the money? It seemed unlikely, given the circumstances. Or was she with him for the money, but guilty of something to do with his death, and therefore unwilling to take any legal action in case it provoked further investigations, which she didn't want? We just didn't know. But we had our suspicions.'

Smith took off his glasses and pinched the bridge of his nose gently. His eyes glanced across at Burton and he continued, 'Soon afterwards, this Marisa dropped out of sight. She travelled to Europe. Now, we're not entirely sure where she went, but we figured it would have been Spain or England. And that's pretty much it. Until now.

'Let me tell you where we are with this. We have no proof that Marisa and Melissa are the same person, and we have no proof that either of them was actually involved in anything illegal. What we do know is that both have had similar relationships with older men which have resulted in the older man dying. What we need is something that would help us prove that a crime has taken place. Can you think of anything, Michael, anything at all that might help us to do this?'

Burton looked at Smith and then across to King. There was nothing. And Melissa knew there was nothing. He smiled and shook his head.

'Nope. I've told you everything I know. If I could think of something else to implicate Melissa I would be glad to share it with you. But I can't. And from what I've heard today, I suspect that there's not much we can do about it. I mean, let's face it, gentlemen, we don't even know for sure that she's involved. If we try and make anything stick, I'm likely to go down for breaking and entering at the very least, and she'll probably still get away with it.'

He sat back and thought about the whole situation. He had the feeling Melissa had planned everything from the start. Every eventuality had been considered. He wondered. Even when she thought she had won, when she told him what she had done, had she told him the truth? Or would part of her have held back information, or given false information, just in case she was caught? He remembered her comments about the drugs.

'You said your doctors tested for GHB. Is that all they tested for?'

'Yes, why?'

Burton could barely contain his excitement. Had he found a chink in her armour? 'Well, what if she was lying? I remember her talking about the drug she used. I clearly remember her saying that Rohypnol would have been better, but it's much easier to detect. But not, most likely, if you're looking for GHB. If I'd been given Rohypnol, would they still be able to detect it?'

'I don't know,' said King, 'but it's worth a try.'

★ ★ ★

'So it was Rohypnol. Come on, Melissa, we all know what happened. You gave Michael Rohypnol, just as you did your husband, and then you set them up. Faced with the idea they'd raped and killed you, you guessed that they'd take the only way out.'

Burton was looking into the interview room through a oneway mirror. He'd asked to be present at the interview, but King had refused point blank. After much badgering, the detective had allowed him to watch.

Melissa sat back in her chair. She was in a similar interrogation room to the one Burton had been in, and the two detectives facing her were the same. She looked calm and comfortable. She looked towards the mirror, and Burton fancied that she knew he was watching.

'I'd like to press charges against the man who broke into my house, please. Whether he was sober, drunk, or on Rohypnol as you are now claiming, I want him charged.'

'*You* gave him Rohypnol!'

'I gave him nothing. He broke into my house, and so I used the gun to make him sit down. He didn't appear drugged, but then I know nothing about drugs, so I wouldn't know. I was about to call the police when you arrived.'

'We can exhume your husband's body and check him for Rohypnol.'

A sad expression crossed Melissa's face. 'I'm sure you can, if you wish to do so. I'd be very distressed to hear that you wanted to do this. My husband died swimming, an activity which he loved. This whole charade which has followed is a distasteful attempt to smear both my husband and myself, and I will be taking this matter to the relevant officials, both in your police force and in Mr Burton's Foreign Office.

'I would, though, ask you to consider a few points before you start on this idiotic attempt to discredit me. It may just save your career.

'Firstly, are you sure that you can detect this drug in the system of somebody who has been dead for over a week? Secondly, even if you do detect it, how are you going to prove that I gave it to him? It seems far more likely to me that your Mr Burton, who appears to have been taking the drug himself, is a more likely suspect. Please feel free to check my house for the drug though.

'I still have powerful friends in the Foreign Office, Mr King. They will honour my husband's name and they will see to it that Mr Burton is fired immediately. I don't suppose your position will be tenable after that.'

Melissa held King's eyes in a cold, hard stare. 'I'm tired of playing games. I've offered to drop the breaking and entering charges if you will stop insulting me and ludicrously trying to frame me for the murder of my husband. If I do, most likely both you and Mr Burton will remain gainfully employed, although I'm not sure that's a good thing. I will make the offer once again. This is, however, the last time. If you want to play hardball, we'll play hardball.'

* * *

'She's right,' King said. 'We're not going to get anywhere. The doctor said that he can normally find Rohypnol in a person's urine up to five days after the dosage, *if* he's looking for it. But even he has no idea whether he'll be able to find it in a dead body, especially one that has spent some time in the water.

'Anyway, maybe she didn't use Rohypnol

on Sir John. Maybe she did use GHB. The doctor confirmed that GHB can be difficult to find, even a day afterwards.' He looked at Burton. 'And, between us, he couldn't even confirm Rohypnol in your case. He tested for it, but it was inconclusive. Not a clear no, but also not a clear yes. I bluffed it with Melissa, hoping she might give something away, but she's a cool customer, that one, no doubt about it. And even if they could find Rohypnol in Sir John's body, how are we going to prove she gave it to him? She wouldn't have asked us to search the house unless she knew it was clean, and even if it isn't, she'll just say she had no knowledge of it and Sir John must have taken it himself. We're in a no-win situation.

'She's right about our jobs, too. If we carry on with this, she'll get away with it, albeit with some negative publicity she won't want, but we'll be screwed. You'll be sent back to England with your tail between your legs, and I'll be looking for a new position here. Heaven only knows what jobs are available for detectives who have been thrown off the force.'

For the first time since Burton had known him, the normally composed King looked exasperated, although Burton had to admit that King's exasperated was equivalent to mild annoyance in most other people. He and

Burton were now sitting next to each other at the interrogation table, and Smith had brought in a bigger chair from an office and was now seated at the head of the table. The air of adversity was gone, and had been replaced with a collegiate togetherness that was nevertheless getting them nowhere.

'So she walks?' asked Burton. 'Just like that, entice one man to kill himself, almost do the same again, and then she walks?'

'Not only that,' said Smith, 'this time she'll get the money as well. We can't do anything about it. The will is valid, we have no evidence that Sir John was murdered, so she'll get the lot.'

'And that's how it should be.' King spoke softly and slowly, but his words carried a certain authority. 'We live in a country where you are innocent until proven guilty. This applies equally to all of us, including Melissa. If we can't prove she did it, she should not have to suffer for our suspicions. As Blackstone said, it is better that ten guilty men escape than that one innocent suffers.'

'It still doesn't feel right,' said Burton. 'She might be innocent, in which case she should be acquitted, but she's not even going to stand trial.'

'Nor will you, Michael, if we take her deal. And you're certainly going to be found guilty.

I mean, you admit you did it. You can argue about why you did it, but the bottom line is that you broke in. Think about it. If we accept her offer, you won't be charged, or at least, I doubt very much you'll be charged. The final decision is with the public prosecutor, of course, but they almost certainly won't charge you if Melissa doesn't want them to.'

'All right, all right. We'll take the offer. Are we all agreed?' Burton looked at the two detectives, both of whom nodded their heads resignedly in sullen agreement.

★　★　★

'Hello, Michael. I'm sorry it had to end like this.'

'Yes, so am I,' responded Burton ruefully.

Melissa smiled at him as they walked towards the exit of the police station. She was a very beautiful woman and, as she smiled, Burton saw everything in her demeanour that he was originally charmed by, and yet he no longer felt the powerful, overwhelming attraction he had experienced when he'd just met her. In his mind he could see only the cold, hard woman pointing a gun at him steadily, and somehow this conquered any feelings of lust that might otherwise affect him.

They'd met outside the interrogation

rooms, both having been discharged. Burton had spoken to the public prosecutor, who had looked bored and admitted to being uninterested in prosecuting anybody 'involved in this sorry tale', citing a lack of public interest in taking anything further. Burton wasn't surprised; he was actually unsurprised by the whole outcome from the first moment he had sat down in the interrogation room. It was at that point he had realized how well she had planned it. At first, he wondered why he was being taken to an interrogation room at all, but he soon became clear to him that she had covered all the bases, and that it was actually he who ran the greatest risk of going down for a crime that day. In a way, he conceded, once he had got used to the idea that she was going to get away with everything else, he was grateful that she had not pressed charges.

'What are you going to do now? You've clearly got away with it,' he asked.

Melissa's smile didn't waver. 'Got away with what, Michael? I think we both know that you were sailing much closer to the wind than I was. Anyway, I'm glad you haven't been charged. And I'm glad that I was able to help you.'

Burton stopped on the steps of the police station. She surely couldn't want him to thank her. That would be too much. He grunted non-committally.

'The only real mistake you made was not noticing the phone on the sofa. Otherwise, I wouldn't be here.'

Melissa looked hurt for a second, and then grinned slyly. 'Well, I don't know, Michael. Maybe it wasn't a mistake. If you weren't here, I wouldn't have been able to use you as a bargaining chip. And if you'd been killed, well, the British would be unhappy, the Bahamians would be unhappy, and your friend Mr King would be unhappy. With those enemies, you can be sure I'd have been charged and tried for something, and most probably something way in excess of possession of a firearm. Nobody wants to have to beat a manslaughter rap, even if you do have a reasonably credible claim of self-defence. Juries are fickle things, Michael. Who knows, perhaps I'd even have been found guilty?'

She walked down the steps and turned to face him, smiling all the more brightly now. 'Anyway, I just hope you're able to put this behind you. I hope we both are. Goodbye, Michael.'

Burton watched as Melissa walked confidently down the street away from him, her beautiful head held high, her long dark hair resting elegantly on her shoulders and her summery yellow frock fluttering with the wind around her shapely legs.

We do hope that you have enjoyed reading this large print book.

Did you know that all of our titles are available for purchase?

We publish a wide range of high quality large print books including:
Romances, Mysteries, Classics
General ~~~~
Non Fiction

Special interest
large p
The Little Oxf
Musi
Song
Hymn
Servi

Also available fr
Oxford Un
Young Reade
(large print edition)
Young Readers' Thesaurus
(large print edition)

For further information or a free brochure, please contact us at:
Ulverscroft Large Print Books Ltd.,
The Green, Bradgate Road, Anstey,
Leicester, LE7 7FU, England.
Tel: (00 44) 0116 236 4325
Fax: (00 44) 0116 234 0205